Agnes Romilly White was born in 1872, and died at Culfeightrin near Ballycastle in 1945; she did not marry. Very little is known about her life, however between 1890 and 1913 she lived at Dundonald, County Down, where her father, the Rev. Robert White, was rector. The life of the village formed the subject matter of both of her novels, *Gape Row* (1934), and its sequel, *Mrs Murphy buries the Hatchet*, which appeared two years later.

Born in Belfast in 1921, Roy McFadden moved to Dundonald in 1922 to escape the worst of the Troubles. He went on to edit *Ulster Voices* and *Rann*; and has published nine collections of poetry, including the *Selected Poems* (1983), and *Letters to the Hinterland* (1986). He lives in Belfast with his wife and five children.

First published 1934 by Selwyn & Blount
This edition published 1988 by the White Row Press Ltd
135 Cumberland Road, Dundonald, Belfast BT16 OBB

The White Row Press gratefully acknowledges the financial
assistance of the Arts Council of Northern Ireland
in the publication of this book.

Cover illustration: *Gape Row* by Joanna Mules
Data conversion by Unitype of Dundonald.
Typesetting by Textflow Services Ltd, Belfast.
Printed by the Universities Press Ltd, Belfast.

British Library Cataloguing in Publication Data
White, Agnes Romilly
gape row
I. Title
823'. 912 [S]

ISBN 1 870132 10 6

GAPE ROW

Agnes Romilly White

The White Row Press

Introduction

Shortly after I was born, we went to live at Dundonald, where I spent my first two years at Daisymount Terrace, a line of small grey houses adjacent to Gape Row, in what was then a country village with an identity of its own. I was too young to remember it clearly, but the smell of paraffin always moves me to nostalgia, and I believe my response is associated with the oil-lamps of that time and place. After we left the village we occasionally returned to visit friends at Boyd's Avenue and the Comber Road; and my grandfather, armed with a kitchen spoon, used to shepherd me to the Moat to dig for giant's bones, not far from the graves in St. Elizabeth's churchyard.

The previous rector, the Reverend Robert White, had retired almost a decade before our arrival, but his daughter Agnes Romilly White, in sketches and short stories, recorded her experience of the village and its inhabitants before the Great War. In 1934, in her first novel, *Gape Row*, she brought together her memories in what her publishers described as an 'enchanting novel about Irish peasant life'. The term 'Irish peasant' would have outraged Gape Row; but its inhabitants scarcely had a chance to reply as the cottages were demolished shortly after the novel was published, and they were scattered to the winds . Now, as a former villager and a local writer, I can, however late in the day, challenge the condescension implicit in those words and attempt to place the novel in a truer perspective.

Gape Row was a line of ten low, whitewashed cottages, which 'started cheerfully with a spirit-grocery at one end, and finished with the post office at the other'. Though set in lush, fruitful countryside, the Row was nonetheless only a brisk walk and a tram-ride from the city centre; and part of the novel's strength is the author's ability to balance the autonomy of the village against its dependence on the city for employment and communications, its slow rhythms against the rush of the brash town, and its close neighbourliness against urban self-containment.

On a literary level, *Gape Row* should be read not as a nostalgic account of village life some seventy years ago – or worse, as a stage-Ulster sketch with a laugh and a sob on every other page – but as a minor classic. The story is simple, and the characters are uncomplicated; but at their best the descriptive passages come within range of the prose of Sam Hanna Bell and Michael McLaverty; and the dialogue, vivid and vigorous, could find accomodation in the plays of Synge:

'Oh my! And did you ask him?'
'I wasn't speakin' till him at all'.
'What kind of fool are you to have missed such a chanst? began Mrs Murphy impatiently. 'If it had a been me...'
'Would you have ripped it out of him, and him going by at the rate of a weddin' behind his da's mare?' asked Mrs Gillespie sourly.

Descriptive prose sometimes runs the risk of being merely ornamental; but Agnes Romilly White economically relates her descriptions to the progression of the narrative or to the mood of a character:

'The afternoon sun, going westward, struck the hillside fiercely, and she sat down to rest for a few minutes on a little grass bank below the hedge. But it was almost five o'clock, and before long she rose and faced the steepest part of her journey. The road grew hotter and hotter. The day was very still, and the high thick hedges on either side shut off the cool little wisps of air that blew about the fields. She undid her bonnet strings, she fanned herself with her handkerchief, she remembered with tormenting clearness certain frosty mornings last winter, and the heavenly coldness of the ice on the water-barrel.'

Living in the rectory ('the big, kindly house'), Agnes Romilly White was a privileged spectator of life in Dundonald. She represents Gape Row as a matriarchy, where strong women – Mrs Murphy, Mrs Morrow, the Widow Gillespie – made the decisions; and where the husbands listened and acquiesced, or as with Tam Murphy, immersed themselves absent-mindedly in tobacco smoke. The men provided meagrely from menial jobs; the women pinched, and supplemented the family income from the sale of eggs and fowl, or by huxtering from a tiny, got-up shop in the parlour.

Whatever the origins of its name – 'It was always on the lookout...
and when it was not intent on the world whirling past its doors, it was
looking sideways at itself' – Gape Row had a place on the map before
it found its way into print. Though poor, it was not impoverished,
attracting itinerant vendors of fruit and vegetables, clothing, delph,
and a variety of junk, together with much heralded visits from the
Herring Man. Beggars abounded: some, like 'Betty-fly-around' were
prepared to work in her fashion, others asked only for a pipeful of
tobacco. Street musicians and evangelists also found the cottages
worth cultivating; and when votes were required, politicians ventured to smile in over the half-doors.

'Great hatred, little room', W.B.Yeats wrote of Ireland. For Gape
Row, smallness engendered intensity of life and speech, where people
and environment were intimately interwoven, and where news and
gossip from the city were sceptically examined and sifted for a local
truth. Belfast was always worth the cost of the tram-ride – 'It would
remind you of the New Jerusalem itself', Mrs Murphy declared, 'and
it just a bundle of dirt' – but to return to the village was always a relief,
and the Newtownards Road and Holywood Arches quickly receded
in importance beside the enduring reality of Meetin' Street and the
protective shoulder of the Moat.

This Dundonald survived as an entity until the mid-thirties, and its
inhabitants were still fresh in the author's mind when she wrote her
novel. Both Joyce and Shaw claimed that they invented nothing in
their writing; and one has the impression that the rector's daughter
also drew heavily from life, celebrating it with a joyous and almost
anarchic vitality that one could hardly fail to be drawn into.

Gape Row is a novel which I have read again and again for pure
pleasure, tinged no doubt by a measure of regret for life at a simpler
time in a simpler place. Thinking of the stream that ran underneath
the cottages, and of my elder brother who attended the local school,
in my poem, *Daisymount Terrace*, I wrote:

I listen, hand at ear,
For a mercy of water, and
My brother's confident shout
In an innocent afternoon.

In *Gape Row*, Agnes Romilly White has given me more than a
semblance of an answer.

Roy McFadden

1

Ann Rainey leaned over the half-door and looked about her. On the other side of the road a green field sloped up to the rectory grounds, and stopped at a high hedge covered with hawthorn. A row of poplars, whose leaves chattered in cool monotones all through the summer, stood on the other side of the hedge. When the poplars were in leaf, the rectory was almost hidden from view, but in autumn, when the leaves fell, and lay in little, rustling drifts on the grass, Gape Row came into its own again, and saw with one well-trained eye all that it wanted to see.

It started cheerfully with a spirit-grocery at one end, and finished with the post office at the other. A straight line of low, whitewashed cottages ran between. The postmaster followed the trade of shoe-making in the room over the post office. He went up by means of a rung ladder and trap-door, and once he was up it was a difficult matter to bring him down. When a customer rapped long enough on the counter with her knuckles a pair of reluctant feet appeared on the top rung, and if the matter was urgent he came a step further and parleyed. For an ordained minister he would descend slowly and with indignation, and once, through the strategy of Mrs Murphy, he came down at break-neck speed. She had sent her little daughter for a pen'worth of note-paper and a postal order, and he had called down to her that this was no time of day to come bothering him, and besides the only postal order about the place had been promised to a man from the hills a fortnight ago. "I'll hould you I'll bring him down brave and smart," said Mrs Murphy grimly, and later in the day she put her head in at the door, and called up in agitated tones:

"Och, Tommy dear, I doubt your goat's a corp!"

He flung himself down the ladder, and passing her in the narrow hall with an energy which almost capsized her, ran as he had not run for years. When he reached the loanin' behind the church, he found the goat browsing peacefully where he had left her in the morning. After that he was harder than ever to dislodge.

The village had flung out little shreds of streets here and there in an effort to expand itself, but Gape Row still remained undeniably the principal thoroughfare. It saw the traffic from the city pass through on its way into the quiet, distant spaces of the country: it gathered facts such as births, deaths, marriages, courtships, quarrels and flittings almost without thinking: it knew who had bought anything from a cow to a new hat as soon as the bargain was completed, and it took a devouring interest in politics. It was always on the look-out, which indeed was the meaning of its curious name. Its eyes roamed hither and thither after the manner of a searchlight, and when it was not intent on the world whirling past its doors, it was looking sideways at itself.

A stream ran under the houses all the way down, and one man was so overcome with the romance of the thing that he called his house Riverdale Lodge, and wondered that he had taken ten years to think of it. The inhabitants of Gape Row did not suffer as severely from the situation as the ducklings. They heard the call of the water at an incredibly early age, and spent a short but stiff-necked youth in trying to evade their owner's eye, and to follow the stream joyfully down to darkness and death. A woman who met with a loss of this kind felt as if a new hat had been snatched from her head, or the children's boots dragged off their feet, for the money made by fowl invariably went to buy something useful for her man, or the children, or perhaps – but very rarely – a piece of finery for herself. She might sit on the bank, and call "*whee*-ty! *whee*-ty!" with her mouth to the opening below the post office till she was hoarse, but she knew the subterranean travellers would never come back.

Old Ann lived midway between the spirit-grocery and the post office. She hung over the half-door this afternoon in the warm sunshine, and looked about her. The road was empty. Gape Row was silent as if it had been asleep. She drew her grey woollen shawl more closely across her chest, and said:

"Blethers and nonsense!"

At that moment Mrs Murphy rolled out of a door further up the street, and continued to roll slowly towards her. In the distance she looked like a large, animated parcel which had been tied somewhat carelessly in the middle. The many bulges and excrescences of her person were more or less due to the number of garments she thought it her duty to wear at all seasons of the year, and when she had got herself firmly tied up at one point she was liable to burst out at another. She had a magnificent capacity for taking to herself any new disease she heard or read or dreamt of. She studied symptoms, invented them, grabbed at them, and wore them with as much pride as other women wear their diamonds. Sammy Soretoes, the baldest man in the country, said actually to goodness he felt the hair rising on the crown of his head when she gave him a full and faithful account of what she had suffered in the past, and what she intended to suffer in the future. As she came up to Ann she put her hand to her throat and said hoarsely:

"Squinsey!"

"Blethers and nonsense!" said Ann shortly, and something in her face made Mrs Murphy ask in a quick, clear voice:

"What ails you?"

"Nothing ails me."

"Dear forgive you for that! You may as well tell me at once, for you know I be to ferrit it out."

"Deed I know rightly! Well, it's young Ann that's annoyin' me, that's what it is. She's goin' with Johnny Darragh, him of the Whinny Hill, and I don't like him, and I don't like the breed of him."

Mrs Murphy looked down the long white road in front of her.

"He has a very nate fut," she said, thoughtfully, and she ought to have known for she had studied feet. More than once a stranger loitering carelessly by on a summer day, had found himself hurrying out of the village because of a large woman who stood in a doorway, with her eyes firmly riveted on his boots.

"I'm quare and onaisy about his feet!" replied Ann witheringly. 'I can tell you what I'm thinkin' of is the years gone by, when his father walked with her mother, and then threw her over for the wee, black-avized witch he took – and my Mary Ann the handsomest girl in the four townlands! God knows I'll never forget that Twelfth!'

"I mind it well myself. It was Ligoniel they were at that year".

"Aye, it was Ligoniel the Orangemen had went to, and they came home late in the evenin', the drums and all, and they were standin' about batein' the drums and carryin' on, and the whole country after them. I was here in the door watchin' them, and I seen her among a wheen of comrade-girls at the back, and I thought her face was quare and white, but sure she might have been tired, the crathur, and her never off her feet from early mornin' and the long road she had travelled that day. After they bate a wee while, the drums went home and everybody scattered. I was boilin' up the kettle, thinkin' she'd be ill off for a cup of tay, when all of a suddent she opened the door and come in, and stood there by the fireboard. She had a pink dress on, and a white hat with pink roses round it, and och annee! they said she was the purtiest thing walked the roads that day! You mind the proud set of her head, and feth, it was a proud head she had that night, but her face was the colour of ashes, and her eyes like coals of fire, and there was a look on her countenance that scared me to the heart – it was that firrum." "Daughter dear", sez I to her, 'what's come on you at all, at all? Are you sick?'

"There's nothing wrong with me", sez she, 'I'm a bit tired, that's all, but I want to tell you that I'm not goin' with Johnny Darragh no more. I'm done with him for good. He never left Bella Blackstock the day, and he never looked wonct at me. I'll never mention his name again. I wouldn't dirty my mouth talkin' about him'. And with that she turned and went up to the room. I had to sit down on the chair in the corner, for my legs near left me with the start I got, and after a bit I gathered myself up and wet a wee taste of tay and took it up to her nice and warrum, and sez I, 'drink this, daughter dear,' and I helped her to take off her things. And then I left her, for I knew she had a mind to be by her lone. That was the curious turn of her, like the father. And och oh! the work she had to get the purty dress ready for the Twelfth, and the good heart she was in startin' off, and it the lovely day and all!"

"It was a quare pity!" murmured Mrs Murphy sympathetically.

"To come home that night, heart-broke and affronted before the whole field," continued Ann, 'the dirty rascal! But nobody ever heard a lament out of her, and she went in and out to her work as high and proud and lady-lookin' as ever, and I never seen a tear in her eye. I knowed rightly what she was comin' through, but I daren't say a word, she was that close. It all gathered in on her heart, the whole sorrowful trouble of it, and she never was the same girl again.'

"I be thinking of our Mary. I trust in God she'll have wit when it comes her turn," said Mrs Murphy anxiously.

"He'd come round here every sunday the whole two years he was goin' with her," Ann went on, 'and he'd plaster me about the terrible fine girl she was, and all he thought of her if he was true. He was a great lick, I can tell you. That done me for licks.'

"I'll hold you what you like," said Mrs Murphy suddenly, seeing light ahead, 'that Ann will throw him up herself. If you remark it, there's a turn in things. Man, but it would be grand! Let her tig-toy with him and keep him off, and carry on with him till her heart's content, and then let her give him the toe of her boot, and tell him to go 'long out of her sight! I'd be right and glad.'

"She will not then," replied Ann moodily. 'She'll stick to him as long as there's a button on his coat, for it's the steadfast kind she is...'

"And not heed a word one of her own would say till her, I'll be bound," interrupted Mrs Murphy. 'Now there's our Mary, and if she doesn't do what I bid her – that's if she ever gets anybody till ask her, for dear knows she has neither my looks, nor my antic ways...'

"What scarrs me is the way she takes after Mary Ann," the old woman went on calmly as if Mrs Murphy had not spoken, 'she has the same deep thoughts her mother had afore her...'

"And the same fut," again interrupted Mrs Murphy. 'Every wee turn of her would put you in mind of Mary Ann, and it was a sore errand she had to the world, the crathur! Look at the man she took at the last.'

"What would have happened him at all, do you think?"

"It's a big odds! He left her afore the child was three months old, and nobody ever seen hilt or hair of him since. Lord knows he may be crawlin' the bottom of the ocean yet for all I care."

"There's some says he went out of the world altogether – to Turkey or Tarsus, or some of them heathenish places where people eat other. It would be a fearful end to come till."

"By my sang, I hope they ate him!" said Ann brightening, 'but God knows they'd be ill off for mate that made a roast of *him!*'

"Broth!" corrected Mrs Murphy, who was well read.

"Broth or no broth, I'm an old woman now at death's door and not fit for troubles and vexations to be comin' on me," cried Ann, 'and wantin' nothing, nor askin' for nothing but a chair in the corner and quietness about me for the short length of my days. Och annee annee!' And she wiped away her tears with the corner of her apron.

"Put your trust in the Lord, woman dear," admonished Mrs Murphy, 'sure there's nothing for you to be yammerin' about yet. If Johnny Darragh was a bad old article, it doesn't follow that young John will be the same.'

"Trot father, trot mother, why shouldn't the foal dander?"

moaned Ann. 'Many a time I heard my mother sayin' that, and you
know rightly it's the way things mostly falls out.'

"When did you hear about this?" asked Mrs Murphy, who had
been watching the courtship with some anxiety for months past.

"Just last night. She says she has been promised since Christmas,
and she was frettin' about not tellin' me, but she didn't want to have
me put about, and me with the heart's disease."

"Deed aye."

"Will he stick to his integrity, that's what I want to know?" said
Ann anxiously, 'or will he do what his da done afore him, and drop
her when he gets her guy and fond of him. There's a low-down
principle in some people, and it's like grey hair, it follows breeds'

"That's the God's truth!" responded Mrs Murphy, 'and he has the
father's way with him, too. But sure maybe it will turn out all right,
and she be to marry somebody.'

"I was married at fifteen," said Ann, 'and I wish somebody had tied
me to the leg of the table that mornin'! They'd have done me the
quare good turn, I can tell you!'

At that moment Nicky the herring-man came round the corner
lustily calling his wares, and the conversation ended. Old Ann and
Mrs Murphy moved towards him as quickly as the weight of years in
one case, and of flesh in the other, would allow. Women hurried out
with plates and dishes in their hands. Gape Row came to life again,
and the joy of the bargain palpitated from door to door.

By six o'clock the smell of frying herrings was everywhere. It met
you in a solid body if you walked down the street, and if you tried to
escape round the corner, it was there, waiting to embrace you. Men
coming home from their work welcomed it on the breeze, and
hastened their steps. It snuffed out the strong, old-fashioned scents in
the back gardens, it floated over the fields, it came in at open windows
and took possession of houses where herrings were not. June, who
was young and innocent, fought it with all her pretty weapons, her
hawthorn and lilac, the faint, sweet smells that hang about her
hedges, and over her deep warm banks, but the day was with Nicky
the herring-man, and the housewives of Gape Row, and their
triumph rose like incense to the skies.

2

"There's young Ann away up the hill with Johnny Darragh and the old woman watchin' them from the door," remarked Sammy Soretoes on the following saturday afternoon as he passed Mrs Murphy's door.

She came to the door and stood looking at them quietly. "There's grand air up on the Holywood Hills."

"Aye, and it's the grand air they're thinkin' of I'm sure!" returned Sammy, 'that's a queer bit of history when you look at it.'

"So you might say."

"To think of them two comin' together after all the bad blood that has been between the parties for years, and the old woman as bitter as soot till this day. It bates all!"

"There's not a girl about the country that's not daft about him, and him not a bit handsome no more nor myself."

"Aye, but he could throw the 'come hither' over you, that's the worst of Johnny." Mrs Murphy turned thoughtfully away and began to prepare the evening meal. She took down cups and saucers from the dresser and laid them on the table. She cut farls of soda bread in half and buttered them, and filled the jam-dish to overflowing. A boundless hospitality was the rule in the Murphy household, and on saturdays and sundays all through the summer a steady run of visitors came out from the city 'to take the air, and hear the thrushes sing' in the country fields and lanes. She opened the cupboard door and took out a handsome pewter teapot. She had been a McSpeddan, and this was the McSpeddan teapot. It was the outward and visible sign of the grandeur which Gape Row had come to believe in more or less. With only the teapot for a start she had built up a romantic family history, in which silk dresses, calves, silver spoons, miskins of butter and stuffed chairs jostled each other recklessly and familiarly. Like a nest in which there are too many young birds, her imagination at times became overcrowded, and some of her brightest fledglings fell over the brim and were heard of no more. But although most people believed in the teapot, and in the teapot only, her artless and inventive conversation had the knack of leaving little wisps and tags of the McSpeddan glory sticking to her.

"Dear bless us, but them pink cups of the pedlar's would go with it lovely!" she murmured, holding the teapot from her and looking at it with almost tears of affection in her eyes, 'maybe when I sell the chickens I'll be able to get them. It's well for them has money and no mistake.' But the next moment her thoughts came back to old Ann blinking over the door in the sunshine, and to young Ann walking away with the air of a queen beside her lover.

"I trust in God it will come right," she said aloud.

Meanwhile Ann and Johnny were making their untroubled way up the Holywood Hills. A narrow road broke off the main road at the village pump, and ran up past the police barracks and the rectory gates. It wandered and curved its way to the top of the hill, and loitered awhile among heather and bracken before it dipped swiftly down into the village of Holywood and the sea. They passed the narrow, overgrown lane where seven centuries ago King John came riding down on his way into the Ards. On a summer evening you may find a pair of lovers lingering there, or a woman from a farm searching for a lost duckling, or a brood of wandering turkeys, but nothing to remind you that a royal procession once passed that way.

There were bits of level road which they walked sedately hand in hand, and steep little gusts of hill which they raced up for the fun of the thing. Sometimes they stood and looked back at the many coloured hills across the valley, and drank in great draughts of air which even on that June afternoon had the cold sweetness of the north country and the hills in it. On their left, Belfast lay at the foot of the mountains hidden in blue-grey smoke. They saw the spires of churches and mill chimneys rising through it, and the funnels of ships in the great shipyards, and they heard the low, musical hum of the city and the lark's song overhead.

Down below them in one of the loveliest valleys in Ulster were farm-houses set in orchards and lawns, and neat little cottages and wooded slopes; and green cornfields and grasslands, and meadows filled with ripening hay. A tiny line of chimneys down there meant Gape Row. Behind it on the hill – for the valley had little hills and dents of its own – they saw the square, dark grey tower of the church, and in the churchyard the dusky yews.

Half-way up the hill they looked back and saw Slieve Donard peer over the shoulder of the Castlereagh Hills inquiringly, and at the summit, the long, blue range of the Mourne Mountains, huddled and linked together, came suddenly into view. They walked on until the road began to slip down suddenly in front of them. Then they turned into a field and sat down among heather and rocks, with Belfast Lough sparkling in the sunshine below them, and the mountains beyond it covered with delicious shadows and shadow-dimples. They could see the coastline stretch away to Blackhead. It was here the great ships came and went to the far ends of the earth. At their feet Holywood was tucked cosily under the hill.

"Do you see thon big house thonder among the trees?" said Johnny, 'that's where you and me will live when we get rich. We'll have a butler and a coachman and a motor-car, and lashins and lavins of everything! And you'll have a woman to redd your hair every mornin' in life.'

"The dear forbid!" returned Ann. 'I'd as lief redd it myself. If you're goin' to live in a house like that you'll have to marry somebody else.'

"But I couldn't do wanting you, and that's the God's truth."

"It's just a wee house with a nice wee parlour I want – when we've saved up money to get furniture for it – and a wee bit of a garden maybe..." Ann looked down the Lough without seeing it.

"Do you know," said Johnny presently, 'I used to think you quare and proud. As sure as I'm sittin' here,' for she had looked up incredulously, 'I used to think you were a stiff, high-and-mighty sort of a girl that wouldn't look at the like of me, and that sunday evenin' – do you mind? – that we fell in with other comin' out of church, and went for a walk up Dempsey's loanin' – I never thought you proud or stuck-up since that – but just a wee bit of a crathur – just a wee girl, Ann.'

He drew her close to him and kissed her. A ridge of bracken fern sheltered them, but there were few passers-by on that high, lonely road. The gulls cried close overhead. Ann's voice was low. She turned her face to him, but she could not lift her eyes.

"Oh Johnny," she whispered, 'I'm that afeerd!'

"What are you afeerd for, honey?"

"I'm heart-afeerd to have you that fond of me." She bent her head and her cheeks reddened.

"Didn't I say you were only just a wee bit of a crathur," he answered fondly. 'Listen to me, Ann, I want to tell you something and you're not to be botherin' your head about it. I'm thinkin' of goin' away out of here for a couple of months.'

"Och, no, Johnny!" Her small hands tightened on one of his.

"But listen here, dear, I want to save up agin our weddin' and have something to start with. Work will soon be gettin' slack here, and I was thinkin' of goin' over to the Clyde for a bit. Sandy's goin' as well as me."

"You were there before a brave while," said Ann quietly. She was not the kind of woman to keep her man back.

"Aye, I was indeed, but I didn't know you then the way I know you now, or I wouldn't have stayed so long. But sure the time will soon go round, and I'll be comin' home with plenty of money in my pockets."

"You'll have to go if it's for your good," said Ann, 'but it will be the sore day for me. I'll be that lonesome wantin' you.'

"You'll not be walkin' with another boy and me away?"

Ann laughed. "Maybe you'll be walkin' with another girl – a lassie."

"By my sang, I will not! I wouldn't have the heart to be lookin' at the side of the road she'd be on."

Presently they stood up and looked out over the sea.

"Listen!" said Ann suddenly, 'it's the soldiers' bugle.' She turned her head and leaned forward.

Down among the trees to the left the gallant Norfolks were stationed in the Palace Barracks. It was in the far-off, happy days before the war.

Ann stooped down and picked a bit of heather at her feet.

"See here, Johnny," she said, 'there's a wee keepsake for you, and here's another for me. Put it in your prayer book and I'll put this in mine, and we'll think of this day and this hour every time we look at it.' And they kissed each other and promised.

As they came down the hill in the soberer evening light Johnny pointed to the church. "Ann!" he said gaily, 'we'll be givin' his reverence a job there afore long.'

"What's this I hear about Johnny goin' away?" asked Mrs Murphy a couple of evenings later at the pump.

"He's for goin' to Glasgow," returned Ann, 'but he'll only be a wee while away.'

"And when's he set for gettin' married?" she questioned with narrowing eyes.

"He's talkin' about August, but dear knows what granny will say. I haven't told her yet. She'll think great long when I go."

"Never you mind your granny, nor nothin' else," counselled the elder woman earnestly, 'just you go the first chance you get. Men's scarce and it doesn't do to keep them hangin' on too long.' Ann laughed.

"Howinever I wish he wasn't going away. I'd rather be dancin' at your weddin'."

"I'm brave and content for him to go if it's the right thing. They say Glasgow is a terrible fine place for work."

"It's the dirtiest hole in Ireland!" said Mrs Murphy, getting mixed in her geography. She turned and walked gloomily away between her cans.

3

The tram ran out to the edge of the green country. It had two passengers, an elderly woman and a young girl. They sat in opposite corners as far from each other as possible.

"As sour as gall!" said the girl, allowing a fraction of her mind to stray for a moment from the pale blue straw hat, trimmed with white wings, which she was wearing with a certain timidity for the first time.

"An impitent, dressed-up hussey!" retorted the woman.

"I hope mamma won't be mad for I do become it," continued the girl, 'and sure they threw off a shillin' for me.'

"Did anybody ever see such a head-dress!" exclaimed the woman, 'dear help the man gets *you*.'

The girl regarded her with steady, bright eyes. "There was nobody ever wantin' *you* at any rate. That's as plain as the nose on your face, and sure it's no wonder – your countenance would sour sweet milk. There was the Lady Ermyntrude, and she got proposals by the dozen. I must say I'd like right and well to get a few myself..."

"Ear-rings – and two brooches – and a low neck! Dear-a-dear."

"I hope she won't murder me about the hat. I never had one on my head I liked as well. Sure it was my own money that bought it. Feth, I'll mind and tell her that! What are you lookin' at me for as if I had horns?"

"I'm thinkin' it'll not be long till you're as old and as ugly and as sour-lookin' as me," laughed the woman.

"Never, never!" sang the girl, and she stood up and looked down the long avenue of trees. She was tingling with life and youth and the glory of the years to be. 'Oh never, never, never!' she sang.

The woman laughed again, and the conductor, looking towards her, did not know she laughed. He would have sworn in a court of law that both women were perfectly silent, which was true. It was not for him to hear the unspoken words that were darting up and down the tram like little arrows with fiery tips on them.

The girl stood impatiently by the door, her hand on the window-ledge. The tram took the last little incline of the road with a joyous rush as if it meant to bound away into the heart of that enchanted country, but instead it came to a sudden stop with a jerk and a grinding of brakes. The girl sprang out and the conductor smiled as she flashed past him. He turned to the other passenger:

"You'll be going out to the cemetery, ma'am?" he surmised genially.

"It's news you want," said the sour-faced woman, stepping gingerly to the ground.

At that identical moment Mrs Murphy was standing in the middle of the kitchen floor remarking to a hen who stood before her expectant of food, that she supposed it was time for her to put on her hat and to go out and milk the goat. She went into a small bedroom which opened off the kitchen, and came out a moment afterwards with a soft clerical hat perched low on her forehead and a clerical coat over her arm. She took a deep breath and began to squeeze herself into the coat. It was tight and there were moments when she would thankfully have pared herself down to fit it had it been possible. When the top button and button-hole had been persuaded to meet in a strained relationship she lifted up her voice and said: "Dear save us!" with emotion.

Being used to the sight Gape Row did not even turn its head to look when she sailed past in milking attire, but strangers had been known to stand and stare and even to laugh immoderately. If it pleased her to take notice of such outbursts she would pause to assure them they were a credit to the mother that reared them and that it was aisy to see when people were come of dirt. Once a venturesome youth, thinking he had found a clerk in holy orders milking a goat in a country lane, crept up behind her with stealthy steps and a camera in his hand. He was not a little surprised when a large, red-faced woman turned and ran at him with a stick, and vowed she would break every bone in his body if he didn't get out of the townland in two mad minutes.

She took a small can from the dresser, and chasing the reluctant hen before her, went out and locked the door. She hid the key in an overgrown wallflower below the room window, and sauntered, ruminating, down the road. A little way out of the village she turned into a lane. Further up, a goat, feeding quietly, lifted its head and saw what it believed to be a clergyman coming towards it. As this was the sight it loved most on earth, it took itself nimbly out of the hedge and hurried towards him. Mrs Murphy seated herself on the grass bank, and Biddy, who would have been in her element at a church congress, or in the company of a bench of bishops, waited ecstatically to be milked.

Ten minutes later she rose stiffly and would have stretched herself but for the ominous creaking of cloth.

"This coat's gettin' wee-er," she said unhappily.

"Maybe you're gettin' bigger," suggested a voice behind her.

She whirled round. "Lord bless us and save us, Mary, is that you!" she exclaimed. 'You scarred the livin' life out of me! You shouldn't be givin' me such a start, and me ketched about the heart the way I am with this old coat. How does it come that you got off the day, daughter? I wasn't lookin' for you.'

"Nor I wasn't thinkin' of comin' out, but the master and mistress are away to Bangor on the boat, and they took Gladys and Enid with them, so that's what has me here."

"It's a wonder to goodness but they took you too."

"Feth, wild horses wouldn't have took me! sure the last time I went didn't the people on the boat think I was the childer's aunt. Catch me goin'."

"Well, and what harm would that have done you? I think I'd have taken a while of a day at the seashore if I'd have got the chanct. Come on up the loanin' a bit. I want to tether the goat furder up. And are you still liking the town, daughter?"

"Oh, dear, yes," returned Mary, with a sudden painful restriction in her manner, 'it's more excitin' and interestin' don't you know. It would be very dull to live out here now, I think. It's only jist the country.'

"It only jist is," agreed Mrs Murphy, in withering tones, 'you're not tellin' a bit of a lie, daughter. Well I never was dull in my life, thank God, and I'm not goin' till start now. If you're not above carryin' a drop of milk maybe you'll take that wee can till I get a hoult of the stake.'

"She never seen me hat!" thought Mary delightedly as they sauntered up the lane, 'and her that has eyes in the back of her head. Dear send that she mayn't see it at all.'

"What do you think, Mary, but I've got a blue bonnet's nest in the wall of old Ann's yard," said Mrs Murphy, who had a child's enthusiasm in such matters, 'it's years and years since I had one, and old Ann won't believe its there at all, just because she didn't find it herself – do you mind that? She's a knowin' old blade, too. And wee Ned, he sat stride-legs on the top of the wall for half a day to see the blue-bonnet flyin' in, but she had more wit than to let on where she was, the crathur! Look at them calves, Mary. Aren't they a lovely sight? Michael will make a fine penny out of them after a bit.'

Mary, bored and indifferent, looked at a group of calves clustered in a corner of the field.

"My, but that's a beautiful sight – them fine young bastes in the grass field, and the big thorn hedge to shelter them from the rain, though thank God there's no sign of it the night. And the price of cattle goin' up steady – but I suppose the like of you would hardly know a calf if you seen one now – not that you were ever any way backward if you were offered a bit of meat – Lord save us and keep us, where did you get the hat?"

"Glory O!" exclaimed Mary, with a sudden collapse into countrified ease, 'sure I was waiting for this! Woman dear, didn't they throw off a shillin' for me, and everybody says I never had anything on my head I become as well. The mistress says it makes another woman of me, and if she had seen it first, she'd have *made* him get it for her should she have gone down on her bended knees to ask him, and dear knows, of all the screws that walks the earth the master bates them all – did I tell you what he said about the soap last week, and me washin' Enid's pinafores? You'd split your sides...'

"Howld your tongue! Take off that hat this instant till I see what it's worth. Where did you buy it? What did you pay for it? Threw off a shillin'? I've made them throw off five before now. What call had you for a new hat and the childer runnin' naked, and food that ill to buy, and your da no good at pushin', and me the half of me time at death's door with one complaint and another, you ungrateful young strap, you!"

"Everybody says I become it something lovely," said Mary, almost in tears, 'and my other hat is all spotted, for the red flowers run in the rain, and I was goin' out a perfect show – who's that comin' through the gap up yonder? Is it Michael?'

Mrs Murphy drew the brim of her hat low on her eyes and peered up at a man's figure a couple of fields off. "That's him!" she said hurriedly, 'that's him, right enough. Wave your hand and he'll see us and come down. I daren't. I'd brust. I couldn't lift me hand to me head to save me life. That's right. There he's comin'. Look at thon wee red heifer standin' there alow the hedge. It's the purtiest in the field I do believe.'

"But sure this isn't Michael's land at all?"

"No, but he's rented a couple of fields extra because that much of his own land was broke up the year that he'd no room for the cattle. My, but that's a lovely wee baste! They're doin' past the common, for all that he didn't put them intil this field for a full fortnight after I bid him. Many a time he drops in for a cup of tea and a crack with me. Two head-dresses this summer! And the childer goin' naked! How are you, Michael, son? I'm just remarkin' the cattle. They doin' the best."

Michael came quickly across the field. He was a tall, broad-shouldered young fellow with a square, pleasant face. In his sunday clothes he looked slightly awkward, but at ordinary times, in his wide, straw hat and shirt sleeves he almost touched romance. A little white terrier with a black mark round his right eye and another on his left ear, bounded after him. His name was Patch, and he was Michael's greatest friend.

As he came rapidly nearer, Mary forgot about her new hat and looked critically for the first time at her mother's strange attire.

"That coat looks awful odd, mother," she whispered, 'take it off you.' Michael was still on the other side of the hedge. Mrs Murphy looked her scorn.

"Whip it off you!" Mary persisted.

"Look, see here, Michael," Mrs Murphy called as he swung over the fence, 'when you're rarin' a family and slavin' for them night and day, I'll bail you, you'll learn what impitence and ingratitude is.'

"What's wrong?" asked Michael, smiling all over his pleasant face.

"It's me that's wrong of course! Mary's passin' remarks on me for the way I have to put myself about to get a taste of milk from that animal there. As if it was any pleasure to me to be squeezed and tortured out of my very life..."

"The goat was petted on a young clergyman before mother got her," Mary began apologetically.

"Howld your whisht, Mary, till I tell Michael the right way of it," interrupted Mrs Murphy. 'Mrs Gillespie was goin' away a brave while back to stop with friends down the line and I bid her look out for a bargain of a goat for me, for I wanted the milk for the childer. And if you please, didn't the young curate down there give her a present of a lovely goat that he wanted redd of. He was *lament*able fond of animals and he'd every kind of livin' thing gathered about him, and the goat was that petted on him it would let nobody milk her only him, and the first time I tried she dunted me half a mile up the road. So when I seen the fix I was in I made Mrs Gillespie sit down and write to the young gentleman, and insense it intil him that that goat of his couldn't be milked good or bad, and what do you think but he sent me an old coat and hat of his own, and wrote in a letter that if that didn't do the trick nothing would, and when I put them on me didn't the poor misguided crathur come leppin' to me. She's as good a goat as ever walked on four legs and the childer's dyin' about the milk. It's quare and good in your tea, too. But I could wish that young gentleman had been a bit broader in the shoulders. I lave it to you, Michael, what else could I do?'

"Nothing," said Michael heartily, 'Mary's only jokin'.'

"Divil a bit of her's jokin'! The town has her filled with notions, that's what's wrong with her. Charlie was bad enough before he went to America and I doubt he's worse now, whoever sees him. The way I've slaved and wrought for them bad, ungrateful childer of mine! Many a time I think I'll be found a corp sittin' on that ditch with the can in my hand. It'll be the quare joke to get me home, that's what I'm thinkin'."

"I wouldn't bother my head about it if I was you," said Michael, smothering a paroxysm of laughter.

"It takes you to consider your latter end," returned Mrs Murphy piously, 'we're here the day and away the morra, and stone dead I'd be weightier than ever. How would they get me heaved intil a cart, Michael, will you tell me that?'

"You're not dead yet," said Michael, 'why you're younger lookin' every time I see you. Come on up the loanin' a piece, and take a look round you.'

They walked slowly along, Michael between them, while the goat ambled leisurely behind at the end of her tether. Mrs Murphy and

Michael talked of crops and cattle, of Dan McIlroy's bad farming, and the way prices had risen last fair day. Mary scarcely spoke. When she was with Sandy and the other boys about the village she chattered all the time. Now she liked to walk quietly beside them, listening. She forgot about her new hat and the pleasing fact that she was looking her best in it. With other people she found herself thinking of these things. With Michael she forgot them. His naturalness seemed to reach and envelop her.

Surely he was lonely up there at the farm with only his dogs and horses for company. Some day, of course, he would marry. Her mother often said he would make a grand match and marry a girl with bags of money. She glanced at his face as he talked, or for the most part listened patiently to her mother. He looked so kind when he smiled. The girl with the bags of money would be very happy.

4

A week later Johnny Darragh went to Glasgow, accompanied, had he known it, by the maledictions of half the village.

Ann went to the boat with him. There were a number of people on the quay, and they moved behind a great stack of wooden cases for a last word.

"You'll not be thinkin' long, Ann," he said.

"No, no," she answered bravely.

"And you'll not forget me when I'm away?"

"Forget you!"

"I'll write to you regular, and I'll come back to as soon as ever I can. As sure as death! I promise."

She had not asked him to promise. She had not even thought of asking him. He kissed her face again and again, and the dark little tendrils of hair that curled so sweetly over her ears.

"I want you to gwan home now, dear, it's gettin' late, and I don't like you to be goin' back by your lone."

"Och Johnny dear, sure it isn't dark at all these nights. I'd rather wait till the boat goes out, and she won't be goin' for another twenty minutes or so. I want to see the last of you, dear."

"But some of these fellas knockin' about will be making up to you the minute I put my foot on her," he answered suspiciously. 'Sure I can see them lookin' at you already. I'd rather you'd go home, dear. I'd be more content-like.'

She leaned her forehead for a moment without speaking against his coat.

"Good-bye," she whispered. There was a lump in her throat.

"It's only for a wee while, dear," he whispered back.

She sped up the quay, and caught a tram on the Queen's Bridge going homeward. In half an hour she was out in the country, walking quickly through the soft duskiness of the plantin'. There had been rain in the afternoon and the air was cool and damp. The wood-doves were moaning in the trees over her head.

Granny would be asleep when she got home. She would make a cup of tea, for she had eaten nothing since dinner-time, and then for a while she would sit by the fire, and sew at her wedding clothes. And all the time she would be thinking of a boat that even now was moving slowly down the Lough. Johnny was going further and further away from her every minute, but her thoughts were only half sad. She was so proud of him for going away to make money for her. Granny didn't understand. He only went because he loved her, and she would have done just the same in his shoes.

The village was very quiet when she reached it. Gape Row went to bed early, and considered it scarcely respectable to hear the ten-thirty train whistle, as it rushed through the station. The windows were severely shuttered outside with heavy wooden shutters, which, during the day, were pinned back against the wall. Late on a summer evening, Gape Row looked like a girl with demurely lowered eyelids. Its air was almost dangerously quiescent. There was in it no hint of the work and bustle that filled it in the daytime, the cheerfulness and gossip, the political fervours that occasionally swept through it, or the shindies that now and then woke the echoes.

A couple of hours later, Ann stole into the little bedroom off the kitchen and undressed noiselessly. Old Ann was asleep under the heavy patchwork quilt that had served a couple of generations. She knelt beside her bed and said her prayers. Tonight they were all for her lover. Girls had lost their lovers before now, and hers was out on a dark sea, full of unseen dangers and horrors. Words she had heard every sunday evening since she was a little child, came into her mind.

"Lighten our darkness, we beseech thee, O Lord; and by thy great mercy, defend us from all perils and dangers of this night; for the love of thy only Son."

She crept into bed, and repeated them dreamily over until she went to sleep,*"for the love of thy only Son – for the love of thy only Son."*

The next morning she could have sung for joy as she walked along the road to the tram. The hills were flooded with early sunshine, and the fields wet and glittering with dew. The Cave Hill was the colour of dark blue velvet, with little wisps and blotches of amethyst light studding it here and there. She stopped for a minute on her way to look into a thrush's nest in the hedge. She had watched it sympathetically since the first bits of moss and twigs were arranged with feverish haste in the tiny forked nook in the thorn. The mother-thrush knew her for a friend and peered at her with eyes that were as bright as jewels. She remembered the night Johnny had first told her he loved her, and how her grandmother had looked at her sharply when she came in, and said: "What's come over you, daughter? Your eyes are as bright as a clockin' thrush's." She laughed to think of it – a laugh with a low, throaty sound that was new in it, and then she looked round hastily lest anyone should have heard. But there was no one on the road.

The neighbours had remarked daily on the change in Ann. Her face had new, soft curves, and a pink colour, like the pink of a carnation, came and went in her cheeks. Her shy aloofness had always made her unpopular, but now, even the children ran to meet her. Old Ann talked to her by the fire in the evening more freely than ever she talked. And for her, too, everything was changed – the dew shining on the little blades of grass beside the road as she hurried to town in the morning, the green light slipping down through the trees in the plantin' – even the ugly machine at which she worked. She saw a new heaven and a new earth, for love had opened all the windows.

She and Mary were walking home from the tram not long afterwards when she heard a quick, shuffling footstep coming behind. She knew without turning her head who it was. A little figure, dressed in clothes of incredible shabbiness, was walking below the hedge on the other side of the road. Her eyes were bent on the ground. Ann turned and spoke to her pleasantly as she passed. She lifted her head, and gave her a strange frightened look as she slid off down the loanin' to her own house, but she did not answer a word.

"What on earth possessed you?" asked Mary. 'Sure you know she's not right wise?'

"Poor Jinanna", returned Ann apologetically. 'I'm sorry for her, the crathur.'

Mary lifted her eyebrows as the heroines in her favourite novels did. "Everybody says she has lashins and lavins of money stored by somewhere," she said, 'and she's that mean and pitiful she won't even buy clothes to put on her back. Did ever you see such a sight as she is?'

"She had on a wee red bow of ribbon at her neck."

"Aye she's daft about a bit of colour. Sure, one time she put on blue ear-rings comin' to church, till she heard the people passin' remarks behind her, and then she quit. She's clean daft."

"I'm sorry for her all the same," said Ann. 'They say she was well off at one time. She has nothing nor nobody to live for.'

"Bah!" ejaculated Mary. The latest heroine had been French, and was given to use the expression. 'You're gettin' soft in the head. Didn't she pass you all the days of your life without speakin', and what call have you to let on you see her now?' And she shrugged her shoulders, and said 'Bah!' again with great effect.

"Tam," said Mrs Murphy, settling herself at her own quiet hearth. 'What do you think I heard the day? A quare bit of news, mind you.' She dropped her work on her lap and looked across at her husband, who was reading a tattered copy of *Ivanhoe* on the other side of the fire.

If she expected to meet with enthusiasm she was disappointed. He glanced at her vaguely over the top of his book for a moment and went on reading.

"Quit readin', man, and listen to me," she said impatiently, 'sure I'm tellin' you what I heard the day! Michael looked in here on his road home from town, and sez he, 'the price of cattle's something tremendjis,' sez he, 'you could hardly face a cow at all' – are you listenin' to me, Tam?'

He looked up again with the same vague disquieted air.

"Aye," he murmured gently into the page.

"Well, before Michael was right in at the door, I seen something was up with him. Thinks I to meself, 'me brave boy has took a notion of marryin' and has come to me for a bit of advice. He looked that light and heartsome it was the first thing would come into your head. And here was me, sittin' wonderin' who in the earthly world he had took a notion of, and prayin' to goodness it wasn't noan of them young McIntyres that's brekin' their shins after him, mornin', noon and night, and the mother layin' traps till all's no more, for if there's anything flesh and blood couldn't stand it would be to see one of them young straps gettin' Michael – the finest boy you'd meet with in a day's walkin'. I was that scarred, that actually to goodness I found me heart beatin' in me breast, and sez I, 'Michael, son,' sez I, 'I hope in the Lord you've done well for yourself. It can't be undone,' sez I, 'and that maybe you'll find when it's too late, like many another' – are you listenin' to me, Tam Murphy, or are you not?'

Her voice, crescendoing with the last words, roused Tam suddenly and he repeated: "Aye, aye," with a fair show of interest.

"Howsomdever, Michael come on in, and sez I, 'sit down off your feet, son dear, till I make you a taste of tay,' but he stood there leanin' up agin the door-post, and sez he, 'I can't stay,' sez he, 'the mare's fresh and she's not over willin' to stand, but I just looked in as I was goin' by to tell you, first and foremost, that my brother's comin' over from the States and I'm expectin' him one of these days,' sez he. 'My alive,' sez I, 'thank God it's no worse, sure I thought you were goin' to be married at the very laste,' and he threw up his head, and laughed hearty. He's quare and uplifted, I can tell you. They say the brother doesn't know what he has – thousands on the top of thousands! I'm right and glad he's comin' for it will be a bit of a change to see a man about the place that *has* something, and *is* something, and not just an or'nary bein' goin' about in his corduroys like the rest of us."

She paused a minute for breath. "What would Andy John McCready be worth, Tam, do you think?" There was no reply, and she repeated the question shrilly.

"If I had married the church tower, I declare to goodness!" she exclaimed huffily, 'or a graven image or even a gate-post, I would think nothing of it, for answer me they couldn't! But I might as well be tied to a corp any day, for conversation the arts of man couldn't drag out of you nohow! Such a man I never seen in all my born days! You can read away there till the Day of Judgment if you like, for I'll spake to you no more!'

Even then Tam scarcely heard her. He was far away. His small tattered library, which she pushed ruthlessly under the bed, or into out-of-the-way corners in the crowded little house, had been picked up on saturday nights off the second-hand bookstalls in Smithfield. He read and re-read them and yearned ceaselessly for more. He had nearly all the Waverley novels in their cheapest form, a few out-of-date histories, some eighteenth century poets, a couple of Shakespeare's plays, and Boswell's *Life of Johnson*. He had always been inarticulate. Few cared to talk to him. None really knew him. Year after year he hung over his shovel, a patient figure on the road, and he never knew that he was of the stuff that scholars are made of, or that his brother is on the staff of every college.

Mrs Murphy took up her knitting again. Except for an occasional snort which she could not repress, and the furious click of her needles, which to the trained ear suggested hostilities in another form, there was silence in the kitchen for a quarter of an hour. And then the door was burst open, and Ned, the little five-year-old son of the house, rushed in, his brown bare little feet scarcely touching the ground.

"Mother," he cried, tingling with excitement and importance.

"Jinanna's lyin' dead at the pump."

"It's a lie!" gasped Mrs Murphy.

"It is not," returned Ned. 'I seen her! She's lyin' dead on her back, I tell you.'

Mrs Murphy flung her knitting on the floor and ran out. Tam came behind her and looked nervously at the crowd which had gathered at the pump, but he went no further than the door.

His wife who was of another temperament, shoved people to left and right of her until she reached the little figure lying white and motionless on the ground.

"Stand back and give her air, you parcel of geese!" she cried and as she loved nothing so much as giving orders, she continued rapidly. 'Throw a wee taste of water on her, Mrs Forbes. That's right. Run down and get her bed ready, Maggie. Dead? Your granny! She's no more dead than I am. She's only fainted. There, didn't I tell you? She's comin' till. Well, if she isn't she should be. Lord save us, such a colour! Where are you, Samuel Robert? You're brave and souple. Get on your bicycle, and go for the doctor as hard as you can. Don't loss no time. Tell him to smarten himself and come on, for God's sake, for I don't know what under the sun is workin' her now. This is no ordinary dwam. There now, she's comin' till at last! You're all right, woman dear, lie quiet till I get a wee taste of whiskey down your throat to warm your inside. It's only a bit of a faint. Sure it's nothing at all, I never know the minute I'll not drop off my feet, meself. Didn't I go slap over into a bed of nettles last year, and they thought I would never come till.'

Jinanna opened frightened eyes and looked about her.

"Feel her hands," said Mrs Gillespie mournfully, 'the could of death's in them.'

"Gwan you down and fill a couple of porter bottles with hot water for her bed," directed Mrs Murphy, 'and don't stand there makin' a fool of yourself. She'll be rightly in the mornin'.'

"If it's the Lord's will," said Mrs Gillespie, hurrying away. 'I wonder who'll get her money?'

When Ann came home that evening she found the village swarming round Jinanna's cottage like bees round a hive. She had fainted again and again and the doctor's report was grave. Mrs Murphy, who had more than once seen fit to sweep him out of her way, and take the patient into her own hands with the happiest results, was in this case content to be head-nurse. Ann met her as she came panting up the street at nine o'clock.

"How is she now?"

"A wee thing better, maybe. But sure she might go off in one of these dwams any minute – and not a soul belongin' to her to come nixt or nigh her! The brother on the hill doesn't bother much about her, and dear knows it's not much wonder, she's that odd."

"It's a queer pity of her."

"Aye, it's a pity of anybody that has no more wit than to be scramblin' after money, and gatherin' the way she has done. They say she doesn't know what she has. There'll be no pocket in her shroud, that's what I could tell her. Good night, Ann. I'm that tired I can hardly trail meself after meself."

Ann stood looking out over the quiet fields. "I'll bring her a wee pot of jelly tomorrow," she said to herself. 'God help them that's lonely in this world!' And she sighed, and smiled and thought of her lover.

5

"If I had corn-coloured hair and a pale, flower-like face like the Lady Ermyntrude, I'd do rightly," murmured Mary in her little attic bedroom, 'but sure nobody would look at me beside Ann. I'm heart-afeerd I'll be an old maid.'

As she pinned on a plain, navy-blue straw hat, she looked at herself in the glass and sighed heavily. Mrs Murphy, who believed in keeping her family in bounds, had often told her she was nothing to look at compared to what she herself had been at her age. Her face had dim hints of her mother in it, but the elder woman's features had been so long concealed under ever-increasing waves of flesh that no one was struck with the likeness.

The Lindens, where she was a 'general', was an unpretentious little villa, exactly like every other little villa in a certain suburb on the outskirts of the City. Here, Mary swept and dusted, washed and baked, and took a more decisive part than their own mother in the rearing of the three young children of the household. She did her mistress's hair on 'At Home' days, and gave her much valuable information about the doings and sayings of a certain Lady Ermyntrude, who was far and away her favourite heroine in fiction and her ideal of all that was beautiful and refined. She also applauded her desire to get on socially and helped her to keep an eye on the tradespeople. When she came out to the village she boasted of 'our children' and 'our silver', for she had the habit, so common in Ireland, of identifying herself with the family she served.

She had promised to meet Ann on the Newtownards Road to help her to do some shopping. She didn't know why. Johnny was to be home in a fortnight, they were to be married immediately, and Ann was going back with him to Glasgow for a few months. He had written hurriedly urging this and Ann had consented. Mary had long ago promised to be her bridesmaid. As she hurried through the little gate she called *Au revoir* to the children in the porch, so that the servant leaning out of the top window in number seven might hear her.

The two girls met on the bridge and sauntered slowly along the Albertbridge Road, stopping now and then to examine the shop windows.

"I'd be married in white, or remain an old maid for the rest of my nataural," declared Mary. 'The Lady Ermyntrude had a robe of white satin with the arms of the De-What-you-may-call-thems done in priceless jewels in the small of her back – Lord bless us and save us, if that isn't Sandy himself on the top of the tram! Look quick, Ann! What under the shinin' sun has brought him home?'

Ann strained her eyes after a tram that was sliding swiftly into the distance. She saw Sandy's red-brown hair and square shoulders, and her heart leaped at the thought of another who might be with him. But he was alone.

"I suppose his time was up on the Clyde," she said, 'but I wasn't expectin' to see him so soon.'

"No, nor me either," replied Mary, adding silently, 'he's here to take a last look at her he loves ere she becomes another's. My, but it's queer and sad and novel-like.'

"Ah, if Johnny had been with him!" thought Ann, 'if he was only home and me takin' care of him, I'd have nothing left to wish for! But he soon will be, please God! He's staying away to put money by for me – oh, Johnny, I wish I could suffer for you, dear.' And she moved quickly along the crowded street, a rapture in her heart like pain.

It was late in the evening when she came home. Her hands were full of parcels, for she had been shopping for Mrs Murphy as well as herself. There was no one on the road when she left the tram, and she walked slowly along through the green twilight of the plantin'. Here the sunlight never came except where it could slide down the branches of the trees in little bars and blots. Ann loved to come home out of the city with its harsh clamours and noises. She loved to feel herself enveloped in quietness and cool airs and dim green lights. She smelled the heavenly smell of damp fields and hedges, and heard with a strange new sensitiveness, the wood-doves' sad lament. The hills, lying on either side of the road, held the last light of the day in their gentle folds, and she saw the narrow lanes that ran up through the fields with little twists and hesitations to the cottage doors. Before long she and Johnny would be sitting at their own warm hearth, separate and shut in from the world.

"Och, but God is that good!" she thought, and the rare tears filled her eyes.

Half an hour later Mrs Murphy heard a light, quick footfall coming up to her door. Ann came in. Her hands were full of parcels and her face was white.

"What on earth has come over granny?" she asked in quick tones of alarm, 'she's cryin' and moanin' like anything and she won't say a word except to bid me go to you. What's wrong?'

Mrs Murphy looked up. Her eyes were red and swollen.

"Och, Ann daughter!"

"Johnny is dead!"

"He is not then!" exclaimed Mrs Murphy in roused tones, 'but I wish to God he was.'

"How dare you say such a thing!" cried the girl, her spirit blazing suddenly in her eyes, 'how dare you?'

"Och, Ann dear, sure Sandy brought the word himself," began Mrs Murphy nervously, 'and him nearly heartbroken when he was tellin' me. Men's a heart-scald from the first to the last, daughter, that's the goodness truth! – they're not worth a body botherin' their head about – here the day and away the morra...'

The words died on her lips. Ann did not speak, but her eyes were fixed with a strength and intensity that compelled her to go on.

"It's Johnny, dear," Mrs Murphy burst out, half-crying. 'Sure he's went and got himself married thursday was a week. He's married on the daughter of the woman he lodged with. Sandy done his best to keep him from it, but the mother and her was workin' early and late to hook him, and now they've got him, and much good may he do them, the dirty, low pup! Sandy says she has a tongue on her would cut cold iron, and I'm thankful to the Lord for that! For the love of God, daughter, don't be takin' it overly to heart. What about a crathur like thon! Sit down in the corner there and cry your fill. It'll do you good.'

She wiped away her tears and the two women looked at each other silently across the kitchen. In those few moments something young and beautiful died out of Ann's face for ever.

She drew her breath sharply. "There's the flannelette I promised to get you," she said, moving to the table and laying down a couple of small parcels. Her lips were white and her voice trembled oddly. 'A yard and a half at sevenpence-ha'penny – and the bit of lace for Bella's dress – and the other things. They were out of the grey wool at Brady's, but they'll have it in next week.'

She turned and went out of the kitchen and down the street. Mrs Murphy sank into a chair, and her tears flowed afresh.

6

"Our Mary's to be home the night", Mrs Murphy remarked across the fire to the occupant of Tam's rush-bottom chair, 'she couldn't content herself in her place after what happened

Ann. She fretted that much that the mistress said she'd let her come.'

"I'm glad at it," said Sandy briefly.

"Aye, they'll be company for one another, goin' in and out of the town. Mary's set for gettin' work in the same wareroom as Ann. She thinks maybe it might be a kind of comfort to her if she was with her back and forrad night and mornin'. Ann never had a comrade-girl only her."

"Mary's the right good sort, so she is."

"She's not bad. But, man dear, will you tell me what is any girl frettin' her life out about Johnny Darragh for! Sure he's the very spit of his da, and we all know *him*. He makes my flesh trimble every time I come anear him, the ojis old rascal! He'd put you in mind of something you'd find under a stone."

"She thought the world and all of Johnny," said Sandy with averted eyes.

"Aye, and she'd have been a sight better with them she overlooked as I could tell her, and many a time did," replied Mrs Murphy significantly.

"What on earth did she see in him at all?"

"It's this love that ruinates the people. It's a heart-scald I tell you. Not but I like a good love story myself. I couldn't be polluted with the trash Tam reads – old books about kings and queens and foreign climes, and the dear knows what. But many a time I wonder at Ann. I wonder she stooped so low to lift so little."

"Does she ever say anything about him to you or Mary?"

"Say anything? Her name him? Lord love you, she'll never name his name if she lives to be a hundred. Sure you know that's the turn of Ann and always was. Thank God I always had the use of my tongue, but there's a queer differ in people, Sandy."

"She'd be better if she could talk to you or Mary."

"Aye, a good talk's right and wholesome. It lifts the mind. But Ann's not made like that and we can do nothing for her. I'm heart-afeerd even to be kindly with her sometimes, for fear of vexin' her."

"We can do nothing for her". For long afterwards the words shot drearily backward and forward in Sandy's mind.

"And her with the weddin' clothes got and the day fixed and everything," lamented Mrs Murphy. 'Surely the ways of man's past finding out. There was a change come over her lately too – maybe you remarked it yourself. She was always that proud and distant in her way – she never let you in on her – and sure lately it would have done you good to see her goin' by. Her face had a sort of a light on it. She never used to bother with the childer about the door, and this summer many a time I seen them wee articles of Mrs Morrow's runnin' to meet her, and she'd lift them up in her arms and kiss them. And she was terrible good to Jinanna after she took bad. There's some that says Ann's hard, but they never seen what I seen.'

Sandy stared into the fire with clenched teeth.

"And she's that hurted, Sandy," said Mrs Murphy with tears, 'she's that hurted! Och annee annee! I wish I had the hammerin' of the villain that done it on her. He'd be a better man when I'd finished with him! But maybe the woman that's got him will be near hand as good with her fists as myself, and I trust in God she may.'

Mrs Murphy picked up the needle she had dropped and resumed the darning of Bella's stocking with immense energy. She glanced across the fireplace at the boy's rough, bent head.

"But she'll come round yet, son dear," she said more cheerfully, 'she'll come round yet in God's good time.'

It was five minutes before evening service.

Ann and Mary slipped into an empty pew half-way up the church. A little behind them three men were already seated. One of them shifted uneasily, and turned away his eyes when they came in. It was not until the lesson was being read that he looked towards them again, and then his eyes rested upon Ann.

She sat at the top of the seat close to the wall. Her head was lifted up so that he could see the outline of her face. As he looked at her he wondered what she was thinking about, and then he remembered sorrowfully that he knew.

The sun, going down behind the hill, caught the stained-glass windows and the coloured lights fell in a glory on the chancel floor.

Ann turned away her eyes. There was a little, latticed window set high in the chancel wall above the vestry door. It was fitted with plain glass and had evidently been put there to give light to the dim chancel. Outside, the branches of an elm tree swayed close against it. The sun never came on that side of the church, and in summer there was a soft, green gloom of leaves, and in winter the bare boughs of the tree pencilled delicately against the panes. Ann thought of a sunday evening long ago, when she was a little girl, sitting there beside her grandmother, and how she had watched through that window a bird clinging to the twig of the elm, as it rocked and swayed lightly in the wind. And at last she had pointed to it in excitement, and her grandmother had put out her thin, hard little hand and closed it firmly on hers. She remembered with a strange distinctness how she had studied the criss-cross lines and wrinkles of her grandmother's hand for the rest of the service, and wondered why the wedding-ring had slipped down so loosely on her finger. How long ago it seemed... St Elizabeth, with the lily along her arm, was flashing lovely lights from the northern window, but Ann's eyes were turned away in pain. The warmth and colour stabbed her heart. Instead she looked up at the little window with the cold, green light of the leaves coming through it, and thought of the long years of her childhood and girlhood, and how she had waited for love to come...

They prayed the old prayers, and the children in the choir sang the evening hymn. The blessing was said over them, and they rose, and came out into the mellow August twilight. The two girls went quickly down the little hill into the village. They carefully avoided the various groups of people who stood about chatting with the leisureliness of sunday evening, and chose a quiet by-road for their walk. Mary glanced back over her shoulder once or twice.

"There was a strange man in church as sure as you're livin'," she said at last, 'a dark, low-set, ferrety-faced wee man. He has a gold ring on his finger too, if you please! Who under goodness could he be?'

"Daisy McIntyre's away over to speak to him now," she exclaimed after another backward survey. 'I can tell you it didn't take *her* long! She'll not be behind hand if she knows it! And she has a new white dress on, and it lovely made. He may be whoever he likes, that wee man, but he isn't much to look at.'

Ann did not answer. She did not seem to hear.

"He couldn't be Michael's brother – thon!" said Mary, continuing her one-sided conversation courageously, 'he's no more like Michael nor day's like night. Mamma has me deeved about that man! You would think the Apostle Paul himself was comin'. There now – there's Daisy walkin' 'longside of him down the village! My, but she done it well that time! Look at the step of her! And do you know, Ann, who he'd put you in mind of? John Smith the pedlar, if ever you seen *him*.'

But Ann was not interested and she did not pretend to be. She had grown very silent since that fateful evening in Mrs Murphy's kitchen. Her face was thinner and it had lost the pretty fugitive pink roses that

came and went in her cheeks. But she held her head at the old proud
angle. She never spoke of her lover. She seldom spoke of anything.
Mary, being a Murphy, could not live and be silent, and talked when
she was not answered. But this was not altogether amusing, and there
were times when she sighed heavily and was still. Ann had not
thanked her for leaving her post at The Lindens, but Mary knew she
liked to have her with her.

Sometimes she scarcely noticed her presence. She grew more
remote and difficult as time went on, but Mary kept loyally at her side.

"Good night," said Ann curtly when they came back to the village
and paused for a moment at Mrs Murphy's door.

"Maybe you'll come in?" Mary ventured.

"No thank you. Granny will be lookin' for me," and she hurried on.

Mary paused on the steps, the latch in her hand. She watched Ann
walking down the street. How handsome she was with her beautiful,
dark head, her pale clear-cut face and pretty hands and feet. Poor
Ann! She would never be happy again. Her heart was broken. Mary
sighed.

Ann went into her house and closed the door, and Mary suddenly
became conscious that something unusual was going on in her own
kitchen. She opened the door a chink and peeped in. It was full of
people. Sammy Soretoes was sitting in the corner opposite her father
who was in his usual place. Sandy and Michael were there, and a
couple of others, and the stranger who had been in the church – the
ferrety-faced little man was seated in the middle of the floor talking in
a penetrating nasal voice. His left hand was raised and she saw the
gleam of a gold ring on his finger. Her mother's face was fixed on him
with flattering attention.

"Why, Mary!" she exclaimed, 'I thought you were never comin' in.
Who have we here do you think, but Mr Andy John McCready, all the
road from America. You'll hardly mind our Mary, Mr McCready. She
was only a wee lump the time you went away.'

Mary came forward and shook hands with the stranger. She hoped
she did not show the surprise she felt. So this was the rich brother they
had heard so much about. Daisy McIntyre could have him and
welcome.

"And he never seen our Charlie, Mary," said Mrs Murphy, two
bright tears glittering in her eyes. 'I would like queer and well to have
heard word of him from them that had seen him. He went out Apryle
was a year, Mr McCready. I've thought terrible long after him.'

"He's many hundreds of miles from my part," said the stranger. 'I guess you folks wouldn't know yourselves if you were out there.' He looked round the little kitchen and laughed. 'This little scrap of earth you call Ireland is a very small place after all.'

"It is indeed, Mr McCready dear – that's what I say," agreed Mrs Murphy.

"I always had a great wish for till see the world," remarked Sammy.

"Aye and so had I," said Tam gently.

"And I spent my whole life followin' a horse and cart for another man," continued Sammy, 'with the day off at the Twelfth and maybe a day at Bangor, and with all I was contented enough. We don't many of us get as far as you, Andy John.'

"Well, no, I guess you don't," admitted the stranger, 'but I had to go – it was in me – it was *here*,' and he laid a short, thick hand on his chest.

"Aye, it was that," said Sammy. A faint regret for his own far-off youth was stirring in him tonight. He held a twisted hand to the fire, 'it was workin' early in the mornin' loadin' wet cabbages for the market gave me the pains terrible bad in my feet' – he pointed to his bandaged feet. 'I never could get redd of them...'

"Sure there's no cure for rheumatic pains, man; anybody knows that," interposed Mrs Murphy impatiently.

"I think maybe I know that as well as you. But as I was sayin', I always had a great wish for till see the world."

"I couldn't have stayed at home," said the stranger genially, 'I couldn't have stayed and worked the farm no matter how it went. It was too small for me. If you could see some of the farms I've seen out there! This place is too dead and alive for me. That's what I've been sayin' to Michael since I came back, but what beats me is he doesn't see it. He thinks that little old farm of my father's the finest place in the world.'

"It is," said Michael shortly.

"You think so because you've never been away from home," his brother assured him: 'You'd change your mind if you had seen what I've seen – or the half of it.'

A fire leaped in Michael's eyes for a moment, and as quickly died away.

"It's the right tidy wee farm, and I seen nothing agin it," said Sammy, 'but if I was a young fella with money in my pockets I'd travel round the map.'

"Feth, so would I!" exclaimed Mrs Murphy. 'Is it any wonder my son went away? He took after me.'

"He's in the very best country in the world for a pushing young man," said the new-comer agreeably.

"I don't know that you would call my Charlie pushin'," returned Mrs Murphy thoughtfully, 'but he's clever if you like. He takes after my side of the house. He had a lock of money left him a while back from his Uncle McSpeddan, and nothing would do him but he'd set up for himself in a wee shop in Ginger Street – papers and cigarettes and one thing and another. But sure he was intil this and that all over the town, and the shop went to pieces in next to no time.'

"Many a young man makes the same mistake," said Andy John, 'he took more in hand than he could manage I guess.'

"He did that!" returned Mrs Murphy earnestly, 'but what I blamed most of all was the back parlour. He had it something lovely! He made a lamp shade of yalla satin with his own two hands, that thick that you couldn't see a stime when it was on the lamp, though what he wanted with a lamp and him with gas comin' out of a bracket on the wall on two sides of the fireplace is more nor I know. But that was our Charlie for you! – and if he was workin' at any article of the kind – and he was never done – do you think he'd bother his head if Lord Gough himself was rappin' at the counter for a bottle of Sars? Feth, no! He'd let him rap there! And it's my belief that's the way the business went from him.'

"I would say so," said the stranger, with considerable astonishment.

"If I was a young fella with money in my pocket," repeated Sammy, 'I'd be off out of this the morra.'

"If you were me, saddled with a man and a parcel of childer, I wonder what you'd do? asked Mrs Murphy crossly. She thought Sammy was inclined to talk too much tonight.

"America would have been the very country for you, Mrs Murphy," Michael told her with a smile.

"I could have been there before now if I'd had any wit," she replied, an indescribable coyness spreading itself gradually over the breadth of her face. 'Lord bless us, I wouldn't like to tell you the chances I had of settlin' in America and in Australia too, if I don't disremember. You'd hardly credit it Michael...'

"It's very lonely up on the hill. It would get on my nerves. I couldn't stand too much of it, I tell Michael. I'm used to life and bustle..."

"You're not lonely up there surely, Mr McCready, and all them lovely bastes about the place!" interrupted Mrs Murphy.

"I guess much of it would kill me: my nerves wouldn't stand it. I'm used to city life. I guess I'll spend a good deal of my time in town while I am here."

"The dear bless us! I suppose it's all in the way you're used. I'm just sayin' to Michael here, I was very near settlin' in America myself more nor wanct, although I don't know how it came about, for I was no beauty, though well-featured and well-complected like all the McSpeddans."

"Your daughter takes after you ma'am, in the matter of good looks," said Andy John graciously. He had glanced more than once at Mary who was sitting beside Sandy in the shadow of the wall.

"She does not, then," returned Mrs Murphy, a shade of tartness in her voice. 'I was very different at her age, as anybody can tell you, and I had more boys in one month than she'd have in a year.' Mary blushed furiously as the stranger's small, dark eyes were turned on her, 'but I was young and impitent and I suppose I missed my foot like many another.'

"Mary," said Sandy in a low voice, when the talk had swung back into less personal channels, 'couldn't you persuade Ann to come with you and me to Bangor on the boat next saturday? We could get away by the half after three and have a good walk along the shore.'

"I could not," replied Mary, in the same lowered tone.

"Why couldn't you?"

"She's set for goin' nowhere."

"You could try your best," said Sandy more earnestly than he knew.

"I say, Sandy, he's not a bit like Michael. I wouldn't know he was a drop's blood to him, would you?"

"I would not. Maybe there's some other place she'd as lief to go. You could try and find out."

"Aye, I could. Look at mamma gazin' at him with all her soul in her eyes. Isn't he the conceity wee article?"

"Whisht, woman! he'll hear you."

"Not him! He's too busy listenin' to himself. Him and mamma's havin' the queer old talk! Do you mind the way he shuts her up every now and then and goes on himself? I wondered to goodness who you had with you in church."

"We wouldn't need to loss much time. The boats will soon be off."

"I know that. You'd never guess who he puts me in mind of? John Smith the pedlar! He's the livin' image of him."

"They'll hear you, I tell you," said Sandy crossly, 'and you're not listenin' to a word I'm sayin'.

"Sure I'm deeved listenin' to you! I'm to get Ann till go to Bangor. Well, she'll not go. Wild horses wouldn't bring her..."

"Why?"

"...nor mad dogs neither."

"But why wouldn't she?"

"Need you ask?" She lifted her eyebrows.

"I don't see it," said Sandy obstinately.

Mary shrugged her shoulders. "Bah!" she said as airily as she knew how.

"What's that you're sayin'?" he asked.

She looked across the kitchen and met Michael's eyes. They were fixed on her with a new gravity. All her lightness suddenly fell from her.

"I'll do my best, Sandy," she whispered.

A couple of hours later Mrs Murphy turned the key in the door.

"After all it's a wonder but he nivir seen our Charlie," she murmured in wistful mother-tones.

7

Mrs Murphy did not sleep well that night. It may have been from unusual brain activity, or the excitement of seeing the stranger, or perhaps she was thinking about Charlie. The next morning as Mary was hurriedly eating her breakfast, she stood at the end of the table regarding her thoughtfully.

"Do you know, Mary, what come intil my head in the dead of night? You don't become that new hat of yours."

"Oh my! And they all said I looked that well in it."

"What would you say to gettin' a new one?"

"Glory be to goodness!" exclaimed Mary, remembering her trepidation the first evening she had worn the hat for her mother's inspection.

"I'll tell you what you'll do," said Mrs Murphy leaning forward, her hands on the table. 'Call in a couple of shops on your road home the night and price them. Don't buy noan till you come on home and tell me what they're like. You want one that's not too light, and the winter comin' on, and not too dark to make an ould woman of you afore your time, and not too many curly-cews on it that a taste of rain would destroy, and whatever you do don't let them palm off an old one on you that they can't get redd of, for that's what they're the sorra for doin', and get one with a bit of style about it, for I've sold the ducks brave and well and I have a couple of shillin's by me for a wonder to goodness, and above all, bate them down in the price.'

Mary looked up with sparkling eyes. "I'll get a veil, too," she said, a thrill of excitement in her voice. 'Daisy McIntyre had one on her yesterday at church, and I'll bail you I'll look as well as her! I'll get a white veil with white spots on it like sago.'

It was scarcely possible for Michael who lived in the open air to spend a sleepless night, but he too was restless. Patch, curled up at his feet, felt that something was amiss and slept with one eye open in case his master should need him. Michael's thoughts and Mrs Murphy's were playing all night round the same person, and the next day in the potato field, he made up his mind to keep out of the village for the present. Sandy and Mary were lovers. He had suspected it before, but now he was sure of it, and although Sandy was his best friend, it maddened him to see it. Last night it was plain they had something important to say to each other. Well, let them say it, but he would look on no more. He bent doggedly to the plough, and called to the horses. If he was beaten at least no one would know it.

Michael and Andy John were brothers with more than a dozen years between them. When the latter was sixteen, his father's brother, who had made money in America, came home for a long visit. He had no son of his own, and having assured his brother that this was not the country for a boy who had brains and push and who knew the value of hard cash, he persuaded him to let Andy John go back with him. He never came home again in his parents' lifetime. At intervals he sent them generous cheques, and he wrote many letters telling of his success in business, his trips with his Uncle, the wonders of his new life. "The child is doing well," his mother would say, as she folded away each precious letter in the drawer where she kept all that he had

written since he went away. To her, he was still the thin slip of a lad
she had watched go down the road that August morning. Perhaps,
with the sublime unselfishness of parenthood, she was satisfied. She
had always been a delicate woman, but her boy would come back, she
told Michael, before she died. They used to sit together in the evening
sometimes, talking of the good times they would have when Andy
John came home for the length of a summer. And then, quite
suddenly, when Michael was eighteen, she died of heart failure.

In the long winter after her death, Michael thought his brother
would surely come in the spring. But he wrote that pressure of
business kept him in New York. After his mother's death especially,
Michael often found himself longing for this wonderful brother of
whom he knew so little. He got sudden aches of loneliness for him, of
which he would have been ashamed to tell anyone. His father, who
was much older than his wife, died a few years later. Everyone pitied
the lonely boy up at the farm, and prophesied an early marriage for
him. But so far Michael had been content with an old house-keeper
and his dogs and horses for company. As soon as he could, his brother
was coming home for a long visit. Michael never ceased to look
forward to that. And now, at last, he had come.

But for a curious fleeting likeness that one saw occasionally, the
brothers were very unlike. Andy John was short and some day or
other would be stout. Michael was tall and lean. His eyes had the look
of a man who was used to scanning long distances across the hills, and
his brother's had the shrewder, narrower, more intent look of the
townsman. Andy John's air of prosperity captivated Mrs Murphy
from the first. It was impossible not to be impressed with his superior
clothes, his jewellery, his habit of jingling money in his pocket, and
above all the unshakable confidence, which he expressed directly and
indirectly every moment of his existence, that money was the beginning and the end of all things.

Mrs Murphy and he had much in common. He got into the habit of
dropping in a couple of times a week, and she, to whom restraint was
difficult, would listen for hours while he told her fairy-like tales of
men who had risen from humble beginnings to positions of wealth and
power in the States. There was one who had gone out from her own
neighbourhood in his early days, and she was never tired of hearing
particulars of him, and his wife and family. "Do you hear that, Tam?"
she would say, turning reproachfully to her husband, and at last Tam
grew so uncomfortable under these recitals, that he sought refuge at

Sammy's hearth when Andy John was expected. If Mary was not out
with Ann – and for some reason Mrs Murphy had begun to discourage
her from going far away from the house in the evenings – she too
would sit listening and saying little. It would surely be grand to have
plenty of money like those people, she thought, and some day or other
to be married to a very nice boy. But he would be different, quite
different from the man sitting opposite. In the depths of her heart she
knew exactly what he would be like. But she did not dare to think she
knew. Once or twice, as Andy John's voice rose and fell, she flushed
guiltily lest her thoughts should have been seen in her eyes – her
timid, half-awakened, fluttering thoughts. Andy John looked
immensely gratified when she flushed all over her fair face. Sometimes
he looked at her with those boring black eyes so long that she grew
uncomfortable, and turned her eyes away to the fire. There were
moments when she determined to jump up and run down to Ann. She
felt a little frightened without knowing why. But something held her
back. The strange power in those dark, keen eyes was already
fastening down on her.

8

"She won't come."
    "Did you try your best?"
    "Of course I did. She wouldn't go if you made a queen of her."
    "I knew she'd be hard to turn. But..."
    "You couldn't turn Ann no more a pig goin' to hoke," said Mary
cheerfully. 'You may just leave her there.'
    "Well, if she won't come, she won't – but I could tell her Johnny
Darragh isn't lossin' his sleep about *her*."
    "Feth, I'm sure he is not! What's the wife like at all, Sandy? Did
you see her?"
    "Aye, I seen her many a time. She's like a fat, ignorant lookin' lump
of a woman, if you know what that is."
    "And Ann the lovely girl she is! What on earth made him take a
notion of her?"

"He didn't take a notion of her. She anchored on till him, and the mother did the rest."

"My, oh, but he was the queer fool! But it's done now and it can't be undone."

"That's what I say." Sandy spoke more cheerfully. 'I suppose she'll quit thinkin' about him some time or other. She had no business to be goin' with him at all.'

"That's what mother says, but what can you do when you fall in love? She says you can fall out the way you fell in. She doesn't think it lasts for ever."

"Well, she ought to know. She was in love wonct herself, I suppose."

"Dear help us!" Mary's laugh rang out. 'Her in love – and her that fat! And who would she be in love with? My father? My alive!'

"She was young wonct like the rest of us," said Sandy, 'and I believe it does last – rightly – sometimes.'

They sauntered down the road together, and after a few minutes' rather grave silence Mary sat down on the bank. "It would be all the same if McKinstrey's bull was after me," she gasped. 'I *be* to sit down! It's me feet. Look at me lovely wee shoes! Aren't they too sweet for words? Oh murder! They have me near squeezed to death!' She slipped them off with some difficulty, and plunged her grateful feet into the cool, damp grass that fringed the road. 'Oh, man, that's grand! Man, but I'm in heaven now! I daren't tell mamma I have them. I keep them hid under me good hat in the bandbox. She'd say – 'what good will the like of them be to you in the winter day?' – or some such foolish thing as that.'

"They'll rise plenty of bunions on your feet before long," said Sandy morosely, 'maybe that will please you.'

"Not at all, man dear! Don't my feet look awful wee in them Sandy?"

"You'll soon burst them," he answered, 'and the sooner the better. Sure anybody with half an eye can see they're no fit for you. You have a brave-sized fut like myself.'

"They're just like what the Lady Ermyntrude would be trippin' about in – the wee buckles and all! That's what I said to myself the minute I seen them."

"Who the dickens is that woman you're always ravin about?"

"She was the daughter of the Duke of Castlemontague, and as beautiful as a rose with the dew on it. And all the young men for miles round were in love with her."

"Some fool trash you've been readin'," said Sandy scornfully, as he seated himself on the bank beside her, 'if it was me I'd rather have a book with a bit of history in it.'

With her feet released from bondage, Mary's spirits rose.

"Do you ever pretend you're in a novel, Sandy? No, I'm sure you don't. You wouldn't know how. Well I'll tell you. When I'm lyin' awake in the mornin' I say to myself, 'James, the butler, is gettin' the breakfast downstairs, and Elise – that's my French maid – (Elise is the French for Eliza) is waitin' in the next room till I press a button at my bedside for her to come on and dress me'; – though God knows, I'd break her legs if she offered to put a stitch on me! And then I think what I'll do all day. The duke of Some-place-or-other calls with a basket of flowers, and says he, 'Will you motor down to Richmond with me, miss?' And a beautiful young man in the Guards that has yellow curls and no money wants me to go somewhere else. And I have to decide which of the toffs I'll go with. It's not so aisy, mind you."

Sandy's face gleamed with merriment. "You bate all I ever come across," he began. 'Hullo, Michael.'

Mary turned her head quickly to see Michael wheeling past on his bicycle. He nodded and called, "a grand evenin." His eyes, blue-grey and smiling, met hers for a moment.

"That's a decent chap," said Sandy, 'if ever there was one. He's worth a shipload of that brother of his. I wish he'd take himself off out of here. Go on with the story, Mary.'

"I can't," she answered crossly, 'you shouldn't have spoke and put me throughother.' She wondered why she suddenly felt inclined to cry. 'Sure I have to carry on a bit now and then to keep myself in some kind of heart. Walkin' back and forrard every day with Ann isn't too lively, I can tell you. Most times we're as silent as the tomb.'

Sandy's face sobered instantly. Mary looked down at her little shoes and wished her last words unsaid.

"Sandy," she said, after a short silence, 'will you never care for anybody only Ann?'

He was silent for a minute and then he lifted up his face. It was still and white like her own.

"I've cared for her for years on the top of years," he said in a low voice, 'and I'll care for her as long as I live.'

Mary stooped down and began to pull on the agonizing little shoes. Tears filled her eyes and splashed down on her hands. "I'm that

sorry," she said hurriedly, 'I'm heart-sorry! Some day or other she'll
be fond of you too, Sandy. I know she will.'

"I'm thankful she has you to look after her. You're the right, good
friend till her, Mary."

"She never had a comrade-girl only me." said Mary proudly, the
strange, unwelcome tears still rising fast as she wiped them away, 'but
for all that she never says a word and she never dropped a tear that I
seen. It all works in on her inwardly, mother says. Och, but she'll get
over it, Sandy dear, never you fear.'

"You're not a bad-hearted crathur at all," and Sandy patted her
shoulder kindly, 'but for goodness' sake, Mary, will you tell me this.
How did you know I was thinkin' about Ann? I never told you. I never
as much as dropped a word to Michael.'

"I'm not as green as I'm cabbage-lookin'," said Mary, a flash of
amusement showing through her tears.

Later in the same evening, Andy John called on his way to town to
say he was going to meet some American friends who were passing
through Belfast, and would not be able to pay them his usual saturday
night visit. He would be down the next afternoon, "and a turn over the
hills wouldn't do us any harm," he said to Mary, with an air of
ownership which delighted her mother, and which sent a thrill of fear
and excitement beating through her.

"That's the right wee man!" said Mrs Murphy complacently, as his
step died away.

"Aye, but I doubt he's inclined to en-bon-point."

"Lord bless us!" exclaimed her mother, 'what sort of a disorder's
that? I never heard word of it. Are you sure he has it?'

"I'm brave and sure."

"Child, dear, he's the picture of health! Don't be scarrin' yourself.
Bon-bon – what do you call it?"

"It means stoutness. He'll be a perfect little barrel of a man after a
bit. Wait till you see."

"Well!" exclaimed Mrs Murphy indignantly, 'you frightened the
senses out of me! I thought it was one of them things that had to be cut
out with a knife at the very laste. It's worth your while to talk! Bon...
aye, indeed! Is there anything else wrong with him? Would you like to
marry a ramrod? I wouldn't moan you if you had a young man half as
good as him...'

"Young man!" interrupted Mary, 'is it young man you're sayin'?
Sure he's thirty-five if he's a day.'

Mrs Murphy glared at her daughter. "I've said it before and I'll say it once again. If death spares you, the men will spare you, Mary. You have neither my looks nor my antic ways. Your father's a poor man workin' for his livin' on the roads. Your mother has let herself down. Andy John McCready wouldn't look at the side of the road you'd be on. There's plenty of girls in the country well-lookin' and well come home, by you. So don't be cockin' yourself up. The McCreadys always married money and always will."

"I'm sure I don't care who they marry. It's immaterial to me." Mary laughed and shrugged her shoulders in her Frenchiest fashion, although smarting inwardly at the thought of her lack of attractions. She knew she was plain, she told herself. She had looked so long and admiringly at Ann she could not help knowing.

"I do believe I have the aggravatinest family in Christendom," said Mrs Murphy, who seemed unusually ruffled. 'I'll stop botherin' my head about them so I will. What need *I* care what happens them? I'll get what will do me *my* day.'

Mary bustled cheerfully about the fire. "I'll put a drop of soft water on the fire and wash my hair," she said carelessly, 'it'll leave it nice and fuzzy for the morra.'

"You can wash your hair till Tibb's Eve, and that's neither before nor after Christmas!" retorted her mother, 'and you can have it stickin' out round your head like the horns of a goat, for your place of worship in the mornin', if you like! Maybe that will plaze you.'

9

One saturday afternoon early in September, Andy John called and brought Mary to the picture house, and afterwards gave her tea in a restaurant. They sat at a little table by themselves. There was a vase of chrysanthemums in the middle of the table and small, dainty silver teaspoons and forks and pretty china. Andy John ordered tea and hot cakes as if he was accustomed to do it every day of his life. He assured her if she saw the tea-shops in New York she would call this a pretty rotten show. To Mary it was like a beautiful dream. She looked shyly about her. It was rather late in the afternoon, and many of the tables were empty. A girl and a young man were whispering in one corner. She wondered if they were in love with each other. She noticed how some of the women took dainty little bits of cake on the end of a fork and put it in their mouths. She thought the Lady Ermyntrude could scarcely have done it better and she tried to imitate them. Others ate more sloppily. She studied them carefully under her half-lifted eyelashes and decided who, according to the standards of the Lady Ermyntrude, were ladies, and who were not.

If she married a rich man she would live like this every day. She would have fine, white tablecloths and silver and china at every meal. It was like a beautiful dream. Andy John had often told them of his silver, his soft carpets and easy chairs, the pictures with which his walls were covered – entirely covered it almost seemed. "The best that money could buy" – that was the expression oftenest on his lips. All he wanted now, he had told her many times, was a wife. She knew he liked her. She thought he meant to ask her to marry him and go back with him to New York. Her mother was thinking of nothing else morning, noon and night. Of course she would marry him. No girl in her position had ever had such a chance before, but she hoped he would not ask her for a long time. She did not want to get married yet. Some day it would be nice to be rich and grand, and be able to do all kinds of wonderful things for her father and mother and the children. Oh, she would make them all so happy! She would buy them clothes and furniture and a gold watch apiece, and even a nice little house at the sea, and heaps of new books for her father. A rush of warm, generous feeling went through her. She changed her mind quickly about not wanting to get married for a long time. She was so eager to fling all these lovely benefactions across the sea to her old home that she hoped he would ask her soon. It was good of him to like her, and to make it possible for her to do these splendid things. She looked at him shyly and gratefully, and the warm glow of her thoughts showed in her eyes. He saw the look and felt a tepid stirring in his veins. She was so young and sweet and lovable. "This girl is getting struck on me and no mistake," he said to himself, and perhaps he too fell to dreaming dreams that, for once, had not the chink of coin in them.

When they came out into the street it was raining. Mary held her umbrella over her new hat with infinite care. There was a touch of swagger in her manner.

The streets were dirty and crowded with workmen and

workwomen hurrying home. She walked through them on tiptoe. She was going to be rich and learn to be a lady. She thought perhaps she ought to begin at once. She would try to drop all the horrid Belfast expressions she was in the habit of using. It was so difficult to remember. And then she stepped into a puddle and splashed herself to the knees and would have cried: "the dear save us! Och annee annee!" had not the Lady Ermyntrude laid her finger on her lips, metaphorically speaking, at that moment.

When they came home Mrs Murphy received them beamingly and bade them sit down off their feet and rest themselves, for there was nothing to her mind so fatiguing as walking on the hard flags of the town. They told her about the pictures and the teashop and the smart ladies, and she laughed at the least joke and felt deliciously to the very marrow of her bones that, after all, she was going to show the world what the daughter of a McSpeddan could do. Her Uncle John's sons had always looked down on her and laughed at her, but when they heard this, they would laugh at the wrong side of their mouths. And presently she made more tea and pressed the currant cake feelingly on Andy John, and begged him to tell her was his cup of tea to his pleasement, or was it not?

Mrs Gillespie came in for a few minutes and looked at the little party with envious eyes, and Mrs Murphy, interpreting the look, beamed the more, and pressed her to take a cup of tea. But Mrs Gillespie sighed, and said she was not in a mood for refreshments. She suffered from a nervous inside, she explained to Andy John. Mrs Murphy said: "Blethers woman!" and affirmed that she had suffered more inwardly than all the village put together. But she said it lightly and airily, and Mrs Gillespie felt that the subject was being profanely treated. She shook her head gloomily and said:

"It'll come agin you yet."

Mary sat up feeling very stiff and genteel, and sipped her tea. She thought the conversation low. She was more than ever convinced of it when Mrs Gillespie turned a watery eye on Andy John, and asked had he heard how that little scrub of a fella up the street had sold her pigs on her, and her a widda-woman with five children to bring up? Andy John had not heard, and she proceeded to tell him.

Mrs Murphy swung her teacup gently round and round until the last sugared sweetness that lay in the bottom of the cup had been dissolved, and then, with a loud, sucking effort, drained it to the dregs.

"Pigs," affirmed the widow, 'is the sicknenest scald on goodnesses earth.'

"That was a good drop and no mistake," exclaimed Mrs Murphy, 'there's nothing lifts the mind like a cup of tea. But I doubt if it would lift yours, Eliza Gillespie, or anything else.'

Late on the same evening, she and Mary were alone in the kitchen. Mrs Murphy sat on a low chair at the side of the fire, leaning forward comfortably, her elbows on her knees. Her eyes were fixed on Mary's face, and occasionally she ejaculated, "Man, that was great!" or 'gawn, Mary, for mercy's sake! Tell us more.' Mary was going over every detail of the afternoon's outing, what Andy John talked about, the pictures, the woman at the next table who had beautiful ear-rings and flat feet, the girl and boy whispering in the corner, the nice things she had had to eat. Mrs Murphy drank it in greedily. 'God bless us and save us, daughter dear, isn't it wonderful!' she said repeatedly, a speech which was vague enough to be safe, and which carried off some of her superfluous excitement. It was better for Mary to be impressed again and again with the grandeur of her future, before there was a definite speech between them on the subject. At the back of her mind she had an uncomfortable feeling that, looked at with unprejudiced eyes, Andy John was not 'a girl's fancy.' Of course Mary would never dare to refuse him. She could not think any daughter of hers would commit an act so sinful. But you had to be careful in dealing with girls. She would say nothing yet. And she put a fine restraint on speech, and bided her time.

Mary sat up very straight with a strip of crocheting in her hand. She pulled the needle daintily in and out. Except for a few sudden and unaccountable lapses she felt marvellously like the Lady Ermyntrude.

At the same moment, a couple of doors away, young Ann was moving restlessly to and fro in the narrow house. She had washed and tidied away the supper things and done all the little odds and ends that needed doing. When she sat down in her usual place by the fire with a book in her hand, she jumped up in a couple of minutes and went to the door to look out. Old Ann was bored beyond words. "Annee, annee, you'll give me my death of cold openin' and shuttin' that door," she kept muttering, but the girl took no notice of her. She did not even hear her. Her face was whiter than usual, and her eyes very bright and wide-opened. Later, when Mrs Gillespie came

in, and sat down on the opposite side of the fire and sighed, old Ann
felt immensely cheered.

"It's a terrible cold night for the time of the year," observed the
visitor.

"Your're dotin' woman! There's a heat in the air I haven't felt for
months. It's done my pains good already."

"Goodness bless me! And only this mornin' after I fell into a kind
of a doze away there near daybreak – for a regular night's sleep's a
thing I may say I never get – I wakened out of it and put up my hand
to touch my face, and didn't I think I was dead it was that cold."

"Blethers and nonsense!" said Old Ann, 'give the fire a poke and
quit ravin'.'

"It's blowin' for rain now," replied Mrs Gillespie, stooping down
for the poker, 'it'll teem afore mornin'.'

"I'll hould you there'll not be a drop the night." Old Ann sat up
and drew her shawl about her. She felt better already.

Young Ann stood for a few minutes in the background, watching
them wrangle agreeably. Then she slipped out and closed the door
gently behind her...

Mary paused for a moment. She lifted her head to listen. She
almost thought she heard a knock at the door – a small, fluttering
knock like a child's. But it was not repeated. It must have been in the
wind rising.

"And then, just when she had made up her mind to marry the
other man," she went on, for she was telling her mother the story of
the pictures, 'him that owned the big castle in the trees – what do
you think, but her old lover turned up – the one she'd loved and lost
when she was a young girl singing in the village choir. Sez he,
'darling, have you forgotten?' and sez she, 'is it my little boy blue?'
and they fell on each other's shoulder as neat as tuppence.'

"They'd a dale to do!" ejaculated Mrs Murphy scornfully.

"Of course she married her old lover – little boy blue, you
understand – and sent the rich one away, crestfallen and miserable
from her side. He was as mad as bunty, but kept it well in. And she
lived in a perfect dote of a cottage, covered with roses and hon-
eysuckle ever after. You seen it in the picture."

"And she'd have time to lick her sores from that on, I'll be
bound," said Mrs Murphy fervently. 'Man, but she was the right
fool.'

"And the rich lover – would you believe it? – never married

anybody, he was that much put out. He just looked before him, proud and lonely, for the rest of his natural. I'd love to refuse a man and have him that daft..."

"Look, see here," interrupted Mrs Murphy uneasily, 'It's a very dangerous thing to do. Many a one has been sorry for the rest of their days...'

"Whisht!" said Mary, 'there's a knock sure enough.'

She rose and went to the door and opened it. Someone was standing in the shadow a little way back.

"Are you wantin' anything?" she began, nervously, 'och, Ann, is that you? You frightened the senses out of me.'

"Come on out for a bit," Ann said, in low, urgent tones; 'put a shawl round you and come out. The house was chokin' me.'

"I'll be there in a minute." She turned back into the kitchen, and put her crocheting down on the dresser. She took a shawl from a pin behind the door and flung it round her shoulders.

"Ann wants me," she whispered to her mother, and then she ran out and closed the door.

Ann was waiting for her on the step. She caught her by the arm, and Mary felt the heat of her hand through her dress.

"Come on up the garden," she said, in the same low, hurried voice, 'it'll be quiet there.'

They went round to the back of Gape Row where the little gardens sloped steeply up the hill, and scrambled through a hole in the hedge. There was a row of sally trees at the top of the garden, and below one of them a rough, wooden bench. Ann sat down on it, and Mary sat close beside her.

The darkness grew more luminous when they had been out for a few minutes. Behind them on the hill the church stood, dim and grey, and in the churchyard the yew trees, darker than the darkness itself. Ann breathed more easily. She hated the day with its sun and light and heat. This cool, dark world did not hurt her so much. They sat close together and Mary put her arm round her waist. But neither of them spoke a word.

Ann lifted her head and felt the fresh night wind blowing against her hair. All day she had been burnt and fevered with pain. If only she could take this cool, soft, healing darkness into her heart she would be happy again. But she would never be happy – life was too full of pain and deceit for happiness. Even little children, and flowers, and

sunsets, and the lights on the mountains – all the innocent, beautiful
things she had learnt to love and notice lately – they had been
deceiving her too. She would never believe in anyone again. She
would never believe in anything.

She looked up and saw faintly against the sky the blurred outlines
of the Holywood Hills. The light from a farm-house far away shone
out. It looked like a star set in the darkness of the fields. She
remembered how she used to go up through those very fields when
she was a little girl, looking for primroses or blackberries or birds'
nests, and when she was a little older to gather moss and 'buckie-
berries' to decorate the church at harvest-time. She knew every turn
and twist of the road up there, every field gate, every crease and
dimple in the hills, the bit of broken wall where the wild valerian
grew. She used to love it all, but now she hated it. She would never go
up there again on a summer evening and watch the boats come and go
on the Lough. There was a heathery field there with rocks pushing
through the grass, and tall bracken, and whins that were soaked
through and through with sunshine. Once on a June afternoon she
had been there... She remembered the gulls crying overhead. She
remembered her lover's kisses on her mouth.

Suddenly something in her heart seemed to break, and she slipped
down on her knees and hid her face in Mary's lap... There was pain in
those tears...

10

The evening light falling over the hills and the grey-green fields,
was the colour of mother-of-pearl – gentle and pale, and veined
with dim blue markings. The wind in the poplars turned the leaves
back, showing the faint, silver underside and setting free the faint,
silver voices, as Mary came up the loanin' from Jinanna's cottage. She
was dressed for a journey and carried a small bundle in her hand. She
was on her way to the Lindens to take care of the children while her
mistress went for a couple of week's holiday. She stood for a minute

looking up and down the Belfast road. Her manner seemed to betray a certain amount of indecision. Then she turned quickly and walked back to the village.

She hurried on until she came to an open door half-way up Gape Row. She stood on the step and called "Ann, Ann," in low, urgent tones. Someone pushed back a chair inside.

"I'm just off," she began, as Ann came towards her, 'come on out here to the street for a minute. I want to speak till you.' They moved away from the door.

"For the love of goodness," said Mary speaking imperatively in spite of the nervous light in her eyes, 'will you go down and see Jinanna. She has me tormented and bothered out of my life about seein' you, and when I run in a minute or two ago to say good-bye, here wasn't she at it again as hard as ever, beggin' and prayin' me for all the sakes to get you to call in. I made your excuse as well as I could – I said you were workin' late and one thing or another – but she's that set on it I could do nothing with her. She got me to promise to come back and see you, and that's what has me here this minute. The mistress will think I'm dead.'

"I can't leave granny," said Ann shortly.

"You can leave your granny rightly! Sure what would ail you? Mamma and Mrs Gillespie and the rest of them are never done runnin' in and out, and don't you leave her every day of your life?"

"Aye, but she expects me to stay with her in the evenin'."

"Mind you, Ann, thon wee crathur's near past herself," said Mary earnestly, 'it's my belief she'll not be a crack alive. And whatever the sense of it she's taken a great fancy till you. They say people takes queer notions before their latter end. If anything happened her and you'd never went in, it would be on your mind till eternity. I'd be far aisier and me at the Lindens if you'd promised me for till go some of these evenin's.'

"Well, maybe, I'll see about it," said Ann grudgingly.

"Man, that'll be grand! I'll take peace to myself now. I doubt she'll not be here when I come back. 'Au revoir', Ann. It'll not be long afore I'm home." She waved her hand airily and ran down the road.

Jinanna was not a favourite in the village. She was socially unimportant for she gave no news and asked for none, and such people are invariably disapproved of in Gape Row. Mrs Murphy had often been heard to thank the Lord that never in the whole seed, breed and generation of the McSpeddans, or even in the inferior family into which she married, had there been one who could scrape money off stones like that wee widda. But from the moment she slipped down at the pump in a dead faint, the neighbours nursed her day and night, after the marvellous manner of the poor.

They brought her food which she could not eat and strong tea which she could not drink, and they would have entertained her with cheerful gossip had she cared to listen to it. But it was regarded as the one entirely hopeless feature of her case, that she could hear unmoved, how many blankets the sergeant's wife had spread out on the hedge last monday to dry, or that Minnie Sloan was after Dicky McKibben, and her cross-eyed and ten years older nor him, and his mother threatening to take the tongs to her if he brought her home. If the worst came to the worst, they sat on the edge of her bed in twos and threes and assured her she was the picture of death.

Jinanna, although immensely grateful for the care that was lavished on her, was true to the habit of years, and lay silent for most of the time. Sometimes she said "I'm that thankful to you!" in fervent tones, or 'I'm givin' you the quare bother and I'm sorry at it,' but even those first evenings when she was too weak for speech, her eyes followed Ann with a special look in their tired depths. Ann would call in on her way home from her work, and nearly always she had a little present for her, jelly or fruit, or a pretty handkerchief out of the big drapery window at the Arches. Once it was a bottle of cheap scent, and Jinanna was so pleased that she kept it for years on her bedroom mantelpiece without opening it. Then quite suddenly Ann's visits ceased altogether.

A couple of evenings after Mary left, Mrs Murphy was sitting alone by the fire in Jinanna's kitchen. She peeped in through the open door of the room once or twice. The invalid was fast asleep. She put coal on the fire noiselessly and swept the hearth. Then she looked round for a newspaper or a bit of reading on the shelves. But there was nothing of the kind. She was bored and impatient. What on earth was keeping Mrs Gillespie? She should have been here half an hour ago, and her waiting to go home to give the children their porridge. Bad wind to her! She rose and slipped to the door to see if she was coming down the loanin' and when she opened it, instead of Eliza, Ann was standing on the step.

"The Lord save us and bless us!" remarked Mrs Murphy, in more or less subdued tones.

"I turned Mrs Gillespie at the head of the loanin'," said Ann stiffly. "She said she'd be down about nine."

"And you're for stayin' here? That'll do the best; I heard her askin'
for you more nor wonct. I'll just run on home now for the childer will
be dyin' for their stir-about. I'm right and glad you come."

Ann moved past her into the kitchen. Mrs Murphy would have
liked to continue the low-toned conversation had she got encouragement. She pointed out a bowl which was filled with milk, and the little
bottle of whiskey in a shady corner behind the flower-pot in the
window. "Mind and give her a sup when she wakes," she whispered.

"Well, after that!" she muttered, as she hurried up the loanin',
'after that!'

Ann slipped into the room, and sat down beside the bed. Jinanna
was still asleep, and even in her sleep, her face had a strange,
quenched look, as if long ago someone had given her a dreadful blow
and she had never got over it. After a little she opened her eyes.

"Och, Ann is it you," she said, 'I'm that glad to see you. Sure I had
the lovely dream! I dreamed I was a wee girl again up on the Heathery
Hill, and my mother was learnin' me to milk the spotty cow. I could
hear her voice as clear as a bell, 'aisy now, lady! chay, lady!' and her
soothin' and talkin' to the cow. Och, dear-a-dear the way the time goes
round! Sure she's dead this many a year and I'm near forty-two.'

"Don't talk," said Ann.

"Talk? I be to talk! It'll do me good, child dear. Do you know I've
had a great mind to talk to you since that evenin' you spoke to me, and
you goin' along the road with Mary. One time not long after that, I
met you by your lone, and I could have found it in my heart to stop for
a bit of crack – but I didn't like – I'd got that odd..."

"I'm sorry," Ann forced herself to say. 'I didn't know.'

"Sure you'd never think, dear. There's nobody would have thought
of stoppin' to speak to the like of me. Ann, I've been lyin' here
thinkin' of old times – old, old times – and do you know – I'd like to
tell you what it was that made me into the odd, withered wee bein' I
am. I'd the queer trouble in my time, och dear but I had!"

Ann had sternly repressed all outward tokens of her own sorrow,
except that one night under the sally trees at the head of the garden
with Mary. And now she feared to meet the surge of emotion which
she felt lay behind the tragedy in Jinanna's face.

"Wait till I get you a wee drop of whiskey and milk," she said. 'Mrs
Murphy told me to give it to you.'

She went into the kitchen and came back with a small cup in her
hand.

"Maybe you'll go to sleep again when you've drunk this," she said hopefully.

Jinanna shook her head. "Sure there'll be plenty of time for sleepin' in the grave! I'm somehow or other on for talkin' this evenin'. I think it would do me good." She drank the milk slowly and leaned back on the pillow Ann had placed under her head.

"Rest a wee while, now," urged Ann.

"I will, dear, to please you. And then I'll tell you what happened me long ago. Many a time I wonder how I come through it all."

Ann looked straight before her, through the open door into the bare little kitchen. A pint tin on the dresser caught the gleam of the fire-light. Her eyes were fixed on it. Her face was cold and set.

"There's things you never forget," murmured Jinanna, 'you never forget – no matter how long you live – no matter what happens... I was nineteen – and Jimmy Murdock, he was twenty-two, and we were walkin'. My father wanted me to marry a man of the name of McKinstrey that lived at the foot of the hill. He had lashins and lavins of money, and his land marched ours, but sure he was an old man with a baird on him and he scarred the heart out of me. I couldn't have married him, not if I'd been hung for it! The worst of it was my father and Jimmy couldn't agree. When he'd come in to see me, they'd have a crack together and they'd be sure to fall out. My father was set for aggravatin' him, and he was red-headed and aisy riz in the temper. They'd start and argufy over a heifer maybe, or a ploughin'-match, and Jimmy, the foolish boy, had a dread on him lettin' the old father get the better of him. I couldn't abear to hear them, and I used to slip out to the fort behind the house, and after a bit he'd follow me, and he'd promise and promise never to let another word cross his lips, but what was agreeable. And neither he would, maybe, for a wee bit. It was spring then, and we had promised other to get married in harvest...'

She paused for a moment or two. Ann's face grew more rigid and she turned away her eyes from the shining tin on the dresser, as if its brightness hurt them. There was an old, faded picture hanging on the wall below Jinanna's bed. A golden-haired lady, in a white frilly Victorian dress, knelt beside a chair on which a pale little girl sat. The words below it were, "My darling is better." Ann looked at it for a long time before she knew what it meant. She was dreading Jinanna's next words.

Presently the weak little thread of a voice took up the story and went on. "We were terrible busy that year, and I mind – och, oh! – I mind the way I used to sit up at night to sew at my wedding clothes. I had a quare lot of nice wee things gathered – I was always terrible fond of nice clothes. And one sunday evenin' I come in from the byre with two cans of sweet milk in my hands, and there was Jimmy and my father tearin' away at each other in the kitchen like mad. My father was standin' with his back to the dresser, and his face was like the livin' coal. Before I knew what had happened he had ordered Jimmy out of the house and told him never to come back, and he just turned in a rage and went... I dropped the cans and ran after him, but maybe he never heard me – sure maybe he thought I sided with my father. I went the length of the potato field and watched him go down the road – he never looked back – he was that headstrong – and then I turned and came home all my lone, and the heart that dead and heavy in me! Och annee, annee!"

Jinanna wiped away a tear or two with her thin fingers. She was too weak to cry. Ann tried to speak but could not. Her lips were dry, and pressed tightly together.

"There was no time for cryin' and lamentin' about our place," Jinanna went on. 'I was busy from mornin' till night, with the calves and the fowl outside, and the bakin' and lookin' after things in the house, and my mother not at herself for many a year before that again. But sometimes when I'd open the door on a warm summer mornin' and the shadows of the bour trees would be tremblin' and movin' round the house like livin' things – something would rise in my heart, and I'd nearly cry out with the pain... You're quare and aisy hurted at nineteen... Long after that I thought maybe it might have been as hard on him as it was on me... I used to cry at night... I suppose one must aye love somebody...'

"Did he ever come?" Ann asked huskily.

"No, dear, he never come back. I never seen him again. He went up the country somewhere, and married a woman out of Scotland that had a power of money. So I heerd tell."

A woman out of Scotland. Ann rose to her feet. She could not bear another word.

"Mrs Murphy will be queer and angry if I let you hurt yourself?" she said hurriedly. 'Lie quiet and rest. Would you like another wee sup of milk?'

"I want for nothing, daughter. Sit down, sure it's doin' me good already to talk to you. Och, don't go away, Ann. I'll be queerly put about if you go away." She put out her hand and caught her skirt. There was a wet gleam in her eyes. Ann sat down reluctantly.

"Where's this I was? Oh, aye! That summer – Ann, I never give up hope, not for a long while. I used to watch for him. I thought he'd be sure to come back at the last. Every mornin' I'd say to myself, 'God knows he might be here the day!' and at night I'd think: 'In the goodness of God he might be here the morra. I'll not let myself cry the night.' I got a fashion for droppin' my work in the evenin' and runnin' up to the fort, and watchin' down the road for him. Sometimes I thought I'd find him there in the fort, waitin' on me. He might have been backward about comin' up to the house, after him leavin' me without a word. Och, but I'd have been heart-glad if he'd have been there! I think the joy would have turned my head...

And then one day, about a year after that, I was feedin' the young turkeys in the yard, and I looked up and there was Molly, the tin woman, comin' in at the gate. You'd hardly mind her, but she used to go about the country, sellin' tins. She'd have them hangin' all over her on wires, dozens of them, and if the sun was shinin' on her, she'd near dazzle your eyesight. I mind as if it was yesterday, the way she stood there inside the gate, lookin' about her. She was a thin, long, harrow of a woman, and she used to gather up all the news of the country and carry it from one house to another. There was them that was glad to see her for what she could tell them. Well, she come over and spoke to me, and looked at the turkeys, and I said she be to come in and rest herself, and I'd make her a cup of tea. She said she'd be glad to sit down off her feet, for she'd walked the whole road from Mrs Murdock's beyant on the other side of the hill, and she was brave and tired. 'They're in great heart over there at the news,' says she. 'What news?' sez I. 'The news from up the country,' sez she. 'Sure the son that went away a while back has made a terrible grand match of it and has got himself married on a woman out of Scotland, that has a power of money, and a farm of land left her.' Och, Ann dear!... Everything in the yard went round and round me like a whirligig, and I stooped down over the wee turkeys and never let on me. 'They're in queer delight, the more they never seen the woman herself,' sez Molly, 'they have her picture framed, and it hangin' on the wall. I would take her to be a brave age too. She's a stout lump of a woman, and the mouth on her a bit tight for my taste. But they're queer and well pleased for all that.' I brought her in and made her a cup of tea. I thought she'd never go. I thought she'd never quit talkin'. The noise of her voice was in my

ears for days... At last she went away. I let her out by the wee gate at
the side of the house. I mind to this day the jing-jangle of the tins on
her back, and her hurrying down the hill... Well, there'd be no call to
be watchin' down the road any more. I thought he must have forgot
me queer and quick – and more times I thought he hadn't forgot at all,
but was afeerd to come back. But it was all over now. After that I used
to take a tremblin' from head to foot when I seen Molly, the tin
woman, comin' over the hill or heard the jingle of her tins."

Ann had been carried away in spite of herself. She put out her hand
and touched Jinanna's arm with a swift fleeting little gesture. "It
wasn't fair," she said between her clenched teeth, 'it wasn't fair.'

"Och, dear, aye, sure that's the way we be thinkin' when we're
young. We'd like to have the sun shining on us all the time. But we
learn different, Ann dear, we learn queer and different. After a wheen
of years my father and mother died, and then my brother took a notion
of marryin'. He was a hard man like my father, only silenter, and there
was no company in him. I wasn't needed there any more, and John he
had been botherin' me for a brave while, so I just went and took him.
He had a wee farm over by Ballymascrawn, but it wasn't nice, rich,
kindly land like ours, and somehow or another we didn't do well. John
wasn't what you'd call a pushin' body, and when I'd get a lock of
money gathered up from fowl or that, it would get a scattermint before
long. He hadn't the best of health, the crathur! We got out of the land
before long, and went into the town and he wrought on the Island. But
I fretted after the quietness of the fields and the room there was about
me everywhere, and I said to him, 'I'd rather die on a ditch out yonder
than live in the best of a house here.' And so I would. You think long
all the time in the town, and sure here you'd never be thinkin' long
and the young things growin' round you in the fields. After a while we
flitted out here, and then the child came – a wee girl- and we were
content beyond all. We hadn't much to spare, but sure what about
that! She was only three years old when the black measles came into
the village and she took them, and they went in on her inwardly and
she died." Jinanna drew a long, sobbing breath. Ann put out her
hand, and let it rest gently on her arm.

"Oh, poor Jinanna," she whispered.

"Aye, dear, it was queer and hard! But sure she's better done for,
where she is. One night, a couple of years ago I was down in Ginger
Street lookin' for an oul' skirt, and I come on that picture there
fornenst you. I couldn't afford it by rights, but I just had to get it, and

the woman behind the counter threw something off the price for me. It was a wee second-handed shop, and I'd been dealin' with her for years. I carried it home and hung it there below the bed. I was queer and proud of it. It makes me think of my own wee girl. It's the very livin' image of her. And isn't that the lovely lookin' lady kneelin' there beside her? Hasn't she the lovely yellow head of hair?"

Jinanna lay in silence for a few minutes looking at the picture with a pleased, wistful expression on her face. The grey shadows of the twilight were creeping into the room, darkening round the mother and child. Ann's thought flew back to her own childhood, and the mother who had died so long ago. This golden-haired woman made her think of her. But her mother's hair had been black. She remembered how she had let it down one night at the kitchen fire, and it had fallen to her waist in great heavy masses. And her eyes had been blue – deep Irish blue. She was beautiful but her beauty had only brought her sorrow. "I wish she had lived," Ann thought.

"If the wee girl hadn't died on me I'd have counted my troubles light," murmured Jinanna.

"It's been the queer hard world to you, so it has," said Ann.

"Aye, dear, but sure we can't choose our lot. It's all sent us for our good. Poor John, I think it come heavier on him than on me – and the next harvest he took a sevendible bad cold, and him workin' early and late in the corn. I couldn't get him to rest. He wouldn't take peace to himself. He persevered on with that cold till he got it right and bad on him, and it turned to consumption in the end. Poor John, he didn't last long after that."

"You were left very lonesome," said Ann gently. She tried to think of a more sympathetic speech, but could not.

"You might say I was! It's an awful thing to have nobody aback of you, Ann – to come into an empty house every day of your life. But I always had my fill of work, thank God! Poor John, he was the best-hearted crathur, but he wasn't cute and people got the better of him. We were behind in the shop when he died," Jinanna's voice sank very low, 'and he had borrowed money at odd times from a cousin of his that has a good farm, over beyant, on the side of the hill. You heard tell many a time of Break-o'-day Andy Sloan. He had a fashion of risin' extra early in the mornin' to get the work pushed on. That's how he come by the name, and he's a hard, hasky man, forby. And mind you, he had neither chick nor child to come after him, and them that will get the money will not think near as much of it as he done. A narrow gatherin' gets a wide scatterin', they say. Well, the night John was buried, Break-o'-day Andy come down here and sez he, 'What about that money he borryed from me? I suppose I'll be done out of that, too. That's my thanks for keepin' him and you out of the workhouse!' I told him I'd pay him the fifty pounds he owed him, if he'd give me time, and he said he hoped he'd have his health till *that* happened. And when he was just going out at the door, what do you think he turned and said to me? 'Don't forget about the interest?' sez he, and I said neither I would, and he went away more contented like. I thought he mightn't have been so hard. After he'd went out, I sat down at the fire by my lone and had a queer meal of cryin' I can tell you.'

"Don't talk any more for a wee while," said Ann urgently. 'Take a wee bit of a rest, or you'll be bad again. I'm that sorry for you! I am indeed!'

But Jinanna could not rest. Ann saw with concern, a strange excitement growing in her face. Her cheeks flushed, and her eyes grew large and bright.

"I'll fix the pillows more comfortable for you," she said, in real alarm, 'and maybe you'll get a wee doze.'

"Doze!" repeated Jinanna scornfully, raising her head, and looking flushed and well. 'Doze! I'd like to see me!' She paused for a moment and drew a long breath. 'I tell you I've done it! I've paid him! I've wrought and slaved and starved, and gathered it up unbeknownst to anybody! Every penny, Ann!'

"What!" exclaimed Ann incredulously, 'you couldn't have done it, surely?'

"I have indeed! I've went to bed hungry many a night, and been starved with the cold when firin' was dear, and sure my clothes are a parable to the world, they're that patched and darned! Is it any wonder the neighbours call me near?" A sob came into her voice in spite of its triumph. 'They weren't far wrong when they said I was an old miser, and do you know, I've heard the very childer passin' remarks on me goin' by. Look at the old shoes I walked the world in, year in, year out! Mind you, Ann, when I was young, I always kept myself nice and fly. Sometimes yet I find myself walkin' up and down the Newtownards Road, lookin' at the shop windows, and pickin' out the fancy-lookin' articles I'd buy if I had the money. It was a quare sin for me! But I've done it, Ann, I've done it!' Her voice rose and swelled with new strength and vigour. 'I paid him the last farden the week before I took bad and there's nobody can say a word agin John or me now.'

"I don't know how you done it," said Ann stupidly. 'It's the greatest wonder I ever heard of. It's queer and grand, and he was a bad old man that took it off you. Poor Jinanna, but you've had a hard life!'

"What about it all now!" exclaimed Jinanna recklessly, as she pushed the damp hair off her forehead. 'What about it all now, when it's over and done with, and I owe nothing to nobody and can take ease and peace to myself for the rest of my days. And mind you, Andy was queerly took aback when I brought him the money. It would have done your heart good to see the look on his face! He never thought to get it.' She laughed weakly, and lay back on her pillows.

"Och, I wish you had told me before. Sure it would have eased your mind to have told somebody. The power of trouble you've come through!"

"Daughter, dear, I couldn't have told you – not till this night. I couldn't have told the sons of man. Do you mind the time when I was bad last winter, the more I never went to bed, but sat at the fire the whole time? His reverence was comin' back and forrad constant to see me – sure the road never cooled with him comin' to see me. And many a time I had it on my tongue to tell him. I knew he'd have the queer feeling for me. But I never did. I had to keep myself hard and close till it was done."

She leaned back on her pillows exhausted. The colour faded from her face, the life ebbed from her voice. "The worst of it was the lonesome house, and me comin' back to it in the evenin's, and sorra a one to say 'you're there!' If the wee girl had lived! I had the terrible bad luck, Ann. I lost everything – Jimmy, my father and mother, and then John and the child. But God knows best..."

Ann bent over her, dry-eyed. Her own lost happiness had never seemed so dear and beautiful as at that moment. She took hold of both her frail little hands and held them close.

"There's them that looks to have all they want. But I lost everything," repeated Jinanna dreamily.

"It's not fair," murmured Ann. 'Oh, it's not fair! To suffer – like that!'

Jinanna raised her eyes for a moment. A faint smile touched her lips. "They say there's many mansions," she whispered.

11

"She's not making much of it," said the doctor gravely. "She is not."

"The house is abominably damp, but it would kill her to be moved at present. Anything likely to be vacant in Gape Row?"

Mrs Murphy ran mentally up and down the street. "Sure, there's old Pat McGrath, and isn't he always threatenin' to go and end his days with the married daughter that lives in a big way in the County Cork, and drives her own machine? If he would take a notion of goin' soon, she could just slip in there, and a right, warm, wee house it is. And she would be next door to me, and I could do her bits of turns for her," she ended triumphantly.

"The very thing!" said the doctor heartily.

Ann had told Mrs Murphy as much as she thought necessary of Jinanna's story, and she in turn had communicated the facts to a few of the neighbours over a cup of tea.

"And that's the wee woman we called a skinflint and a miser," she wound up, 'we'll get many a surprise on the Resurrection morn, mind I'm tellin' you!'

"Many a time you heard me sayin' what a widda woman comes through, and you never heeded me," said Mrs Gillespie in mournful tones.

"But nobody ever heard her yammer, and the worst of you is, you never quit," replied Mrs Murphy frankly. 'You'll not die aknownt, Eliza. But here was this poor wee bein' starvin' herself to death to pay that old ruffian on the hill and us thinkin' she was pilin' the money by her. Bedad, it's little ye know! As long as God spares me, I'll never say a word agin a livin' sinner again.'

"I've passed the remark to Billy before now, that if I had what she could spare, I could do queer and well for him and the childer," said Mrs Morrow, 'dear-a-dear! It's little I thought. I can har'ly believe it yet.'

"Aye, indeed! It's like a leaf out of a book."

"I seen her many a mornin' last winter goin' to her work with har'ly a shoe to her foot, and the weather fit to freeze fairies," continued Mrs Morrow remorsefully, 'poor crathur! No wonder she's been at death's door. I'll wash her bits of things this week, Mrs Murphy.'

"Indeed you'll do no such thing, and you with two childer not able to travel the floor."

"Sure it's when they begin to travel they're the heartscald," remarked Mrs Gillespie.

"They're not a bit of trouble at all," said Mrs Morrow proudly, and she held her baby's pink cheek close against her own, 'and poor Jinanna lost her own wee one too, the crathur.'

"She's not long for this world at any rate," said Mrs Gillespie.

"How do you know, Eliza?" asked Mrs Murphy tartly.

"Well, if ever I seen death in any wuman's face I seen it in hers."

"You're ravin'! She'll be rightly yet. But for mercy's sake don't you go near her with your die-a-loney face, for it would near kill anybody to look at you. We'll pull her round. She *be* to get better, she *be* to mend," said Mrs Murphy firmly, and from that hour the remorseful kindness of Gape Row washed like a tide round Jinanna's little cottage.

"Has Pat any notion of flittin' out of here?" said Mrs Murphy to Sammy Soretoes a day or two afterwards.

"Noan whatever."

"The creature would be better with his own."

"Maybe he would and maybe he wouldn't. What do you want Pat away for?"

"Did anybody ever hear such a man?" exclaimed Mrs Murphy, turning her eyes up to the ceiling, 'dear knows I'd be quarely put about if I heard he was goin', and him the kindliest old crathur you'd meet in a day's walkin'.'

"Well, you may take peace to yourself, then. Pat's not the sort that's aisy lifted."

"Feth, no!" She turned and looked thoughtfully into the fire, 'and where under the sun am I to get a warm wee corner for Jinanna?' she asked herself.

"I wouldn't be interferin' with the ways of providence if I was you," said Sammy quietly, across the hearth, 'but as long as you're above the sod, you'll hardly quit.'

"Sure man dear, I'm doin' nothing..."

"There's them that's deeper, I'll allow, for I can mostly tell when some new notion's workin' you."

"Quit, man! You're talkin' nonsense!" she interrupted hastily, 'it's a wonder but Mr McCready isn't here yet. I'm expectin' him down every minute.'

"It's time for me to be goin' then," said Sammy, 'for I'm not overly fond of that young man.'

"He's a queer fine fella, I think."

"Sure I know you do. My, but there's a terrible lot of changes about here since the time he left the country."

"There is that! And most of all, up at the farm, too."

"He should have come when the mother was alive," said Sammy, 'I never forgive him for it. She used to talk by the hour about him when I'd drop in for a crack in the heel of the evenin'. She was aye lookin' for him comin' home. I think she leaned most to him because he had been that long away. I always blamed him heavy for it. My, but Michael was the good son to her.'

"He was that! But who'd have thought she'd have went that sudden at the last, and her a young woman, you might say?"

"I mind her goin' up the hill as light and quick on her foot as a bird," said Sammy thoughtfully; 'that was the year she was married. She never had much health after that. It's a brave while back now – a brave while back!'

"Aye, dear, aye! They say this man has a terrible lot of money..."

"I don't care what he has," said Sammy, rising and reaching for his sticks, 'he can come home now, and blow and blast about his money as much as he likes, but he didn't come when the mother was alive, and her thinkin' long for him the way she done. He'd never be the boy Michael is, not if he had the full of the Royal George.'

"Och, well, I wouldn't be that hard on him..."

"Sure I know you wouldn't. But what I say is he didn't come when he ought to have come," reiterated Sammy, going out into the dusk and closing the door behind him.

"As sharp as a briar," soliloquised Mrs Murphy in the solitude of the empty kitchen, 'he'd near read your very thoughts, that old fella! Where in goodness' name am I to find a wee spot for Jinanna?'

But to everyone's surprise, Pat McGrath went away suddenly after all. Each spring since his wife died he had been heard to say: "I'll be lavin' this when the harvest's in," and later in the year, 'I'll hardly get away now afore Apryle,' but both he and Gape Row were not a little startled when he received a letter one morning from his married daughter saying she had come as far as Dublin to meet him, and meant to wait there until he joined her. Pat looked round the little kitchen helplessly, and sighed. He would have to go now. But not even the grand house in the County Cork would make up to him for the old dresser, with its chipped and blackened delph, and the low chair in the corner where herself used to sit, patching and mending for the children after dark. He hated to leave these things. 'God be with the old times!' he murmured – he was from 'up the country,' and had up the country ways – and then he rose and went out into the sunshine shakily, to look for a young Murphy to answer the letter for him. Before the week was out he had gone, and everyone said the village was a colder place without him.

"You done that well!" said Sammy severely to Mrs Murphy, 'my, but you did! You might have let the old man die in peace in the house he lived in this fifty year and more. I knowed rightly what you were up to.'

"Oh, murder!" exclaimed Mrs Murphy, who was secretly horrified at the speed with which Pat left, after she had thought of his house for Jinanna. 'I had nothing whatsomever to do with it. Why Sammy dear, I'm that sorry about poor Pat. I just couldn't tell you.'

"You grudged him his house and room, and the dear only knows what else you done. Nobody could get it out of my head, that if it hadn't been for you he'd be sittin' here yet, and him as content as you like, the more he was by his lone. I wouldn't put it past you to have wrote to the daughter in Cork, and got her to send him that sharp bit of a letter bidding him come to her or stay for good."

"May I drop dead before I reach the pump!" wailed Mrs Murphy, who had stopped for a moment at his door, with the cans in her hand. 'May I never stir hand nor foot again if ever I done the like! Why, I'm as innocent as that child. Sure I didn't expect he would go this dear knows the time. I'm terrible put about, so I am.'

"Chickens come home," continued Sammy moodily, 'and them that lives longest 'll see the most.'

"I'm heart sorry I ever passed the remark to you at all. Sure all I said was that if he happened to go, the house would be the very ticket for her, and the doctor never done lamentin' about the fusted wee hole she's in, and you mind I said I hoped in my heart he would live and die where he was, for I wouldn't like to see him shifted at his time of day. That's the goodnesses truth."

"You grudged the man his house," said Sammy obstinately, 'you may argue till you're black in the face, but you know rightly you done it. There's them it's not lucky to have their ill-will and it's my belief you riz him.'

"Oh, murder, murder!" cried Mrs Murphy tearfully, 'and me decent and respectable come, and rared the way noan of yous was rared! Me unlucky! I never heard the like. You'll know the rights of me on the Resurrection morn, Sammy Soretoes. Unlucky I may be, but I'm not that unlucky that my feet had to be tied up under me in bundles and rags, and I'm not cripplin' along to my place of worship every sunday on two staves, like them that I could name, for doin' what, the Lord only knows, but it wasn't for building churches any way.' And she took up her cans and resumed her interrupted journey to the pump with tearful dignity.

The day before Pat left she had taken the precaution of sending a message to Red Abel the agent. "Billy will see Red Abel on friday in the market," she said to Mrs Morrow; 'tell him to say I sent him word he is to keep the house for a particular friend of mine, and tell him Pat will lave the key with me.' And having settled the matter to her satisfaction, she turned and hurried away.

But on that friday afternoon Mrs Morrow might have been seen walking down the street in an agitated manner, which did not altogether arise from the fact that she was carrying two children in her arms, and that three more were eddying round her skirts. She had calamitous news for Mrs Murphy. Red Abel had sent her a bald message to say the house was already let.

"What?" exclaimed Mrs Murphy incredulously. 'What?'

"That's the truth! Billy tried to put in a word for Jinanna, but he cut him off very short. And he said the name of the new tenant was a secret for the present."

"A secret?" repeated Mrs Murphy stupidly, 'a secret!'

"That's the very word he said."

"Lord bless us and save us! That's over all! A secret! The next time I take the light from his door ther'll be two moons in the sky. The impitent scut! A secret!" And she screwed up her eyes and stared intently before her as if to see through it.

"It's a bit hard, and her so bad. I bid Billy tell him about her, but he never let on he heard him."

"I never was so affronted in all my livin' life," declared Mrs Murphy angrily, 'if he was a bit nearer hand he'd soon get the weight of my tongue on him, but how is a body to get at him, and him cocked up there on the top of the hill? A secret! my alive!'

"I must run back, for I left the griddle on the fire," and Mrs Morrow engineered her family through the door with great skill.

Mrs Murphy took some plates down from the dresser and laid them mechanically on the table. She had been preparing the dinner when Mrs Morrow came in, and she stood in the middle of the floor, rapt in thought for a couple of minutes after she went out.

But the children would soon be in from school, and would be looking for something to eat. She took a small, black-handled fork from a drawer in the dresser, and lifting the lid of a pot which was boiling merrily on the fire, stuck it lightly and deftly into a potato.

"They're hardly done to the heart yet," she murmured, 'agin I have the bacon fried, they'll be ready.' She lifted the frying-pan down from a nail on the wall and laid it on the hob. But her thoughts were far away.

She was used to authority. She had boasted openly that Red Abel would refuse her nothing, and in reply to her simple demand for the house, he had sent her a refusal – and a refusal that had neither a why or a wherefore attached to it to soften its curt edges. The man must be clean mad. If he thought she was going to lie down under such treatment she would show him something different. Providence intended that wee house for Jinanna and Jinanna would get it, should she have to fight rings round with Red Abel and all belonging to him for it. But how was she to get at him? He lived far away on the top of the steepest hill in the neighbourhood, and she was not as good at the walking as she had been. She would try to find the new tenant, and she would wrest the cottage from him by fair means or by foul. Only in this way, she felt, could her dignity be retrieved in the eyes of the world. Jinanna would then be safe and sheltered under her wing for the rest of her days, and she would have succeeded in her efforts to turn a pin in the unsuspecting nose of Red Abel. If the first thought gave her pleasure, the second was sheer intoxication.

She was often heard to say in those days that her head was more full than it could hold, and that it would be a world's wonder if it didn't turn before all was over. It was really what made her happiest. She had so many people on her mind – old Ann, weak and ailing and in forlorn unhappiness, who expected her to sit and listen from morning till night, while she called heaven and earth to witness that *she* had always said what the Darragh's were; young Ann going in and out to work with the same proud bearing as her mother in the same tragic circumstances more than twenty years before; Jinanna in anxiety about her future, and lastly her own little Bella, who had burnt her foot severely a week ago, and was still in bed.

Mrs Murphy grew tired and a trifle cross.

"You're brave and fat on it, at any rate," said Sammy consolingly, when she complained, 'and cheerful too, I'll allow,' he added, thinking she needed a word of encouragement for once.

"Feth, Sammy, you'll not find me yammerin' no matter how it goes, and me heart-scalded more than most," she answered, with a child's eager pleasure in being praised. 'Do you know what does me good if I'm in bad heart? You'll hardly believe me, but it's Gillespie herself! As sure as you're livin'! The sight of that woman's thrawn face somehow lifts me. Of all the yammerin' crathurs, did you ever know the like? It's yammer, yammer, yammer with her from mornin' till night, and mind you Sammy, she'd ate more at one meal than I'd ate in a week – and there's not a crow's fill on her. She has the right health by me, for sure I never know but I might be in my coffin before night. But yammer, Sammy, I will not. Gillespie has me cured.'

She had her moments of relaxation, however. Her mind often turned to Michael's brother. The thought of him fluttered her strangely. He had brought a touch of excitement into the cramped life of the village. If only Tam had been like him they might have gone away long ago when they were young, and have made a fortune too. She had often wanted to go. But Tam did not care for these things. He was content to hang over a shovel on the road all his days. She was different of course, for she was a McSpeddan born. All the McSpeddans had a rise in them, and Mrs Murphy admired nothing so much in any family or individual as this strange, yeast-like quality.

Tam had yearned secretly and silently for books, education, college. But his wife did not know this and he would have been afraid to tell her. It was the pageantry of life that appealed to her. In dreams she saw herself mingling with the gaily-dressed throng, or driving on her own outside car, with her own servant boy sitting in the dickey. At other times she was sailing magnificently up the aisle of the church, the eyes of the entire congregartion fixed on her clothes. If only Tam had been different, all this might easily have come to pass. Her mind roamed back to the time when Michael's uncle went away. She remembered a dance that was given for him in McKinstrey's barn, the night before he sailed. She had been there in a white muslin dress, with a pink bow at her neck and a waist not more than twenty-two inches. It did not take her long to build up a romance on the history of that half-forgotten gathering. He had danced with her several times, had squeezed her hand, and now that she came to think of it, had muttered something behind her all the road down the ladder when the dance was over. It might have been as sweet as you like, but she had paid no heed whatsoever, for with him having a fish's throat, it wasn't altogether aisy to lift what he said. And forby that, how was she to know he would come home at the heels of the hunt, a rich man? She asked the question with indignation. Dear save us! She had missed her foot again.

She went up and down Gape Row, and back and forward for her goods to the shop at the Holywood Arches, which were incidentally neither arches nor in Holywood, but flat railway bridges spanning the road to the city; and everyone she met knew her to be a poor woman. What they did not know, and what she would have liked to tell them, was that she was the rich Mrs McCready, home on a visit from the United States of America, and worth a power of money – if she had not happened to be a born fool. This very day she might have been driving in her carriage, behind a pair of prancing steeds, instead of trudging, weary-footed along the dusty road. She saw the villagers flying helter-skelter to their doors to see her pass. She heard a burst of envy and admiration from every throat. Would she bow her head to the old friends and neighbours, or let on she had never seen them before? She could not make up her mind, but she saw with an inward eye, the stupefaction on Gillespie's face, and chuckled audibly.

And then the practical side of her nature would re-assert itself. These daydreams were at once a solace and an aggravation to her, but the future was filled with hope. Her mind turned feverishly to it. She would never be rich herself, but if all went well, she believed her daughter would. Andy John had taken a notion of her the first sunday evening they met. She had seen sparks in his eye before he left the house, and day and night she planned and plotted how to help on the match. She would never rest till they were married. Sometimes a vague fear overshadowed her, for Mary did not seem to have fallen in love as foolishly as one might have expected, seeing the man was made of money. But she would take him of course and be delighted to get him. The thought of her refusing him never seriously entered her mother's mind. She had meant to make a grand match herself in her own young day, but it had somehow fallen through. "And what man has *not* done, man may do," said Mrs Murphy in determined tones to the kitten for want of a better audience.

"Have you heard anything about the house next door?" asked Sammy, one morning at the pump.

"Don't bother me! If Fillmacool himself took it, I wouldn't turn my head to look at him."

"It's a wonder Tam never hears word of anything, and him constant on the road."

"My goodness alive, is that all you know!" cried Tam's wife with energy, 'sure he wouldn't raise his head to ask. That's the curious turn of him. Many's a time I tell him if I had his stand there on the road, I'd lift the queer lot. But he lifts nothing, God help him! Poor Pat, I wish he was back. He was the brave, quiet, ould crathur. I doubt he finds the County Cork odd by here.'

"I doubt he does."

"I seen John James Flanigan goin' by the day," said Mrs Gillespie, coming up with her cans, 'he might have knowed something. The father's land marches Red Abel's.'

"Oh my! And did you ask him?"

"I wasn't spakin' till him at all."

"Whatever Red Abel knows John James Flanigan knows," said Sammy decisively. 'Him and him's very great.'

"What kind of a fool are you to have missed such a chanst?" began Mrs Murphy impatiently, 'if it had a been me...'

"Would you have ripped it out of him, and him goin' by at the rate of a weddin' behid his da's mare?" asked Mrs Gillespie, sourly.

"Och, sure, I thought he was on his feet. Well, I needn't care, but there'll be Home Rulers, or Dippers, or the dear knows what landed on the top of us some of these days. Wait till you see!"

"I'm bad with the toothache and I was up the half of the night puttin' one combustible after another intil my mouth to deeve the pain," said Mrs Gillespie, 'it's a little odds to me who's comin' or goin'.'

"Keep up your heart," replied Mrs Murphy as she moved away, swaying between her heavy cans, 'it's a trouble you'll soon be redd of. Sure you've hardly an ould stump left in your head, woman dear.'

As she walked down the road with her husband's tea that afternoon, her air was unusually reflective. Rumour fleet-footed and variable as an April day, was in full possession, and more than once lately rumour had mentioned a certain unappropriated blessing of the name of

Miskimmins, for whom she had a special aversion. As she walked down the road she could not but think of the villainy of Red Abel.

Tam took the basket from her and sat down on the ditch below the hedge. Mrs Murphy, with her hand to her eyes, stood and looked across the country.

A little boy, his hands in his trouser pockets, his eyes intently fixed on the ground, wandered slowly backward and forward over a grass field. It was the field in which Michael's young cattle had been grazing that afternoon in June when Mary had come home wearing her new hat, and Michael came down to meet them in the lane. He was pushing about disconsolately with his bare little toes among the tufts of grass. He seemed to be in search of something.

Down on the road Mrs Murphy shaded her eyes with her hand and looked about her.

"Dear save us, Tam, is thon our wee Ned?" asked Mrs Murphy at length.

"He's been perusin' over that field for the last hour," answered Tam, 'and him by his lone, too.'

Ned's head was bent in search. Here in this very field, one day in early spring he had found a lark's nest tucked deftly into the track of a cow's foot. He had rushed home to tell Jimmy Forbes who wanted a young lark to bring up in a cage, and they had both hurried back to the field. But they did not discover the nest. They searched for many days, but some kind, invisible St Francis must have shaded their eyes, for they never found it. Even yet Ned sometimes wandered about the field, thinking to find at least the remnants of a lark's nest. It would have been some slight consolation for the violence of Jimmy's language when the subject came up.

"Well, of all the childer!" said Mrs Murphy, 'whistle on him, for dear sake, and give him a sup of your tay.'

At the sound of that whistle, Ned turned very quickly. He darted over a couple of fields and flung himself through a hole in the hedge. They watched him as he raced across the meadow towards the road.

"Of all the souple wee crathurs!" exclaimed his mother, 'och son dear, you'll have yourself kilt runnin'. Sure you're swatein' like the mischief!' And she wiped his damp, little forehead with her apron.

"I could run twict as hard!" panted Ned. Mrs Murphy opened the basket and gave him a well-buttered piece of soda-bread while Tam poured some tea into a mug. At that moment she thought of a pot of water she had left on the fire. She turned quickly to go. If she did not hurry it would have boiled over. Before she had taken half a dozen steps, a strange desire to ask Tam a question came into her mind. She had long ago given up trying to get sense out of him – much less to put any into him – but at that moment some evil spirit prompted her to make another effort.

"Tam," she said, turning back for a moment, 'did you happen to hear anybody drop a word about the house today?'

"What house?"

"What house do you think? The empty house, of course."

There was silence for a quarter of a minute. Tam seemed to think he had answered, or perhaps he forgot to answer.

"Look see," she persisted blandly, 'sure you might hear from somebody comin' or goin' along the road what noan of the rest of us would be likely to hear – who it is that Red Abel has give the house to – mightn't you now?'

"I might."

"Aye, that's what I say. Sure man..."

"Mamma, Jimmy Forbes called me a liar!"

"(I'll break his back for him, then, the young rascal!). Sure if you were like another man, you'd find out. Somebody be to know something. The next time you see anybody that lives near hand Red Abel's for the love of goodness send them down to me..."

"I had the lark's nest right enough at my very feet," interposed Ned, 'and Jimmy Forbes says he doesn't believe a word...'

"Hould your tongue, you impitent little divil, and let your mother spake for once. Here I am workin' and slavin' for you and the childer from mornin' till night, and you take no heed to the way I'm affronted, and put about over that house. I wonder at you, Tam Murphy. Sure any old villain might come in there beside us any day and you'd know nothing about it. That's what will happen yet – it'll be one of them old cut-throats out of the town and we'll be murdered in our beds as like as not. Boys! If I had a hoult of Red Abel."

"He went by the day at the Cross-roads," Tam murmured gently into his mug.

"What!" exclaimed Mrs Murphy. 'What! Red Abel went by! What did he say?'

Tam paused. "I don't mind," he said at length.

"Lord bless us! Didn't you ask him about the house?"

"I did not."

"Oh, murder!" cried Mrs Murphy, 'you ravin' lunatic! You fool of a man! Such-in-a-chance!'

There was a moment's tense silence. Ned leaned his little head against his father's arm and munched soda-bread. His eyes were following a flight of wild geese far away towards the horizon.

"Da", he said suddenly, 'what blue-ens the sky?'

"I've said it before, Tam Murphy, and I'll say it again," Mrs Murphy called witheringly over her shoulder, 'if you're a man, many a one the cat ate.'

"Da," said Ned, pulling at his sleeve, 'what blue-ens the sky?'

12

When Mrs Murphy came back to the house, she found the pot of water had boiled over, and the fire almost out. She drew a low chair closer to the hearth, and taking a handful of sticks from a bundle in the corner, sat down and broke them into small pieces which she pushed into the half-drowned embers. There was an unusually dark frown on her forehead.

"It's enough to set a saint mad!" she muttered, 'the Angel Gabriel couldn't work with that man!' She took down the bellows and blew the fire steadily. The kitten with subtle feminine intuition had retired hastily to the sofa on her entrance and lay watching her with green, half-opened eyes. When the fire had been persuaded to blaze again, she rose and hung the bellows on the wall. She felt uncomfortably warm after her exertions, and stood for a while with her arms crossed on the half-door, leaning out. The air blew soothingly against her forehead. Further down, old Ann was sitting in the sun, on the grass bank opposite her own door, with her grey woollen shawl drawn closely about her.

A little man with a large basket, heavily piled with delph, came along the road, into the village. He saw Mrs Murphy in her door and steered straight for her. He had sharp blue eyes, a thin red face and a thin red little nose. He went up and down the hills, supplying the country people with crockery, and according to them was 'a gatherer and bound to have money by him, the more he was a dacent ould crathur enough.' His greatest commercial asset was undoubtedly an unfailing urbanity of manner, which no amount of bargaining could ruffle.

"How are you, Mrs Murphy, dear?" he chirruped amiably, as he came towards her. 'Are you quite well the day? Is Mr Murphy quite well? Is Charlie quite well? Is Mary quite well and agreein' with the town? Is-'

"Look here, me fine fella!" interrupted Mrs Murphy, 'the half of the manners would do you when you come to my door and you an old torment paddlin' the roads and thievin' and roguin' the world with the price of the delph in your basket twict as high as Hoggses or McBurneys the oldest firrums in the lamps of Belfast, let alone the dacent shops on the Newtownards Road and your old jugs and mugs fallin' to pieces in people's hands, did you think we were all dead with your soft soap and your how are yous?'

"Lord bless us!" exclaimed the pedlar, staring at her, 'that's a salute and a half! What has you put about, woman dear? Who done it on you? – and you my best customer, and the one I think the most of from one end of the country till the other.'

"None of your blarneyin' for me," returned Mrs Murphy tartly, 'you'll not come as much speed as you think maybe. I don't want none of your old cracked china the day. So you may gwan wherever you were goin'.'

"Just as you please, Mrs Murphy dear, just as you please," said the pedlar, stooping to lift the basket which he had put down on the doorstep. 'Any word from that fine, handsome young son of yours in America lately?'

"Have you never sold them ones yet?" asked Mrs Murphy, pointing to the corner of the basket. There was a subtle change in her voice.

John Smith stooped down, and took out a cup which he held at arm's length for her inspection. It was ringed round with roses of a fervent pink.

"I could sell them every day in the week if I wanted to, but I've a notion for keepin' them in the corner of me basket for a wee while yet," he said significantly. 'I'll keep them there for a wee while yet, Mrs Murphy.'

"The people's not goin' to be robbed by the like of you," she answered crossly, 'sure man, you ask two prices for the laste thing. How you put the face on you! I wish you'd stop comin' to my door, pollutin' me with your old trash! I don't like them pink cups, I tell you. White china with a gold rim is the proper thing for company. Forby that, I've no money. It's the childer's boots I'm thinkin' of, and the soft weather near here.'

"Everybody had a great grah for them cups," returned John, 'I can hardly keep a hoult of them at all. Sure I'm in no hurry for the money, ma'am, dear.'

Mrs Murphy lifted her eyes and looked wistfully round her. She would not watch him settling the cup back into the basket.

"I mightn't be round this road again. We never know when our time will come," said the pedlar.

"It's that hard to keep them dry-foot!" murmured Mrs Murphy. 'Johnny's comin' thro' at the toes already, and wee Ned on the ground, I might say.'

"I'll bid you good evenin', Mrs Murphy, dear."

"When I sell the chickens, it's the childer's feet I'll be seein' to, man, dear. Them wee cups is the purtiest things my eyes has lighted on this many a year, but what call have I for grandeur of the kind and me with one foot in the grave, and goin' fast where nothing of the sort's required? I don't want them, John. But they're lovely, darlin' wee cups, I'll not deny it."

The pedlar lifted his basket on his arm. He was satisfied.

"What's your hurry?" she asked, 'come on in and have a cup of tay. You be to be dry walkin' the roads and it a warm day for the time of year.'

"Not the day, thank you, Mrs Murphy dear, not the day. I've a long piece to travel yet before the heel of the evenin'. It's quare and cold-lookin' that house beside you there empty so long. Who's comin' to it?"

"Is the man mad?" asked Mrs Murphy, addressing the poplars on the slope of the hill, 'is he clean away in the mind? Who's comin' to the house? My alive, man dear, that's a secret. A secret, mind you! That's the very word Red Abel sent me back, when I sent and told him who he was to give it till. It *had* been given, but *who* it was give till was a secret! What do you think of that? Mind you, I was surprised myself. I thought he knowed more. Such-in-a message till send me.'

"And can't you find out some other road?"

"Amn't I near heart-broke tryin' to find out. Nobody knows

nothing about it, as far as I can hear, and I'm too lusty to travel far meself. It might be the death of me."

"What about Betty-fly-around?"

Mrs Murphy's face lightened. "I never thought of her. Do you ever see her about the roads? There's not much misses her. She might have heard word."

"Feth, if there's anything to hear, she's heard it." answered the pedlar. 'I meet her many a time. I'll tell her you want to spake to her most particular.'

"Tell her," said Mrs Murphy urgently, 'tell her to come on for her life! Tell her I have a grand petticoat waitin' on her.'

"I will, that! Good-bye, ma'am. I'm proud to see you lookin' so young ..."

"Don't bother me! Bring a couple of mugs the next time you're by."

The pedlar had gone a few steps from the door, when she called suddenly. "I say – have you been up at Michael's lately? Did you hear the brother had come home from America – the rich man?"

John Smith turned and leaned his basket against the room window-sill.

"Aye," he answered laconically.

"They say he has a power of money. He come in for all when the uncle died a while back, there."

"Sure Marget was tellin' me the whole piece. She's ratherly put about."

"What's put her about?"

"Sure, she says, Michael was never done before he come home, makin' the terriblest preparations – you would think the Prince of Wales was for comin'! You wouldn't know the place. He has the house white-washed and every one of the out-houses, and he painted the very windys. Marget says they done his father before him, and they might have done him. And he's laid down a load of gravel on the avenue, and has the hedges nicely clipped. It's the changedest place! You wouldn't know it."

"I always thought it was a nice, kindly wee place, lyin' in to the side of the hill that comfortable-like."

"Well, I wish you seen it now. And she doesn't like this man that's come home at all. She allows he's ill to attend, and very close with the money."

"He's a terrible fine young fellow," said Mrs Murphy in her serious sunday voice, 'oh, terrible fine! Rich and grand you know, and used different to us. But she's a crabbit old crathur and always was. Michael's too aisy on her altogether.'

"I declare to goodness she kept him standin' there this last half-hour, and never bought a ha'porth," murmured old Ann from her nook under the high hawthorn hedge. 'If it had been me I'd have took a wee plate or something for shame's sake.' She watched the pedlar going from door to door, and heard him ask for each member of the household in his thin, high voice, with a healthy scorn. 'The right old lick!' she said, half-aloud. When he had come to the end of Gape Row he looked round and saw her, and even took a step in her direction, but she drew her shawl about her with such a defensive gesture and said 'Blethers and Nonsense!' so fiercely, that he turned and went down the road instead. That evening she told Ann exactly how much he had sold in the village and the price of each article, and how Mrs Gillespie had beaten him down in the matter of spotty bowls.

Mrs Murphy came to the door and looked up and down the street after he had gone. Ann was still sitting there. She came out a few steps and called to her.

"John Smith's just away by," Ann seemed to be half asleep, and did not answer. 'He has the loveliest set of china you ever seen in your life! Wee, low cups with pink roses runnin' round the lip, and a wheen of wee roses round the ear. I had a big notion of buying them.'

"I'm sure!" muttered Ann into her shawl, 'I seen what you bought.'

"It wasn't the want of money," continued Mrs Murphy airily, 'but the want of a quate place to keep them. The childer would have them destroyed on me. They're terrible like a set my Aunt Susanna Jane McSpeddan got when she was married, and went on a weddin' trip to Warrenpoint for a week. But she had a good house of course, and a parlour to keep them in, for she made a right good match. More betoken, I was thinkin' of gettin' married at the same time myself, for you mind Aunt Susanna Jane was my mother's youngest sister, and there wasn't that much differ in our ages – and if I'd taken the man that was daft about me *that* time, I'd be rollin' in riches now, for the Lord knows it's not for the want of offers I am the way I am, but when you're young and innocent it's aisy to miss your fut, that's what I say!'

Although Ann repeated the speech in its entirety to her grand-daughter when she came home that evening, she seemed to have lapsed into utter unconsciousness long before it came to an end, and Mrs Murphy went back to her house, and shut the door.

13

"Have your da's supper ready for him at half after six. Don't scald yourselves with boilin' water. Be good childer till I come back and stay about the doors. Take care of Bella and give her her tea. You'll find a wee cake for her behind the green bowl on the dresser. If you ate it I'll murder you. Maybe the yella hen will lay. If she does, see that you get the egg. If I come home and find anything wrong it'll be a pity of you. Take good care of that child, whatever you do."

Mrs Murphy made her way slowly out of the village and turned into a by-road which led to the hills. The day was warm and close, and she was unused to walking. If her errand could have been entrusted to other hands, she would have been glad, but was there anyone else who could wring the secret out of Red Abel? She had waited for Betty-fly-around, the beggar-woman, to call, for a whole week and she had not come. She would wait no longer. She would climb the hill herself and interview Red Abel. If it killed her, her death would be on his head and it would be so much the worse for him in time and in eternity.

The grey, narrow road rose and fell elusively, and the summit of the hill seemed to be reached, only to fall away and to rise again. Presently it would turn and twist to the right, and the sea, washing round Black Head would come into view. She feasted her eyes on the rich hillside, the fields of ripened harvest and sloping grass lands. The hedges had grown a trifle dusty, and the leaves on the trees were darkened and thickened. The sweet, virginal beauty of the year was over.

She was thinking all the way up the hill of Jinanna. If only they could get her out of that damp little hole of a house she might begin to mend yet. There was no room to spare in her house, and the neighbours were equally crowded. Something would have to be done for her and done quickly. They would not let the creature die. Now, more than ever, they could not let her die, for they had to make up to her for all the long years of coldness and neglect. She would talk very plainly to Red Abel when they met.

The afternoon sun, going westward, struck the hillside fiercely, and she sat down to rest for a few minutes on a little grass bank below the hedge. But it was almost five o'clock, and before long she rose and faced the steepest part of her journey. The road grew hotter and hotter. The day was very still, and the high thick hedges on either side shut off the cool little wisps of air that blew about the fields. She undid her bonnet strings, she fanned herself with her handkerchief, she remembered with tormenting clearness certain frosty mornings last winter, and the heavenly coldness of the ice on the water-barrel. At times she turned and stood, a large and cumbrous figure in the middle of the road, and scornfully surveyed a village lying in the sun-clad valley below, wherein dwelt trollops, hussies, lazy lumps, and other strangely-named beings, who had allowed a woman of her age and dimensions to be 'basted livin'.

In the cool of the evening, his reverence, sauntering up the village street, dropped in at Mrs Murphy's to inquire for Bella. He stayed chatting for a while with Tam in the kitchen before he went into 'the room'. When Bella saw him she sat up in bed and said eagerly, "we'll catch the wee fishes." He had brought her the game of fishponds a couple of days before. She opened the box and arranged the fish in little hollows in the quilt. In a few minutes they were both equally engrossed.

A little later, Tam, who was sitting reading in the corner of the kitchen, heard a familiar sound and lifted his head. It was Mrs Murphy, trumpeting her woes, as she came down the village street.

"Boys oh! I'm near dead! I'll soon be in my coffin! Och anee anee! Where are you, Tam?"

She came in with Ned in her wake, crying: "Ma, your face is the colour of a red peony rose. Do you think will it ever come till?" Her bonnet and strings were flung back over her shoulders, and her hair clung damply to the forehead.

"I wish to God I had thrown off a couple of me winter petticoats before I climbed thon hill," she groaned as she flung herself into a chair, 'the swate's teemin' off me! I knew rightly I'd come home a corp!'

"What took you such a journey in the heat of the day, and you the size you are?" asked Tam mildly.

"If I waited to go anywhere till you bid me, I'd wait till eternity," she retorted, 'but dear knows maybe it's well I went this time. I've suffered tight and strong this forty years, but Red Abel's wife says I'll not suffer much longer. She says the coatin's off me stomick, clean and clever, and she's on for me goin' to a new doctor – a wee shillin' fella that has set up fornenst the potato market in Belfast – och, the burnin' pain that has me ketched about the heart!'

"Maybe he would give you a bottle till help you," said Tam.

"What's the good of buying bottles when the coatin's wore away?" asked his wife tearfully. '(Who's that goin' by the windy?... Och, her!) I'll soon be in a better world, and needin' noan of their bottles. But who do you think's comin' to the house?' Something keen and vital came into her voice and eyes as she spoke, 'you wouldn't guess if you guessed till Tibb's Eve, so I may as well tell you. It's Jinanna herself! The very wan, There now, Mr Murphy, there's a sensation for you! And who do you think seen to it all, and made Red Abel promise not to let on till us for fear she would hear word of it, and get herself excited? His reverence himself! As sure as you're livin'! I never heard more since I was born! And him in here constant seein' the child and never lettin' a word drop, and actually to goodness, a face on him as innocent as a lamb! I hope with all my heart,' and Mrs Murphy's voice rose in shrill crescendo, 'I hope and trust that if anybody has left me a black silk dress, let alone a fortune, there's nobody keepin' the news off me for fear I'd be workin' in nerves afore the night! The very first time he takes the light from this door, I'll let him know there's no underground ways in Sarah Murphy! What are you makin' faces at the room door for, you insane idiot?'

A low, sibilant "Hush!" fell from Tam's lips.

"Hush!" exclaimed Mrs Murphy indignantly, 'hush indeed. I'll hush when I'm dead and not till then. That's a nice thing for you to say to your wife, Tam Murphy, after her murderin' herself climbin' them burnin' hills all to satisfy *you* and the curiousness of you...'

The room door, which had been slightly ajar, was flung open and his reverence came out and bade her a pleasant good evening.

"The Lord save and defend us this night!" prayed Mrs Murphy, in tones of horror.

14

The Lindens was deluged with tears when Mary finally left. The three little McComishes hung round her crying in the hall and Mrs McComish had tears in her china-blue eyes.

"I'll miss you something dreadful, Mary," she said. 'I don't know how I'll have another girl in your place, but the Johnstones at number seven keep one – such as she is – and I won't let them beat me. I must think of Mr McComish's position.'

"We must keep ourselves up no matter how we feel," agreed Mary, through her tears; 'mind you, I'll be thinkin' queer and long about you, mistress dear. You'll be sure to bring the childer out to see me some saturday evening till I show them Samuel Robert's guinea-pigs, and mamma will give them their tea. Och, the wee crathurs! Come here and give us another kiss, Cyril darlin'!'

"You do become that hat, Mary," said Mrs McComish fervently, 'it's awful good style! Mind and wear it on all particular occasions.'

Mary kissed the children many times and Mrs McComish kissed her. At length she reached the gate, and when she had gone a few yards beyond it, she turned and came back suddenly.

"Watch the milkman for your life!" she said, in earnest tones, 'he'll cheat like the mischief the minute my eye's off him, and take no impitence from little Brady that goes round with the buttermilk, and don't murder yourself workin' till you get a girl, and for God's sake have nothing to do with that one at number seven, for she's a clart if ever I seen one, and watch yourself when you're lettin' down the scullery window for the cord's nearhand broke, and you'll find the hammer and the turnscrew in a hole in the garden hedge – I left it there the day I was mendin' the gate, and I'll be demented in my bed at night thinkin' the master's searchin' the world for them, and if you can't manage your chignon that new way I'll come in and do it for you on your next at-home day, and mind and have nothing to do with them new people at number fourteen, for they had the miserablest wee washin' out last week I ever seen in my life, if you don't believe me take a careless saunter up the garden next monday about eleven. 'Au revoir', and God be with you till we meet again!'

She kissed her hand to the children and hurried out through the gate. In a few minutes she was walking along the Newtownards Road, her face turned towards the country.

An hour later, Mrs Murphy came panting up the loanin' from Jinanna's cottage, a bolster thrown over her shoulder and her arms full of bedding. She was proceeded by Bella and Johnny, equally laden. Mrs Morrow came behind with the baby and a frying-pan. As they reached the road they met Mary, looking fresh and cool and wearing her new hat.

"My back's broke," announced Mrs Murphy, 'we're flittin' Jinanna.'

"This is as good as the pictures any day," giggled Mary. 'I do declare I never come home but I find you doin' something that would make them scream with laughter in the town if they could see you. Such a sight! He-he!' and she giggled in a way that had a peculiarly maddening effect upon her mother.

"Look, see here, Mary, quit that noise, and take thon chair from Johnny before I break your back with it, and bring it up to the house, and then come back and get the kitchen table. You done well to wait till we were near about finished. Maybe you could make the bed till we get the poor crathur flitted intil it. It would answer you better than makin' fun of your betters," and she hitched the bolster higher on her shoulder, and moved off, looking more mountainous than ever.

"We're that busy, Mary," said Mrs Morrow, bustling up, 'and you're just in the nick of time to give us a hand. I'm that glad you're comin' home for a while. It will be heartsome to have you knockin' about the place.'

"But I really don't know how I'll put up with the country after the Bohemian life I'm accustomed to in town," sighed Mary, who always took a little while to settle down into the bright, country girl.

"Och, but you've come back for Ann's sake, and I thought it quare and good of you. Your mother told me. Poor Ann."

"Wasn't he the dirty brute!" cried Mary, lapsing suddenly into naturalness again. 'I don't know what she seen in him. Many a time I could have shaken her. I wouldn't have touched him with a forty-foot pole.'

"I hope you'll have better luck when your time comes."

"But sure this has given me such a scunder at the men, I don't believe I'll ever bother my head with one of them. There's my mother lookin' back at me. I must run on."

She hurried down the loanin' and found Jinanna sitting on a patchwork quilt which had been spread on the grass bank opposite her door. She looked white and ill and Mary bent over her sympathetically:

"I suppose you're feelin' bad at leavin' your wee house?" she said.

"I'm feelin' powerful grand, that's what I'm feelin'," returned Jinanna, wiping the sweat from her brow with a hand that trembled. 'Isn't it a grand thing altogether to be leavin' that old barrack of a buildin' and goin' up to live in Gape Row beside your mother and the rest of them. Though God knows what I'm goin' to live on I know no more nor that cat! Sure if it hadn't been for his reverence and the neighbour-women I'd have been in the poor-house long ago, let alone my grave. But I'm not goin' to fret or bother my brains about anything any more. I'm going to enjoy myself. The Lord will provide. I have the world before me now.'

Mary, who had never heard her say more than a dozen words in her life, stared in astonishment.

"As soon as I get my strength back, and gather up some money from the dear only knows where, for I don't," gasped Jinanna, 'I'll get a lift to the tram and I'll be off to the town to buy myself a bit of dress. Look at me! Sure I'm in rags and tatters! It's sittin' among the potatoes I ought to be to scarr the crows. I want a new dress and a new hat and a new pair of shoes, and plenty more forby. What's in Brady's window these days? Did you ever notice a blue...'

"Shut your mouth, for mercy's sake!" implored Mary. 'I never heard the like of this in all my days! If you don't quit talking you'll die in that ditch before my eyes. There's plenty has killed themselves talkin' before now, and you're not used to it. The excitement of flittin' has took to your head, woman dear.'

"It's not excitement, and it's not flittin'," explained Jinanna in a small voice, 'but it's keepin' myself bolted and barred and locked up all these years, like an old chist in the corner that has me now I can't stop. Gwan and tell us about Brady's window. Do you know a shop on the Albertbridge Road -Mac-something-or-another – I disremember the name. They used to have lovely things in it. I mind one year they had the loveliest dresses and ladies inside them, would you believe it? Some sittin' and some standin' and some lookin' side-ways. There was no gentleman, of course. They said they were wax weemen, but I dunno. I don't think it, somehow. I've seen wee fellas in sailor suits before now, and they're wax right enough. But those lovely gerls! You would just think they were goin' to speak till you. If they're made of grease, it's a queer thing till me.'

"Maybe I'd better call mamma..."

"What for, child dear? Some says Brady's is the best, and some says what-you-may-call-thems. I don't know. I never bought in neither. It was in a wee second-handed place in Ginger Street I got my bits of things. But now I'm goin' up in the world, and I feel I'd like a bit of grandeur before I die..."

"Do you mind goin' to sunday-school when you were young?" said Mary, in a voice of alarm, 'and did you ever learn a hymn that begins, 'Calm me, my God, and keep me calm?' If you would keep sayin' it over and over intil yourself, it might save you from goin' to the asylum.'

"Asylum, your granny! It's my new house I'm goin' to, and it's my new clothes I'm thinkin' about. (Mind the clock, Ned, son. Och, but you're the right wee man!) Your mother says she'll make your father put in the garden for me next year, and I'll have a wee strip for flowers, the way we used to have up at home. I was always that fond of a bit of flower. And what do you think, Mary, but Samuel Robert has papered the room with his own two hands, and they tell me it's something lovely! I'm fair dyin' to see it! And Red Abel kept the house for me, and the dear knows how many were lookin' for it. Aye, indeed! And I'm alive and well the day, and nobody would believe it that seen me awhile back. I'm thankful to God to feel the air blowin' on my face again."

"I thought I sent you for the kitchen table?" a stentorian voice called down the loanin', and Mary dived into the house.

"Are you feelin' bravely, Jinanna?" asked Mrs Murphy, as she drew near, 'would you like another cup of tea? I'll send Bella up for it.'

"No, thank you, Mrs Murphy dear, I'm wantin' nothing. It's yourself that's kilt. Sit down here on the ditch and take a bit of rest."

"I've a dale to carry, I'll not deny," said Mrs Murphy, seating herself with a sigh. 'Many a time I'd like to send for a thing I read about in the paper called 'Antipon,' if I wasn't afeerd. When I ask Tam, he says, 'have wit,' or maybe he says nothing at all. It's my firrum belief that man of mine doesn't hear the half I say till him.'

"Sure a man's an odd thing, altogether," said Jinanna soothingly.

"Odd!" exclaimed Mrs Murphy, turning her eyes up to the sky, 'odd's not the name for my man – he's dyin' with oddness! And me as open and unsuspicious as a child! Sure you can see through me at a glance. Many a time when he was comin' back and forrad to our house, my mother said to me, 'For my part,' sez she, 'I like to know what's workin' in a man's mind, and what's workin in *that* man's mind you'll never know, should you and him be married, man and wife a hundred year.' And it's the truth! I can drill nothing out of him. I might as well not try.'

Mary's voice was heard talking volubly to someone inside.

"Mary," her mother called, 'bring out the kitchen table and give your tongue a holiday.'

In a moment she came out, carrying a small, deal table. She put it down, and took off the blue hat, which she hung carefully on the sloeberry bush in front of the house. Then she swung the table upside down, and placing it on her head, went lightly up the lane.

"You'll mind to tell me about Brady's window this evenin'?" Jinanna called after her weakly.

"She'll ruinate her brains with carryin' things on her head," remarked Mrs Murphy, 'and she's all for it now. She says it's done in the best boardin' schools. The notions of her!'

A few hours later, Jinanna was brought in triumph to her new home. Although it was barely a ten minutes' walk it took her a long time to get there. She talked all the way, pausing only to gasp for breath.

"Take it aisy, woman, dear," advised Mrs Morrow, 'take it aisy the first day you're out. Sure it's enough for you to travel without sayin' a word.'

"There's the old thorn tree!" piped Jinanna. 'I mind it when I was a wee girl goin' to school. Did you see the blackthorn in flower in the glen this spring, Mary? And the blue-bells and primroses and cherry trees! I used to think it was a lovely sight. But sure my nose has been kept that well to the grindin'-stone, it's years on the top of years since I went anywhere, or seen anything. I declare to goodness there's the church…"

"My mother's comin' to meet us," interposed Mary, 'she'll be ragin' if she hears you. She says you're talkin' yourself into your grave.'

"Och, Mrs Murphy, dear, isn't the air something lovely, and isn't it a grand thing to be out walkin' the roads on your own two feet? Sure it's wonderful! And the place is just the same. I feel as if I had been away a hundred years. There's Sammy Soretoes leanin' over his door. I'd go to speak till him if I was able. My, but sickness is a terrible thing! The way it takes the legs from you."

"It doesn't take the tongue from you at any rate," returned Mrs Murphy grimly, 'and you're not fit to talk – you're just cheepin'! When you're better you can talk to Sammy as much as you like, but I suppose by that time you'll not have a word till say.'

"I'd like to meet everybody I ever knowed, and shake them by the hand this day," chirped Jinanna hoarsely, 'and I'd like to walk to the top of thon hill, and look over on the other side, and see what is to be seen. Catch *me* sittin' in the house for the rest of my days! Catch me workin' and worritin' and grindin' and starvin'...."

"This is before something," said Mrs Murphy, turning solemnly to the others, 'it's before something. She's goin' to take another brash. And mind you Jinanna, if you take another brash, you'll *die*.'

Jinanna cried with rapture over the new house, and the wallpaper with its stiff little baskets of red roses. She entertained the village in sections, and talked until Mrs Murphy implored her for the love of God to quit. She drank strong tea and ate indigestible buns, and at eight o'clock she fell asleep in the middle of a sentence.

"Maybe she'll quit now," said Mrs Morrow gently.

"God forgive me!" muttered Mrs Murphy, as she rolled wearily into bed that night. 'God forgive me, and not comparin' the one to the other, but I couldn't get Balaam's Ass out of my head this day!'

15

"Mary," said Mrs Murphy, unusual gravity in her voice, 'you'd have been heart-sorry for Jinanna if you'd seen her the day.'

"Why? Is she sick again?"

"No, she's not sick, but she has a great notion she'll be in the poorhouse yet."

"Oh, poor Jinanna!" exclaimed Mary in horror.

Mrs Murphy shook her head. "I don't want to be dubious-minded, but it looks very like it. Who's goin' to keep her? Never marry intil poverty, daughter, if you can help it."

"I'm not likely to marry intil anything else."

"How do you know? Jump at the moon and you'll maybe ketch one of the stars." Mary laughed, and Mrs Murphy continued in firm tones. 'Before I'd marry into poverty – if I was a girl – I'd throw meself down the well, or I'd even be an old maid for the rest of my life, and God knows, I wouldn't be *that* for a dale.'

"I was born a poor girl, and I've a notion I'll never be anything else," said Mary lightly.

"Maybe you might. There's plenty no better nor you has riz in the world."

"Dear help your wit! If I was as good-lookin' as Ann..."

"I'm losin' my patience altogether with that Ann! It's time she was lookin' round her for somebody else."

"She'll never do that. She was terribly set on Johnny."

"I'd be the last to blame her if he was all that was wantin' her," said Mrs Murphy, 'for you be to get somebody, if it's only to take the bare look off you. But anybody with half an eye in their head could see that Sandy was droppin' off his feet about her, and him as good a boy as ever walked the earth.'

"She had eyes for nobody but Johnny."

"She drove her pigs to a nice market! Let it be a warnin' to you, daughter, dear."

Mary leaned her chin thoughtfully on her hand. "I'd like riches," she said, 'and I'd like love...'

"Aye, but sure you could love a man with a bit of money as well as them that had nothing," returned Mrs Murphy, eagerly. 'I could love him twict as well if it was me! Look at the way I've been workin' and slavin' and scramblin' to get you all well reared, and I'm not a bit forrader than the day I started. I've hardly a shoe to me feet at the present moment, and sure I never went anywhere, nor seen nothing.'

"Poor mother!" said Mary, in conscience-stricken tones, 'it is a shame.'

"The day I left my father's good house and come home here," continued Mrs Murphy, 'I mind goin' to that door there, and lookin' round me and seein' the poplar trees up there with the leaves just fresh on them – I was married in spring – and them with the fashion they have of shiverin' and shakin', wind or no wind. Did *I* think that mornin' that I'd be sittin' here my whole blessed life, with nothing to look at, year in year out, but them blessed ould trees? Feth, I did not!'

"Poor mother!" Mary reiterated humbly, 'it *is* a shame. You've worked awful hard for us.'

"I think I have that! And what good has it done? I'm not gettin' my family fetched up in the way I had a mind to fetch them up, or the way my mother fetched up hers before me. And if all was knowed I'm gettin' behind in the shop at the Arches, but don't let on to your Da, for he'd be ragin'. Why, if it wasn't for the fowl I'd never have a penny, and sure me back's broke rearing them. All he brings in goes straight intil the childer's mouths. Dear aye! You look for something very different when you're young."

"You do that!" said Mary, a world of sympathy in her voice.

"The want of money's an awful bad want! Marry intil poverty, and you'll soon larn where you are! I haven't had a new rag to put on my back for the last five years. I'm ashamed to go to church on sundays with the clothes I have on me. Not but that we're all the same in the house of God."

"Mother, I'll save up and get you some nice new clothes, indeed I will! I'll put something by every week..."

"Nonsense, child! It's my grave-clothes 'ill be the first clothes I'll be seein' about, I'm thinkin'."

"Anee, anee!" wailed Mary, tearfully.

"It's no matter about me at my time of day," said Mrs Murphy, rising heavily from her seat. 'But it's my childer I'm thinkin' about.'

"Never mind your childer for wonct," pleaded Mary, 'promise to come to the picture-house with me next week. You'd love it mother and it would lift your mind queerly.'

"Is it pictures?" asked Mrs Murphy, her eyes on the ceiling, 'is it pictures and tomfooleries and flagaries, and me with one foot in the grave? To see my childer doin' well is the only picture for me. Sit where you are, child dear, and mind the house, till I take a race down to the shop, till I tell Maggie Maguire she may get somebody else to buy her bad butter but it'll not be me!'

Mary sat very still by the fire. The shadows grew dark in the corners of the kitchen, but she did not light the lamp. She thought of the Sunday evening she had come in, and found Andy John sitting there for the first time, and Michael and Sandy.

How often he had come in since that, and wrested the conversation from her mother as he did that first evening. But Michael had not come back... not even once...

She understood perfectly the underlying meaning of her mother's words. A thrill of exultation swept through her. To be rich, to live in a two-storied house, to have servants and fine clothes, to be able to make her parents' life easier, to give innumerable presents to the children – she glowed generously at the thought. She had never had any money she had not earned with hard work. Her hands were hardened and thickened with work. She bent down and examined them critically by the firelight. Every night she rubbed glycerine carefully into them according to the directions given in 'Boudoir Bits'. So far the results had been disappointing, and she sighed. She had even made an heroic effort to wear gloves at night, but found to her amazement that she took them off in her sleep. The Lady Ermyntrude's hands were always as white and soft as a lily.

And then she thought of Andy John sitting there in the chair opposite her, as he always sat. He had smooth black hair, and small black eyes that seemed to look through her. Of course he was old – quite old – thirty-five at least. The thought of him depressed her. It was as if a pailful of cold water had suddenly been flung over her and over all her beautiful, vague, half-dreamt young dreams. But she would not let herself be depressed. Money, money, money! She would have plenty of it all her life. She would raise the family fortunes, and make every girl in the parish green with envy.

And would he always be sitting there, on the other side of the fire – always looking painfully alert as if he might bounce to the ceiling at any moment? Always so pleased with himself, and happy and talkative? – not like Michael – oh, not a bit like Michael! And pailfuls of cold water, healthy and stinging, poured over her.

16

"That wee woman will drop off among your hands some of these days."

"Away out of that with you."

"Well, you'll see! She's gone like snow off a ditch this last week or two."

"It's the mind," sighed Mrs Murphy; 'if she'd keep a contented mind, she'd do rightly.'

"It's not aisy for a widda-woman to keep a contented mind, and her maybe not knowin' where the next meal's meat's to come from," returned Mrs Gillespie. 'But if she was me, with a parcel of childer and every one of them fit to ate a man off his horse, she might talk. I can't get over what happened my pigs. Billy Morrow sold them for next to nothing on me.'

"Are you yammerin' about that yet? It's all rubbish, woman! He got very near the top of the market."

"Oh, murder!" exclaimed Mrs Gillespie, 'thon the top of the market! Did anybody ever hear the like!'

"There's people couldn't be plazed in a price..."

"My lovely pigs were give away," lamented the widow, 'they were made a present of! After all the boilin' and feedin' and slavin' I had after them! I'm not the same woman since. I'm all away from me clothes.'

"If Jinanna had the price of them pigs comin' in till her this mornin', she'd be brave and thankful, I can tell you. She has a great dread of the workhouse on her at the present time."

"That's where she'll be yet," said Mrs Gillespie, with increasing gloom, 'and meself, too, as far as I can see. I've had no other notion since Thomas James Henry died, and now I'm used to it too. And the students will get her when she's corp – you can tell her that too if you like.'

"The Lord preserve us this day!" exclaimed Mrs Murphy, recoiling in horror, 'did *ever* I hear such a woman! You make my very flesh trimble!'

"But sure it's the truth! Did you hear what happened old John..."

"Whisht!" commanded Mrs Murphy, 'tell us no more! I don't believe a word of it. It's all whigmaleery! You'd put anybody astray in the mind. But Jinanna's not goin' to the poorhouse, if I can help it.'

"You'll not be able to help it. Nor you couldn't do nothing if it was me that was goin' either."

"Feth, I wouldn't try," said Mrs Murphy heartily. 'I'd say, go in and welcome, and peace behind you, and the dear help anybody has to listen to you there or anywhere else! Such a woman! Isn't God above us, and isn't His good air blowin' round us, and hadn't you your fill this mornin', and aren't the childer in the best of health, and didn't Johnny cough up the farden he choked on last week, and haven't you a right to be thankful if ever a woman had?'

"Aye, but it's aisy for you to talk, and you with a brave, quate crathur of a man bringin' in his money reglar…"

"Balderdash! Maybe if you had him awhile you'd be heart-scalded too! God bless us! the bread's burnin'!" and Mrs Murphy turned and whisked through the door.

As she went about her household tasks that morning her thoughts were continually with Jinanna. She would never work again. Last week she fainted after trying to do a small washing. Every penny she had in the world has gone to pay the debt to Break-o'-day Andy Sloan. After the proud fight she had made it was impossible to think of her living on charity for the rest of her life. She knew she would make a struggle to go back to her work before long. "But to the workhouse she'll never go as I'm a livin' sinner," Mrs Murphy exclaimed, turning towards the fire, with a large, flat piece of dough in either hand. 'Go long out of that with you, or I'll tramp on you. I never seen the like of you for gettin' among people's feet!' for the kitten, thinking itself addressed, had risen to meet her. She slipped the bread into the griddle which hung over the low fire and stood up and wiped the sweat from her forehead with her apron. Presently she was leaning out over the half-door, as her custom was when she was heated and tired. The poplars were shivering in the dull haze which hung over everything this morning. Where she stood she could hear the low croon of their leaves. She looked away across the fields, dotted with cattle. It was a sight she loved, for she had the true countrywoman's passion for the land. There was grey mist on the hills and wisps of grey dew lying thickly on the grass. Grey and mellow and beautiful it was, and the air against her face brought little tags of damp field smells, and damp hedges and damp brown earth.

"God help them that's livin' in the town!" murmured Mrs Murphy, 'God help the wee childer on the street!'

A couple of days later, Betty-fly-around spent a lengthy afternoon with her, and incidently mentioned that Break-o'-day Andy had been very ill for some months, and was not expected to recover. Mrs Murphy merely said, "The old rap!" and dismissed the subject. But the next morning, when the children had gone out to school and she had the house to herself, she was walking across the kitchen floor, when she stopped and stood perfectly still for a couple of minutes, caught, as she afterwards explained, by a direct inspiration from heaven. Her arms hung by her sides and she stared fixedly at a red geranium in the window. A light gradually broke over her face. 'God bless us and save us!' she exclaimed, for the occasion seemed to demand the safety-valve of speech. She chuckled and shook her fist at some imaginary opponent. 'You be to do it! I'll make you, you old villain! You'll not get redd of me so aisy! Man, but I'm thankful I was born with brains! Goodness grant he may live till I get at him.'

It was barely a month since she had climbed the hill to Red Abel's, and Mrs Gillespie, who was feeding a family of late chickens on her doorstep, lifted her head in astonishment when Mrs Murphy went past early in the afternoon, dressed in her sunday best.

"My goodness!" she exclaimed, 'where are you off to now?'

"To see a friend."

"It will be teemin' before half an hour. The clouds are gatherin' for it."

"What about a taste of rain?" said Mrs Murphy, over her shoulder. 'I'd go if it was rainin' creepie-stools!'

She followed the winding road across the valley, and mounted a little incline from the top of which she looked anxiously away to a group of trees which surrounded a small farm-house on the brow of the hill. The road before her slid down and at the foot of it a grey stone wall bore the startling legend, 'Eternity – where?' in large, whitewashed capitals. "That's more of Happy Bill and his capers!" she thought scornfully, referring to a wayside preacher who came and went in the neighbourhood. Then she turned into another road, and began slowly to mount the long hill which shut in the valley on the south.

There were broad, luxuriant hedges on either side, and a little margin of grass growing along the edge of the road which made a soft pathway for her feet. A dark cloud came over the sun, and before long a shower was falling. She stood under a tree for a few minutes.

"Why, it's passin' already," she thought, scanning the sky carefully, 'this is what Gillespie calls a teem! The thrawn crathur, it's well for the man he died!'

From this height she could see the city lying in the circle of its violet mountains, the great gantries standing in the Queen's Island which at a distance looked like delicate lace-work, the long lines of red suburban villas running out into the fields, the dull silver of the Lough. As the rain cleared off a sudden ray of sunlight flashed on the heavy cloud of smoke which lay low on the town, and shot it through with amber and gold and mother-of-pearl. Mrs Murphy stood looking down at it thoughtfully.

"It would mind you of the New Jerusalem, itself," she murmured, 'and it just a bundle of dirt!'

Presently she walked on through the rain-sweetened air, and on the brow of the hill, stopped at a low farmhouse. She opened the gate into a square, roughly-kept piece of ground, half-garden, half-orchard, which at present was overrun with hens. The green hall-door was shut and she knocked a couple of times before anyone came. At last an old woman with a white-frilled cap opened it.

"Och, Peg McCourt, is it you I see before me!" she exclaimed. 'Troth and you're not a day older-lookin' since the last time I seen you and that was at Mick McKinstrey's wake, three years back agin July. Sure I didn't know it was you was takin' care of him at all.'

"Come in, Mrs Murphy, dear, come in," returned Peg, 'you're as welcome as the flowers in May! Aye, I mind poor Mickey's wake well. Take a chair near the fire.'

"No, thank you, I'll get back out of the hate. There's a brave fire inside me after travellin' thon hill. I'm not as young as I was, nor as souple on my feet. Tell me, how is he? I heard he was powerful bad."

"He is that, the poor ould crathur!" returned Peg, in lowered tones, 'and the appetite has got very poor on him this last wheen of days. It's my belief he'll last no time.'

"Well, well! It's what we all must come to, rich and poor alike. I suppose the relations are brave and attentive now that they're near hand gettin' the money."

Peg threw up her hands expressively. "You couldn't believe it if I told you," she said, 'they're in here, the Sloans and O'Grady's, at all hours of the day and night to see if the breath has left him, for that's all they want for till know. But for God's sake, don't be lettin' on that I dropped a word, or they'd throw me out on the street.'

Mrs Murphy assured her she wasn't born yesterday.

"They're never done arguin' and wranglin' over the money that's comin' to them" continued Peg, 'and many a time I say to meself, and me goin' back and forrad through the floor, it's a mercy to goodness to have nothin'. They'll be fightin' rings round over his coffin – wait till you see! The Angel Gabriel couldn't lave the money to plaze them.'

"Poor old man!" sighed Mrs Murphy, 'poor old crathur. His money will get the quare scatterment, if he but knowed it. He was always a lonely bein'. There's nobody comes as near you as your own when you're lyin'. It's a pity of them has neither wife nor child, as many a time I tell my man.'

"Aye, indeed," said Peg, as she stirred the fire below the kettle. 'I'll wet you a taste of tea, Mrs Murphy, for you're bound to be tired walkin' the whole length from the village. Did nobody offer you a lift, at all?'

"Oh, divil a lift! There's not a heap of traffic on these by-roads at any time. How many of a family has Terence O'Grady's wife now? Wasn't the last one twins?"

They slid into intimate family matters, and discussed Andy's illness in detail. When the tea had been drunk, Mrs Murphy, who was considerably revived, suggested that she should be taken to see the invalid. Peg led her down a short passage, and opening a door, went in before her.

"Mr Sloan dear, sure here's Mrs Murphy come all the road from the village to ax after you," she said, bending over the sick man, 'didn't I tell you there was a straw to the hen's foot this mornin'? I knew rightly there'd be some stranger here afore night.' Mrs Murphy whispered that she would like a word with him alone. Peg nodded. 'I'm goin' to give the hens their feed,' she said, as she went out of the room and closed the door.

"Mr Sloan dear," said Mrs Murphy, after a few preliminaries, 'you've quarely failed – my, you've quarely failed.'

Andy looked up at her. He was a shrivelled, little old man with deeply sunken eyes, which were curiously near each other.

"Aye, I'm failed," he said, 'and is it any wonder? It's livin' on sups of milk and corn-flour has done it on me, and the doctor allows I'd be worse if I had stronger mate. Never had a doctor in my life before. Never lay in bed an hour.'

"You're not as young as you were. Maybe that has something to do with it," suggested Mrs Murphy.

"Aye, maybe that. But if I could get a bit of strength back, and get round the fields for the while of a mornin' I'd be rightly. There's great strength in the air."

"But man, dear," expostulated Mrs Murphy, 'you're not fit to stand on your two feet, let alone walk. You're better lyin'.'

"I tell you if I could take a turn round the fields, and see how everything's goin' I'd improve," persisted Andy. 'Sure it's lyin' has me weak, and worryin' about the work and things goin' behind on the land.'

"Don't you bother your brains about nothing of the kind at this hour of your life," said Mrs Murphy earnestly, 'it's not worth your while for all the time you'll be here. We brought nothing into the world with us, and will take nothing out of it, and how hardly shall they that have riches enter into the kingdom of heaven – that's what was workin' in my mind as I come up the road, Mr Sloan, dear.'

She drew her breath, and turned to look if the door was closed. She began to talk. She went back a long way... Andy put up his hand to stop her. He tried to call Peg. He swore feebly. Then he sunk lower and lower among his pillows, and his face grew pinched and miserable. Peg, who came to the door several times, found herself dismissed with a wave of Mrs Murphy's arm. She talked for a long time, and as her object was certainly not to kill him, at last she rose to go.

"Peg," she said, on her way out through the kitchen, 'have you a sup of whiskey in the house? Give him a taste, for the love of goodness!'

She walked slowly down the road until she came to a cottage with a large garden in front of it. Instead of going in at the gate, she leaned over the wall, and peered up and down among the gooseberry bushes and the dahlias and the late gladioli. "If I go in at this hour of the day, and he starts his gabblin', I'll never get away," she thought. 'Are you there, Mr McQuade?'

A small, spare man rose slowly from the middle of a bed of flowers. He had a trowel in his hand, "it's a fine evenin', sir."

"A grand evening, ma'am," he said, coming towards her. 'Why, Mrs Murphy, is it you? I hope you're well, ma'am, and all belonging to you, including my old friend, Charlie, although he was never able to acquire much education at my hands...'

"Charlie's rightly and doin' rightly," interrupted Mrs Murphy tartly, 'and acquirin' plenty of money in the United States of America, I'll have you to know.'

"He was the one member of your family..." began Mr McQuade.

"Whisht, man, if I'm to get home the night," said Mrs Murphy, impatiently, 'it's not my childer, past or present, I want to talk about this evenin'. I want you to take your mind off your ould bees, and your ould garden, and your ould flowers, for wonct in your life, and do something that's some way useful to your fellow-bein's. You've got to help me to rescue the perishin' and care for the dyin', Mr McQuade. No, thank you, I won't go in the night. I be to get home. Now listen, man, and for the mercy of goodness, don't speak till I'm done.'

She leaned forward, her arms on the wall, and began to talk in a hoarse whisper, although no living thing was near them but the robins and the blackbirds hopping fearlessly about in the dahlia-bed. It was a long story. When she showed signs of flagging, Mr McQuade opened his lips and adjusted his collar, and at these symptoms she seemed to become so alarmed, that new strength arose in her and fresh torrents of speech burst from her. When she had finished, she gave him some explicit directions, and he found himself promising to obey almost without knowing.

"Surely, ma'am. I will do what I can," he said, and he wondered as he said it.

"I'm quare and obliged to you," she said, in a sudden, flat voice, 'I'll be gettin' on home now. I'm about done out, so I am.'

"And I never as much as got showing her the garden," he thought regretfully, as her bonnet disappeared round the hedge, 'and the dahlias looking a perfect picture this evening.'

The next afternoon, as Peg came round the corner of the house with the afternoon sun blazing in her eyes, something large and black and massive loomed unexpectedly before her.

"You weren't thinkin' I'd be back so soon again Peg, I'll be bound," said Mrs Murphy pleasantly.

"The Lord save us, is it you?" exclaimed the little woman, in a voice of terror, 'you're not comin' back here after yesterday surely to goodness! He was nearly out of his mind after you left whatever you done on him – and he told me to hunt you from about the place if ever you darkened the door again. I never thought of you comin' the day. You'll not go in, Mrs Murphy,' and Peg caught her by the arm, 'there'll be murder done if you go in to that house the day.'

"Your granny! Would you have that old man to die with a terrible sin on his conscience? If you take my advice, you'll folly the turkey that I seen a minute ago goin' off down the cornfield in a quare, artful lookin' manner. Maybe you'd find the nest, and I'm goin' in to see Mr Sloan, with or without your leave, Peg McCourt."

"We'll be havin' the polis up after this," began Peg, in a shaken voice. 'I wish you'd heerd him last night...'

"Gwan for goodness' sake, and quit talkin'," said Mrs Murphy, 'I'm in a hurry home. Who's afraid of the polis? Not me! I don't care if every mother's son of them was standin' there! It's a scandal to have that turkey layin' away, and eggs the price they are. You'll not keep me out of that sick man's room – mind that. I'm twict as strong as you, and more nor twict as big – and you'd better not anger me, maybe.'

When Andy, propped up on his pillows, opened his eyes at the creaking of the door and saw a large, red face, surmounted by a large, black bonnet appearing, he gave himself up for lost.

"I've just dropped in to see how you're doin'," she explained cheerfully, 'and I'll be in the morra afternoon, and the day after and the day after again. Bolts nor bars wouldn't keep me out, Mr Sloan, dear! If you're goin' to die, you may as well die dacent, that's what I say. We'll have plenty of time for a crack, for Peg is follyin' the turkey down the cornfield, and I told the childer to look after the father if I wasn't home to make his supper. So think it over, Mr Sloan dear, think it over...'

Andy wondered vaguely would that voice ever cease... It pictured the next world for him, as he had not seen it since he was a small child listening to a stray preacher at the crossroads, preaching on hell. He remembered how he had rushed home in nameless terror, and hidden his face in his mother's skirts. He had forgotten the incident until her words brought it back to him. He wished he had a stick and could hit her. He wished he was young and strong, and could put her out and set the dogs on her. He wished – and still the maddening voice at his elbow went on and on.

17

One evening, about ten days later, Mrs Murphy was sitting alone by the fire. Even Tam was out. She had been sewing, but now her work was lying on her lap, and she was looking idly before her. The heat of the fire lapped her round with warmth and comfort, and before long her head dropped forward and she slept in the chair. She did not hear a slow step coming down the street, or a knock at her door. The stranger knocked again, and waited. Then the door opened and a voice said, "Good evening, Mrs Murphy." She stirred slightly in her sleep, but did not answer.

"Good evening, Mrs Murphy, ma'am."

"You'll get no more bread and jam from me, ye brat ye," she said drowsily.

"Do you wish me to retire..." asked a strange voice. She opened one eye and saw a small, bewhiskered man standing over her. 'Glory be to goodness, is it you?' she cried with a start, 'sure I thought it was that wee wasp of a Ned, lookin' for more to ate. Take a chair, Mr McQuade, dear.'

The old schoolmaster drew a chair near her and sat down.

"I'll put on the kettle and make you a cup of tea."

"No, thank you. I've taken my last meal for the day and I never eat after it."

"I've heard tell of people like that, but I never met them," she said thoughtfully; 'what I say about our ones is, you *couldn't* fill them.'

"I have news for you," said Mr McQuade in his usual slow manner, 'important news, if you wish to hear it, do not speak till I have done.'

"Gwan, man, gwan!" She leaned forward, impatiently, her hands pressed on her knees. But she knew it would be useless to try to hurry him. He told his story with a wealth of microscopic detail and a circumlocution that was maddening. It was the only way he could tell it. She listened as patiently as she could.

When he had finished she leaned back with a sigh of relief.

"Well!" she said, 'that was a good day's work! Thanks be to God Almighty! And to you too, Mr McQuade. You were the quare help.'

"Not at all, ma'am, not at all. But the trouble may not be all over yet. Something may leak out, and it's possible you may have a visitor."

"Me? A visitor? Who?"

"The Sloans and O'Grady's have to a great extent intermarried."

"Is it married through other, you mean?"

"Precisely. One or other of them may come to see you before long. Something may leak out. Mrs Terence O'Grady is a strong-minded, over-bearing woman. Terence himself is a mild man..."

"A soft, ould slabber," interrupted Mrs Murphy.

"She is said to – er – wear the breeches. If she hears anything, it is more than probable she will come down. And I have no doubt she will speak her mind in an abusive manner..."

"Well dar she abuse me!" exclaimed Mrs Murphy, 'if she comes down here, and starts givin' me any old lip, she'll get more nor she bargained for. I'll not take any reddin' up from the like of her I can tell you.'

"Well, well, it may never happen, and everything has turned out well so far."

"The very best, thanks be to God!" she laughed, and her shoulders heaved with merriment. 'Man, but it does me good till think of it! What'll they say at all? They'll be ragin'.'

"There is no doubt of that at all. But we have done our duty, Mrs Murphy. Our conscience is clear. By the way, I was sorry I did not take you round the garden that evening you called, and show you my prize dahlias the the gladioli. They were in the zenith of their beauty that week."

"It was a queer pity," said Mrs Murphy piously.

"You'll have to come again before the frost sets in, and see them..."

"If it wasn't that I'm the size I am, I'd take a race up thon hill many a time till see you – I'm that obliged till you – and forby that the air of the hills does me good. You have the right wee garden, thonder. How on earth you're polluted..."

The schoolmaster spent his years of retirement in a little garden, not more than a couple of roods square. It lay sloping to the south, on the brow of the hill, and he loved every inch of it, and lived in it from morning till night. Perhaps it filled the place in his heart left vacant by the family who had married and left him, and the scholars who had grown up and gone away.

He began to talk to her about his flowers. He talked for almost an hour, and she listened with scarcely an interruption. She could not but listen to him tonight, for had he not helped her to wipe a great debt off Gape Row?

When he rose to go, she went to the shelf and took down a pot of jam, which she wrapped in a piece of brown paper.

"See here," she said almost bashfully, 'I gave that old fella a terrible hammerin' with my tongue. Take him that wee taste of jam from me, and tell him I'll be proud to shake him by the hand on the Ressurection Morn. My mother always said the soft way was the best way, but feth! it never was my way.'

"He's a terrible fine old man, Mr McQuade," she said to Mary that night, 'but he talks too much. It's an awful thing when people can't control their own tongue. He doesn't know when to quit.'

"But mamma," returned Mary, 'sure that's just like yourself. You go on and on...'

"I may be a good talker, Mary, but I know when to quit," said Mrs

Murphy loftily. 'My mother larned me. It's all in the way you're larned.'

Mary laughed.

"And my oh! but he's round-about, and long in the wind! Sure if you meet him anywhere out by, you can't get away from him. I wish you heard him started about the garden. I'll never forget the day I met him alow the Crossin' Bridge, and I declare to you, if the Lord hadn't sent a shower of rain I'd be standin' there yet, and that was two years ago."

"Maybe he's sayin' the very same thing about you."

"No fear! There's Andy John, now, he's something like a talker. I could listen to him the night round. But then he's a travelled man, as I always tell the people."

"I don't like the way he talks through his nose," Mary said.

"Don't you? Well, I do! I think it carries style. Andy John's not like the common run of people about here. He talks different and he thinks different and his income's different – that's what *I* say."

When Break-o'-day Andy died a little later, Jinanna was sorry. He was a hard old man, but he never had anything to soften him, she said – neither wife nor child, and she had had John and the wee girl for a few years at any rate.

18

"After all, God's good!" Mrs Gillespie said, when the power of speech returned to her. The news that Break-o'-day Andy had left Jinanna a legacy of forty pounds a year, swept through the village like a whirlwind. Mrs Murphy saw the post-boy call next door, and immediately pushed the frying-pan, in which she was cooking the family breakfast, to one side in order to hurry in, and enquire casually of Jinanna, who, under goodness, was sending her a letter. Ten minutes later she came out and called the news in tones of intensest excitement to Sammy Soretoes, who was hobbling painfully across the road to the pump. Sammy turned and stood staring open-mouthed at her, the can in his hand.

"Run for your life and tell Mrs Morrow," shouted Mrs Murphy. 'Where are you, Mrs Morrow ? Praises be to the Lord this day!'

Mrs Morrow, hearing her name, came running out and nearly threw the baby in the air for joy. She lifted up her voice and enlightened Samuel Robert's mother, who was standing at some distance, and she in turn, tossed it round the corner to the postmaster, in his own door, and from thence it reached Mrs Gillespie, by way of Mrs McIntyre's wee lump, Sarah Ann.

"After all, God's good!" Mrs Gillespie repeated, and it was the profoundest expression of faith that was ever heard to fall from her lips.

Jinanna was dazed by the news. She cried for three days and then she rose up and began to thank God in more cheerful tones, and to plan her new clothes. Each time she tried to thank Mrs Murphy she wept afresh.

"Mary, will you bring me a couple of patterns out of the town, for dear sake, till I see what kind of a dress I'll get. Do you mind a lovely blue was in Brady's window, back there in the summer? It was the colour of blue-bells, and it had a wee black sprig on it. If they haven't it, maybe you could get a nice lively lookin' blue in What-you-may-call-them on the Albertbridge Road. I never can mind that name – but Mrs Murphy dear, do you think it's all true? Do you think the money will come?"

"It's as true as the Gospel."

"I'm in great dread of the relations comin' down. I know the bitter sort they are. They'd ate me alive."

"Send them in to me if they come near you."

"Maybe they'd bring a lawyer along with them. I'd be heart-afeerd of a lawyer."

"Send the lawyer to me," said Mrs Murphy grandly. '*I'm* not afraid of him.'

"You're a wonder to me," exclaimed Jinanna admiringly, 'is there any mortal thing you *are* afraid of?'

"Not a ha'porth! What would I be afeerd for? It's all in the way you're made. If you're born afeerd, you'll be afeerd, and if you're not, you'll not be afeerd. So there you are. But it's not for us to be cocked up with ourselves, no matter who we are or what we are..."

"You'll be gettin' proposals, now, by the dozen," said Mary, 'you're an heiress, Jinanna.'

"I'm an independent woman, thank God, and that's far better.

Proposals, daughter? I'd scald any man with boilin' water that comes near me to propose," answered gentle little Jinanna.

"After all, this place *is* alive," said Andy John, a couple of evenings later, in Mrs Murphy's kitchen, 'upon my word, I've sometimes had my doubt of it lately. But such a fuss as they're all making over this legacy – and *such* a legacy. It's nothing at all.'

"Aye, but Mr McCready, dear, we're in very different circumstances to you and very different used. Forty pounds a year is a dale to a poor woman that's alone in the world, though very dacent come. You mind old Dan O'Dougherty that lived on the Heathery Hill? Well, she's a daughter of his. A hard old rascal he was too, that put her from makin' a good match when she could have done it. But I wouldn't have heeded him if it had been me."

"The parent worship that goes on in this country amazes me," said Andy John; 'in the States we strike out for ourselves, and do as we like.'

"And you're just right, too," replied Mrs Murphy, who was ready at a moment's notice to embrace any and every opinion that was in favour with her visitor; 'let everybody please theirselves, if things go wrong.' Mary looked at her mother in astonishment.

"If Mary here wanted to please herself, you wouldn't have a word to say against it, would you?" said Andy John smilingly.

"Feth, I would not, Mr McCready. Live and let live, sure what else are we here for? The longest day is but as grass, and we be to make hay when the sun shines!" she replied, almost hysterical with joy.

Mary blushed hotly, and bent over her darning in a shady corner by the fire. Andy John saw the blush and felt gratified. He opened his mouth, and lectured for the next half-hour – with him the conversation often took this unnatural form – and Mrs Murphy was so filled with admiration that she made little or no effort to take the field from him. He described his house and furniture minutely, and compared it to the little farmhouse on the hill in a way which jarred on Mary, while it thrilled and interested her, and which made Mrs Murphy's teeth water as they had never watered before.

"I wanted Michael to sell out at the time my father died," said Andy John, 'and to come right over to me. I would have given him a chance, and a position that he'll never have here. But, no, he would stick in the old rut, do things in the old way, and die no richer than the man that went before him. That's his way, but it's not mine.'

"Feth, it is not!" said Mrs Murphy admiringly.

"He rises early, and works all day in the fields, and what does he make by it? Not much. I worked hard too, but then I made money, plenty of it. I need never do another stroke if I liked, but I want more – I guess I'm the kind that's not easily content. I have ambition, and Michael has none. That's what's wrong with him. I gave him the chance of dying a rich man, and he put it coolly on one side. The man that does that, is in my opinion an idiot."

"An insane idiot!" chimed in Mrs Murphy.

"It's a wonder mamma doesn't hit him on the side of the head for talkin' like that about Michael," thought Mary indignantly. 'I'll not go for a walk with him the next time he asks me if he doesn't quit. I wish Sandy heard him.' But the talk soon veered into safer channels, and Andy John had not the faintest idea that he was being criticized by the girl sitting demurely at her work in the corner.

"That young fella knows a thing or two," Mrs Murphy remarked a few days later to Sammy Soretoes, who was smoking by the fire.

"He knows everything, and the price of it!" Sammy took the pipe from his lips and spoke with extreme heartiness.

"His uncle had a great notion of me at one time. If I had took him it would have been better for me," sighed Mrs Murphy.

"I never heard any word of that before."

"There's many a thing you never heard word of, Sammy dear."

"As far as I mind him, he wasn't the kind to take a girl's fancy, no more nor this boy…"

"Whisht man! There was nothing wrong with him except for a stoppage in his speech – they said he had a fish's throat, wherever he got it – but sure what about that! Deil a hair I'd have cared if I'd have got the money! There's many a thing you miss when you're young and green."

"I mind you young well enough, but I never mind you green," said Sammy, 'the lodgin' you're cheated in, I needn't go till. I think the man you got is a good man, the more he's not pushin' the world afore him like some I could name, and you ought to be thankful for him. Tam has a fine head on his shoulders.'

"His head's full of history, and one kind of gorbage and another," replied Mrs Murphy, 'but the like of that's not much use to you when you go to the shop.'

"But sure you might have got nobody at all, and that would have been worse."

"Me get nobody at all!" she exclaimed indignantly, 'are you right wise, man? I could have got them by the dozen! Not like Mary here.'

Sammy smoked in silence for a few minutes. "I don't much care about that boy," he said at length.

"What boy?"

"What boy do you think?"

"Is it Andy John?" she asked innocently.

"He's never off your doorstep, it appears to me."

"Aye, he's in brave and often. He likes to have a crack with me now and then, and with Michael away constant at the markets and that, it's middlin' lonesome for him up there. And between ourselves, it's my belief him and him didn't agree too well at the first."

"I wouldn't wonder. But I'd rather have the turn of Michael. This fella's too full of himself."

"Michael's a brave boy, I'm not denyin' it, but this is a travelled man, Sammy, and it makes the queer differ. What would do you and me, wouldn't do him." Sammy grunted. 'There's some of the neighbours that jealous-minded and ill-wishin'! The bad-heartedness of the people about here's wonderful.'

"Old Ann would take her oath that he has a wife and family in the States he's not lettin' on about," said Sammy.

Mrs Murphy laughed. "She was always a dubious-minded bein', and what good has it done her? Look at me, as open and unsuspicious as a child, and not gettin' on so bad either. The people's jealous because he has the money."

"Money's not everything in this world."

"Maybe not, but it's a good deal. There's a queer change in Jinanna since the money's been left her, I can tell you. She's another woman. Do you mind thé state she was in before that, daughter?"

"I do," said Mary soberly.

"Aye, dear aye! I've seen a heap of things in my time, but I never seen anything much worse than poor Jinanna when she thought she'd have to go to the poorhouse – and her dacent and respectable. The want of money's a terrible sore want, as I know well."

Mary, who had been ironing at the table, lifted a neat pile of clothes on her arm and carried them into the room. In a few minutes she came back, and stood looking down into the fire. Sammy watched her with kind, scrutinizing eyes. She smiled across the hearth at him. She was so young and light-hearted, it was impossible for her to look at anyone without smiling.

"You done well for Jinanna, I'll allow," said Sammy, 'it bates me how you done it. Your mother is a brave cliver managin' sort of a woman, Mary.'

"I was born with brains," Mrs Murphy explained with dignity, 'it was brains that done it. The McSpeddans all had them. Aye, it wasn't a bad day's work, though I say it myself.'

Presently Sammy rose and knocked the ashes from his pipe. He smiled at Mary, and all the kind, grave little wrinkles about his mouth and eyes came into view.

"Lord love you, but you've little wit!" he said, looking back at her as he went out.

Mrs Murphy ran her hand along the mantlepiece, and searched among spotted dogs, graven images and fancy tea-canisters for the matches. "The evenin's are droppin' down brave and quick." she said. ('Who under goodness, has lifted the box of matches? I can lave nothing down on this fireboard – oh, here they are.') 'Did I tell you what old Ann said the other evenin' when I was kindlin' the lamp? You know the fashion she has of sayin' 'Thank God for light,' when she kindles the lamp? Well she was sittin' there in the corner, and I put a match to the lamp and sez she, 'thanks be to God for light.' I passed no remark for I'm used to her, but Andy John, sez he, 'I guess that's a real old custom, belonging to a bygone age,' sez he, quite quiet and polite, 'that's something of a relic,' sez he. 'If I'm a relic,' sez she, as cross as two sticks, 'I wonder what kind of a cornerpiece you are?' I tell you, Mary, I was ashamed. I'd have checked her for it there and then, but I was in dread of her sayin' something worse. He'll wonder what kind of manners the people here have on them at all.'

"Och, sure Ann's an old woman, and it's no matter what she says," replied Mary easily, 'she's put about these times.'

Having cleaned the wick with a deft movement of her finger and thumb, Mrs Murphy lighted the lamp, and drew her chair hastily up to the fire.

"My feet's like death!" she exclaimed; 'break up the fire, daughter, for dear sake,' and she took off her heavy, elastic-sided boots and held her feet to the blaze.

"It's the world's wonder to think of old John McCready's son gettin' up in the world the way this boy has done," she remarked carelessly. 'I suppose he'll marry some Americay woman. He'd hardly look at anybody else. My, but she'll have the fine time. She'll never have to wet her finger. She'll have servants, and silk dresses, and a trip to the salt water when she takes the notion. The life of a lady! My alive,

but it's wonderful! Old John McCready's son, and him rared beside
us.'

She was itching to say more but restrained herself. Mary was
unusually silent. "Who's this was tellin' me that Michael and Daisy
McIntyre are for makin' a match of it? Somebody was sayin' it the
other day. Who's-this-it-was-now? It'll-come-back-to-me – maybe -"
She leaned forward, and peered into the fire, lost in thought. 'Och
aye! it was Betty-fly-around – the very woman! She says it's goin' all
over that side of the hill. They were out walkin' last sunday evenin'. (I
hope in the Lord it's not true!) Michael's mistress will have a very
different time from the other woman – workin' early and late, and
never an hour to call her own from monday mornin' till saturday
night. She'll not be sittin' in the drawin'-room, takin' her tea like the
quality, of an afternoon. Not but that Michael's a fine boy, and
everybody has the best of a word of him,' concluded Mrs Murphy,
who loved him in her heart, and hated to compare him with anyone,
'but what I'm sayin' is, Andy John's wife will light on her feet!'

Mary was sitting on Ned's little stool in the corner. The lamp hung
on the wall behind her, and the light fell on her fair hair. She was
staring into the fire with grave, wide-opened eyes.

19

A few days before Christmas, Jinanna put her head out of the
door and beckoned mysteriously to Mary who was passing. She
led her into the bedroom, and opening a drawer, took off layer after
layer of soft paper.

"It's a present for your mother for Christmas," she breathed, her
eyes shining with excitement. 'I've had them here sittin' waitin' for
the last month. John Smith and me had the queer piece gettin' them
in without her seein' us. Do you think she'll like them?'

"My goodness alive!" cried Mary, 'you don't mean to tell me it's
the pink set? Why, she's daft about them! I say, Jinanna! She'll be
the proud woman when she has them sittin' in the cupboard. Are they
really for her?'

"They are indeed."

"She'll not call the King her cousin, when she has them I can tell you."

"Look what she has done for me? Neither gold, nor nothing earthly could repay her, but I thought this would be a nice wee Christmas box for her."

"If you'd searched Belfast from one end to another, you couldn't have found anything would have pleased her half so well. Sure she's not at herself for a couple of days after John Smith's been round and she's seen them again, and hasn't had the money to get them."

"The crathur!" exclaimed Jinanna, 'the crathur! Well, she'll not have to fret about them any more, at any rate. It's not often your mother thinks of what pleases herself, Mary. She's wrought hard to bring you all up.'

"Aye, she has that."

"Be sure you don't tell her about them till I bring them in till her on Christmas Day. It'll be a bit of a surprise for her."

"Feth, it will that! She'll be queer and pleased. They're lovely wee cups. I never seen as nice."

"Aye, they're brave and nice." She closed the drawer gently, and opened the one below it. 'This is where I keep the blue dress,' and again she took off many wrappings of soft paper, 'isn't it the lovely blue? It's the very colour of the bluebells that grow about the Giant's Causeway. I was there for a day the year I was married. It was the only big day I ever had in my life. We could see the banks just covered with them, and us sailin' along in the tram. I think that's what put me in such fashion with the stuff when I seen it in Brady's window. It all came back to me. But that's many a year and day ago now.' She knelt down and began to cover the dress up tenderly again.

"It feels that nice to have a bit of money to spend on them you like, and on them you have an obligement to," she said, pausing for a moment, 'it feels awful nice! But if you marry a poor man the way I did, what chanct have you? What do you think, Mary, but Samuel Robert was tellin' me the other night how much he thought of you! He said he doubted you'd look higher, and I said maybe you might.'

"Well, really I think so!" replied Mary in a scornful tone, 'a labourin' boy! I'd die an old maid first! Why he has only sixteen shillin's a week! What's sixteen shillin's a week when the glamour's wore away?'

"It's not much," agreed Jinanna, 'dear me, no, he wouldn't do at all. You'll get better nor him, dear. Maybe you'll marry a rich man yet.'

"Not likely!" said Mary, reddening in spite of herself. 'I'll not get the chanct.'

Jinanna bent down, and began to tuck the paper carefully round the blue dress. "Aye, money's a lovely thing!" she began, 'there's nobody knows the want of it better nor me, and I thank God every time I go down on my bended knees for the riches He has sent me. But Mary dear, I'm old now, you know – I'll be forty-two next birthday – and I'm tellin' you dear – money's powerful grand, that's what it is – but love's better! It's afore all, dear, no matter what they say.'

Mary stooped down, and fingered a little frill of the blue dress. "My, but it's queer and pretty the way she put the frills on the body," she said, 'it's queer and nice! Mamma says love is all fiddledeedee.'

Jinanna shook her head solemnly. "It's not fiddledeedee, whatever it is."

Mary stood up quickly. To her horror two tears had slid down her cheeks and splashed on the paper.

"I must be off," she said, 'I'm in a hurry. It's awfully good of you, Jinanna. Mother will be queer and proud of them cups. They're just grand.'

"You'll not let on you seen them till I walk in on Christmas Day, will you, daughter?"

"Indeed no! Good-bye. A happy Christmas to you, Jinanna."

"The same to you, dear!" She hung over the half-door watching her until she was out of sight. 'I wish in my heart it had been Michael,' she thought, 'there's nobody like him, search the whole country through and through.'

On the afternoon of Christmas Day when she carried in a basket filled to the brim with rosy-pink china and laid it speechlessly on Mrs Murphy's knee, she could have cried for joy. There were undoubted tears in Mrs Murphy's eyes.

"What's this at all, at all?" she cried, in bewilderment, 'my wee pink cups? This bates all! A Christmas box! Are you right wise, Jinanna.'

"I wish they were better and nicer and grander altogether, for it's you deserves the best that money could buy, Mrs Murphy dear, it's not many has a friend like you," said Jinanna breathlessly.

"Lord save us and bless us! My lovely wee pink cups – the whole set

– two bowls and a wee jug – plates and all – did anybody ever hear the like? It's over-all! I never did anything for you, woman dear – you're dotin' – why wouldn't we give a hand when we can? My, but they're beautiful! Many a time I've committed a sin the way I've pined after them darlin' wee cups! I'm fair dyin' about them! There's not a lady in the land has a purtier set of china now nor me. Sit down Jinanna, and Mary will make us a wee cup of tea by ourselves. I'm dry after my dinner, and the baker left in a lovely Christmas box of a cake. Cut a slice of it, daughter."

Mary stood watching them for a minute or two, and then turned away quickly to get the tea. She loved to see her mother look so pleased. It gave her a warm, happy feeling in her heart. If she married Andy John – and by this time she knew everyone expected her to marry him – she would often be able to bring that bright look of pleasure to her mother's face. That in itself would be enough to make anyone happy. She hummed a little tune as she poked the fire to the kettle and got out the baker's cake, with the grand, white icing on it and the red flower in the centre.

"I could have told you all about it, mother," she said, smiling. 'I was in the know, wasn't I, Jinanna?'

"Mary," said Mrs Murphy, handling the cups one by one with deft and loving fingers, 'didn't I always tell you Jinanna was the height of dacency from top till toe? Glory be to goodness, such a present till get.' And to emphasise the confidence and regard she felt for her visitor, she gave her a dig in the ribs, and throwing a significant, sidelong glance at her daughter's back, whispered, 'they'll do the weddin'-party grand.' Jinanna nodded in a gratified manner and Mrs Murphy smiled and winked and pursed up her lips as if some huge, secret amusement had taken possession of her.

"The luck that's flowin' in on me these days has me right and thankful to the Lord," she said piously and aloud, 'and mind you, I count these pink cups of yours not the least of all His mercies, Jinanna – not by any manner of means! The kettle's boilin', daughter – wet the tea.'

Late in the evening she took a cup and saucer in her hand, and hung the fragile little cream-jug on her finger, and went down the street. Old Ann had been ailing lately and she blamed herself for not having gone to see her earlier in the day. It would not be a very cheerful house, this Christmas Day, she thought.

Old Ann sat by the fire, gazing aimlessly before her, and young

Ann, with a book in her hand, sat opposite. She rose and gave Mrs Murphy her chair and presently went out.

"I thought you were dead and buried, Sarah Murphy," began the old woman querulously. 'I never seen hilt nor hair of you today, and me bad since mornin'. You'd have been in right and early if I'd wanted a bit of peace.'

"Sure I haven't had time to bless meself since I got up this mornin'," explained Mrs Murphy, 'with gettin' the childer ready for church, and makin' the dinner and one thing or another.'

"It wouldn't be you but you'd have an excuse handy, at any rate," grumbled Ann, 'this is the miserablest Christmas I ever mind in all my days. My chest is that ketched on me with the cold, I can hardly spake, and her lookin' as if all belongin' to her was dead. She ought to be down thankin' goodness on her bended knees she got rid in time.'

"Aye indeed. So she ought."

"I wish I was dead," said old Ann, 'that's what I wish. Where did you get that cup from, and what are you bringin' it down here for?'

Mrs Murphy explained rapturously.

"A fool and his money's aisy parted," commented Ann. 'I seen that many a time before.'

"Aren't they something beautiful?" exclaimed Mrs Murphy; 'did ever you see a cantier wee cream-jug in all you life? The sugar-bowl...'

"For goodness' sake, quit botherin' me about your old chiney, and me with a load of could on my chest fit to destroy me and no peace in me mind. Ann couldn't go to her church this mornin'. I was angry at her."

"Never you mind Ann. She'll be as merry as a cricket before May Day in the mornin', as the sayin' is."

"She will not then, for that's not her turn. There never was such merryin' in her, but she was content enough till that rascal done it on her."

"It'll be the worse for him yet," said Mrs Murphy consolingly, 'wait till you see! It's all before him, like the man with the wheel-barrow.'

"Aye, but I doubt I'll not live to see it," replied old Ann, a mournful cadence in her voice, 'that's the worst of it. I bate you what you like, he's walkin' the streets of Glasgow in the best of health after all he done on me and mine, and I'm sittin' here with one fut in the grave. Feth, I'm not a bit afeerd but he'll catch it, but I'll not live till I see it.'

"I had a long letter from Charlie this mornin'," said Mrs Murphy, hoping to divert her thought, 'and a nice wee Christmas box of money in it too.'

"It's well but he minded to send you anything."

"I've missed him quarely this Christmas Day! You can't keep your childer round your feet always. It was the lovely letter! He says he's fell in with a family of Coburns lately and had got very great with them. There used to be a lot of them round here, you mind, but the name has nearly died out now. There's a pair of twins, two fine boys..."

"They were always the sorra for twins – them Coburns!" muttered old Ann.

"But I hope to me goodness there's not a daughter, and her after him hot scud!" continued Mrs Murphy anxiously. 'It's the dread of me life that he'll be ketched unbeknownst to himself. I gave him a good caution before he went away and sez I to him, 'Charlie,' sez I 'if you can do nothing else, you can run,' sez I, 'run your hardest – run like the divil!' sez I. 'I will mamma,' sez he, and for all that I'm quare and anxious when I think of it. Girls is that ould-fashioned.'

After an hour's conversation she rose to go. "I think I'll come in when you're in bed, and clap a bit of a blister on your chest," she said, 'it might, maybe, do you some good.'

"I find my cough very hard on me when I lie down," replied Ann, 'but I'll have none of your blisters, thank you. Johnny Darragh has me rightly blistered – it'll do me, my day, I'm thinkin'.'

Mrs Murphy stood hesitating, her hand on the door. She looked back anxiously. Ann was sitting crumpled up by the fire, ill and wretched. A desperate situation required desperate remedies, and perhaps she was in a venturesome mood.

"I can't say I've ever tried it myself," she began with her usual frankness, 'but they do say if you've anything workin' in your mind agin anybody, it's a great aise to put up a bit of a prayer for them now and then. Maybe if you could manage a word or two for Johnny Darragh ...'

But Ann replied with some heat that she thought more of her knees.

20

One cold evening at the end of January, Ann was hurrying home along the Newtownards Road. For once she was alone. Mary had gone to Brady's shop with a message from Jinanna, who was still as excited as a girl over her first dress allowance, and happiest when her lap was full of patterns. She had begged Ann to go with her, but she had refused and Mary had gone off alone, her head in the air.

"I might as well have went with her," Ann was thinking remorsefully. She had been working late, and she was tired and cold. The tall windows of St Patrick's were lighted up as she passed, and she stood for a minute in the shadow of the wall to rest and to listen to the organ. A touch of cold rain hit her face. It was going to be a wet night, and granny would scold her again for not having her umbrella.

Men and women, with seared and hardened faces, passed her, and little children, ill-clad and old before their time. In the pauses of the traffic she could hear music. It was full of pain and trouble, like a cry in the night. A sob rose in her throat. Then the rain came lashing down, and she turned up the collar of her coat and hurried on.

At the corner of the street she stopped to wait for a tram. The windows of a public-house flared behind her, and she moved quickly out of the light lest someone who knew her should pass. Her old reserve, intensified a hundred times, had come back to her, and the children of Gape Row ran to meet her no more.

A man pushed past her, talking loudly to a girl whose arm he held. At the door of the public-house the girl drew back, giggling foolishly. Ann turned to look, and the full light fell on their faces. In an instant she had stepped forward and caught the girl's arm.

"What are you doin' here, Minnie?" she cried, 'let her go, Big Archie. She's comin' with me.'

The man turned to her with an oath, "Who is it that's darin' to interfere with me? Why if it isn't Ann herself!"

Ann looked at him scornfully. "You're not goin' to learn Minnie to drink, if I can help it," she said. 'Let her go.'

"Whisht, you, for mercy's sake!" the girl leaned forward whispering. 'Sure you know he has the very divil of a temper! He'll have your life! I'm only goin' in for a bottle of fizz,' she added in louder tones, 'and then I'm goin' with Archie to the Hippodrome.'

"Look, see here miss," said Archie, coming nearer, 'for very little I'd knock that impitent face of yours in the gutter! I'll larn you to interfere with your betters. Lord knows, it wasn't for nothing Johnny Darragh threw you up. Sure I was hearin' the whole piece the other sunday when I was out in the village.' He laughed. 'It's a nice story, that! Feth, it served you right.'

"I'm in a hurry, Minnie," said Ann, whose face had grown deadly white, 'come on, quick.'

Archie lifted his arm threateningly. "Look see..." he began.

"Don't you say a word till Ann," Minnie broke in suddenly, 'she's a friend of mine and if you're not more agreeable in your manners, I'll not go with you to the Hippodrome at all, maybe,' and she smiled up at him, and shook her long earrings which were sparkling with glass jewels.

"Feth, I'll make you if it's only to spite that hussy."

"It's just for this wonct," said Minnie, turning pleadingly to Ann. 'I'm out of a place, and sure it's lonesome walkin' the streets your lone. Sure what's the harm?'

"If you go, mind I'll never speak to you again," said Ann grimly; 'didn't I help you when you got into trouble in the wareroom two years ago, and didn't I stand up to the other girls when they were down on you? You listen to me now and come on.'

"Go in, and have your drink, Archie," said Minnie, smiling into his scowling face. 'Leave me to talk to Ann. I'll be here at the corner waitin' on you when you come out.'

Ann tightened her grasp and drew her away. Archie stood looking after them in sullen rage.

"Hurry up," Minnie called cheerfully over her shoulder, 'go and get your drink, and don't keep me waitin' on you the half the night,' she laughed gleefully, 'he's fair mad! I'll keep him waitin' a brave while just for darin' to say such nasty things to you.'

"He's a right bad man, Minnie," said Ann, as they moved along the street. 'You musn't go with him. No decent boy will look at you if you go with Big Archie.'

"Och, sure it's only for wonct," replied Minnie easily, 'it's a month of sundays since I went anywhere, and when he came along and asked me I said I'd go. A bit of fun does nobody any harm.'

"How is it you're out of a place so soon?"

"It's them mistresses," explained Minnie, 'they're the crabbitest crathurs on God's earth! The last one come in and found me playin' the piano, and she was neither to hold nor to bind! It wasn't the first time either, for I had picked out a couple of tunes and learned them by ear, if she'd but knowed it. She raged that much I just got up and left her, and she had visitors comin' the next day and wanted me to stay on, but I just wouldn't.'

"You're in lodgin's now, I suppose?"

"Aye, down in Prim Street. Such a hole, but the way it runs away with your money is something dreadful. I never have a farden saved, whatever the sense of it is. I'm awful glad I seen you Ann, but I must be goin' back now. Archie will have my life if I keep him waitin'.'"

"You're not goin' back to him, you're comin' with me."

"Och, but Ann, sure I promised him..."

"Well you shouldn't have promised him then," said Ann firmly. 'Do you know what I've been thinking? We'll run down to Prim Street, you and me, and pack your things, and you can take whatever you want in your hand, and you'll come home with me the night, and stay till you get a place. Sure it would be company for granny when I'm away, and it would save you the price of your room.'

"It's awful good of you Ann, but I couldn't be givin' you the bother."

"It'll be no bother at all."

"I thought I had a place the day, and nothing to do but step intil it, but somehow it didn't come off. I blame that old wasp of a mistress. They have went to her, and she has give out the hour about me and the piano. Bad wind to her!"

"You'll soon get through your money if you're much longer out of a place."

"I don't know where on earth the money goes to," complained Minnie, who was wearing four brooches, as well as bangles and earrings, 'it's a perfect mystery till me.'

"We'll be drowned if we don't hurry," exclaimed Ann, 'there's the rain on again. Come on.' She turned down a side street. Minnie followed her, hesitated, and finally stopped short. 'What's wrong? Isn't this a near cut?'

"I could come the morra night just as well," she said, her bright eyes pleading eloquently for her, 'and I'd have the evenin' at the Hippodrome all the same. It's queer good fun Ann, and the music's lovely.'

"I'll take you myself, some of these nights."

"But I promised Archie..."

"If you don't come home with me the night, you don't come at all. Mind that!" said Ann, 'hurry up or granny will think I'm lost.'

Minnie bent like a reed to the stronger will, and led the way through several smaller side streets until they came to a door which stood open.

"Come on upstairs and say nothing to nobody," she whispered, leading the way. She lit the gas in a small bedroom which she shared with several girls. In a few minutes she had picked out her own untidy belongings and was quickly wrapping them up in a piece of crumpled brown paper.

"Everything else I have in the world is at my uncle's," she said, giggling shamefacedly. 'I was thinkin' I'd have to go round with these jewels in the mornin',' and she shook her long earrings again.

"You'll have something to pay downstairs," said Ann, pushing her worn little purse into her hand. 'I'll wait for you out by. Don't be long.'

They hurried down the narrow, dirty staircase, and Minnie ran into the kitchen and paid her bill with a sudden access of dignity. She had Ann's purse in her hand, and Ann was waiting for her outside on the kerb.

"I'm off to the country with a lady friend," she explained to a slattern-looking woman, who was sitting by the fire reading a novelette.

The rain had stopped, but heavy clouds hung over the plantin' as they stepped out of the tram. It was very dark. Minnie shivered.

"My goodness! I nearly fell off the footpad that time!" she exclaimed, 'I might as well have broke me leg. I can't see a stime. How on earth do you know where you're goin' here? I'd lose meself.'

"I could go anywhere in the dark," answered Ann. 'I've got country eyes and I'm country used. But we'll soon be out of the plantin' now. Look, there's a star.'

"Star or no star, give me Ballymacarrett!" said Minnie crossly, 'You might say there's a bit of life there! This is a terrible ould hole of a plantin'. Sure anything unearthly might rise out of that ditch there any time and scarr the heart out of you! Big Archie thought he seen the divil here, one night.'

"It was no wonder," said Ann coldly.

Minnie laughed. "There's no love lost between yous two. It turned out to be an old goat he seen, with a chain rattlin' after it. Maybe he had a drop in. That's what I told him."

When they reached home they found Mrs Murphy and old Ann sitting chatting by the fire. Ann briefly introduced her friend and her grandmother bade her welcome, and veiled her surprise as best she could. Minnie sat down in front of the fire, and the three women slid into easy conversation by way of the soft weather.

Mrs Murphy leaned back in her chair and examined the newcomer critically. Then her eyes followed Ann, who was moving about the kitchen, preparing supper for herself and Minnie. There was a change in her face. What could have happened? Mrs Murphy opened her lips to speak, but closed them wisely. "Glory be to goodness would Johnny's wife be dead so soon?" she asked herself, 'and would Ann look at him if he came after her again, and him a second-handed man, forby the way he treated her wonct?' No, it could not be that. When Ann laughed at something Minnie said, her astonishment increased. She sat on while the girls ate their food, hoping for an explanation. Afterward, when the supper things had been washed and dried, Ann put on her hat. 'I'm goin' out for a minute or two Minnie,' she said, 'I'll soon be back.' Mrs Murphy opened her lips to ask where she was going at this time of night, but closed them speechlessly. At times Ann's dignity had this strange effect on her.

She hurried up the dark road to the rectory. She turned in at the gate and walked up the short avenue. Her eyes, unlike Minnie's, were so accustomed to the darkness that she could almost see in it. The heavy clouds had passed over to the horizon, and a few stars shone in a grey sky. Long ago, the poplars had lost their musical little leaves, and now they were waving strange, gaunt arms against the sky. The big, kindly house stood back among the trees and grass. A couple of yew-trees loomed up, inkily-black, and behind them a great belt of Portuguese laurels heavily-leaved and green. A collie lay on the step. He rose and came to meet Ann, and sniffed at her skirt.

She knocked at the door, and a few minutes afterwards stood hesitating on the threshold of a large, austerely furnished room. There was a reading-lamp on the table, and a bright fire burning in the grate. Books and papers were heaped untidily on the table, and on most of the chairs. Great, worn, threadbare patches on the carpet, gave it a curiously dappled appearance in the firelight.

His reverence came forward to meet her with outstretched hands. "Why, Ann!" he exclaimed, and in her mood of exultation she did not notice the intense surprise in his voice. 'Come in! I'm rejoiced to see you.'

He gave her a chair and poked the fire to a blaze. Then he went back to his seat on the other side of the hearth, and talked about her grandmother's health and the rainy weather. He would have set her at her ease. But in a moment he knew this had not been necessary. He glanced across at her resolute face. Sooner or later she would speak, and not he. So he turned away his head and waited...

"I've been in trouble." Ann's eyes grew dark for a moment.

"I know." It was all he said, and it was enough, for there was in his voice such music and sympathy, that when he read you old words like, 'Come unto Me, all ye that labour, and are heavy-leaden,' they sounded new and beautiful, as if they had just been made.

"It had me nearly beat," she said, almost piteously, at last.

"It won't do that, Ann," he answered, 'it will do a great deal for you, with the help of God, but it won't do that.'

"I want to tell you what I seen the night," she said presently, and then she told him about Minnie. Outside St Patrick's in the rain a couple of hours ago she had felt the dumb misery of the world beating about her, and when she had rushed forward to shield Minnie, some strange, new force which she did not understand had seemed to rise up in her and take possession.

"There's a queer lot of people in the town, needin' a hand," she went on quickly; 'there's some has no friends like Minnie, and some has them they'd be better without. I've seen the queer wonder of things since I went in there! Ladies don't know what workin' girls come through – they hear tell – but I know. I'm one of them."

His reverence leaned forward in the firelight listening, and his face was divinely kind...

Outside his parish he was scarcely known. He was painfully shy. He listened while others spoke. But down there in the little valley between the hills, he gave himself to his people. It was easy for a girl to tell him the innocent secrets of her heart, and there was that about him which made a tongue-tied country lad turn to him with love in his eyes. They knew he had seen God. It was written on his face.

Late that night when the others were asleep, Ann crept out into the kitchen and lighted a candle. She took her prayer book down from the shelf, and opened it where a little spike of faded heather lay between the leaves. She raked the fire over and pushed it into the hottest part. And then she stood and watched it burn away.

21

"Are you there, Jinanna?"

"Aye, son dear."

"You're awantin' for your tay. She bid me tell you." Ned was standing on tip-toe outside the half-door. 'She's makin' potato-bread.'

"The dear oh!"

"And the new pink cups is all spread out on the table," he whispered cautiously, 'and she's tuk down the big, shiny tay-pot out of the press. Aye, indeed! But don't be lettin' on I tole you.'

"No fear!" returned Jinanna, looking up from her sewing, 'open the door and come on in.'

"I haven't the time. I'm goin' down to the tram-head with Jimmy Forbes. She gave me a penny, and sez she, 'gwan out and stay out,' sez she. I might buy a glassy marble. Jimmy Forbes has three. He's queer and set up, to! But I'll soon have more nor him, for my da has promised me a penny agin this day week. Mind you, she said if I showed me nose inside the house for the next two hours she'd have me life – and her makin' potato-cake and all."

"I'll put some by for you when I go in," said Jinanna, soothingly, 'never you mind, wee son! I'll keep some nice and hot at the side of the fire.'

"Just do and never let on you!" said Ned eagerly, 'she had no business to put me out, and me never off my feet, runnin' errands for her! They were comin' off the griddle, mad hot – and the butter swimmin' down the sides of them. Mind and keep a brave wheen for me, Jinanna.'

"I will that!" she promised, 'don't be afeerd, and wait till I go to the town and you'll see what I'll bring you home.'

Ned stretched himself to his utmost. His broad, little forehead and blue eyes were visible for a moment over the half-door. He winked at her with rare skill.

"Thon's the glad eye," he said graciously, as he sunk back and disappeared.

When she opened Mrs Murphy's door a little later, she was met with the dry, pleasant smell of newly-baked bread. The kitchen was full of friendliness and warmth. A pink geranium in a jam-pot flowered in the back window near the fire. The brass candle-sticks glittered on the mantlepiece, and even the delph dogs, with their long sleek, yellow ears, looked more festive than usual. The table was covered with the best white cloth, and on it were laid the pink rosy cups and saucers and the McSpeddan tea-pot, which long ago Mrs Murphy had brought with her when she came to the village, a young and slender bride.

"Oh, my!" exclaimed Jinanna, staring in stupefaction at the table. 'Such-in-a-sight! My-a-my!'

"Isn't it now?" said Mrs Murphy proudly. 'I ask you, where would you see the like? I put them every one out, though there's only you and me here, (the father is cleanin' out the hen-house, thank God,) just till you'd see the lovely table they make. Actually to goodness, I'm in dread of putting my lips to them. It's not right someway. And I owe them all to you, Jinanna, daughter.'

"Dear help your wit, not at all!" replied Jinanna modestly.

"Feth, I do! Many a time, do you know I could have cried hearty when I seen John Smith turnin' round from the door, and them in his basket. It was a sin for me. But I thought they'd go that lovely with the tea-pot."

"Aye, and so they do."

"Draw up your chair to the table, woman dear. I have the tea wet and all, but I was just givin' it a bit of a simper to take the good out of it." She lifted a tea-drawer, which had been bubbling on the red embers at the side of the fire while they talked, and poured its contents into the tea-pot. A dish, stacked with hot, well-buttered potato-cake, stood on the hearth, and the kitten, crouching under Tam's chair, licked its lips and looked on with a green fire smouldering in its eyes.

"It's my belief," said Mrs Murphy, beaming across the table at her guest, 'it's my belief these wee cups here is goin' to bring me the best of luck! There's them it's lucky to get anything from, no matter what it is. Many a time I heard my mother remarkin' that, and I wouldn't say, Jinanna, but you've brought luck to the house with them wee cups of yours. I wouldn't say but a darlin' fine young man might be takin' his tea out of them darlin' wee cups, at an extra special time before very long either, so I wouldn't!' And she winked, and nodded, and screwed up her eyes ecstatically. 'When there's more to hear you'll hear more, Jinanna, for there's nobody intimater nor yourself, nor has more of a feelin' for me and – Lord's sake, is that Gillespie?'

But the footsteps which threatened interruption at that moment went past the door.

"I can hardly put a bite in my mouth that's she's not in, and dear knows I'd rather have her room nor her company, many a time I could tell her. Jinanna daughter, you're atin' nothing. Sure there's plenty here and the more you ate the better I'll be plazed."

Mrs Murphy loved feeding people. She made tea at all hours of the day, for beggars or chance visitors, or weary-footed passengers who came to her door for a drink of water or to ask the time of day. She was a very poor woman, and perhaps that was why she was so often what she called 'behind' in the shop at the Arches.

"Are you sure it's agreeable to you?"

"It couldn't be agreeabler. And the potato-cake's something lovely! Isn't it nice the way the wee plates is nicked round the rim, and the bunch of roses in the middle. They're that antic lookin'."

"I never seen anything to come up till them I tell you, nor never will," replied Mrs Murphy. 'Gwan, woman – ate something. Give us your cup till I fill it – don't tell me there's that woman again.'

She listened for a minute, the cup poised in her hand, but again the steps went past the door and died away. "Thanks be to goodness! We're havin' the right luck this day. There's nothing like a quiet hearth, Jinanna."

"There is not," said Jinanna, and her eyes were sad for a moment.

"I dreamed the night round last night," said Mrs Murphy, handing the brimming cup across to her, 'and who do you think I dreamed about? Terence O'Grady's woman. They say she's the bitterest pill of them all.'

"The dear look down on us!" exclaimed Jinanna nervously, 'I wouldn't like to dream about her, as much as it would frighten the heart out of me.'

"Peg McCourt says there's noan of them aisy done with, but she's the worst. She has a tongue on her would clip a hedge."

"Aye, she's one you would be afeerd of…"

"Blethers, woman I'd be afeerd of noan of them. I wouldn't care if they were all standin' in the floor fornenst me there. What would you be afeerd of? Sure they're always fightin' through other, the whole jing-bang of them. Billy Morrow tells me they're for atin' other regular in the market."

"They were bound to be mad about me gettin' the money. Many a time I think it."

"So do I," said Mrs Murphy joyously, 'and it's more to me than my meat. Boys oh! but it was grand.'

"I know rightly what they said, the more I never heerd a word," continued Jinanna, 'but I declare I'd near-hand forgotten all about them. It's a world's wonder they haven't raised some sort of a disturbance before this.'

"They're afeerd of me," said Mrs Murphy complacently, 'that's what has kept them quate. They know rightly if they said a word, they'd get more nor they give. Mind you, there's some in this village, and I have them right and afeerd. It's not a bad plan either. Me tongue's brave and useful to me.'

"It's well to be you! The very thought of O'Grady's ones has me trimblin'."

"I'd look well! I wouldn't trimble for..."

A loud, peremptory knocking at the door interrupted her.

Mrs Murphy, who was pouring out a cup of tea, grasped the tea-pot firmly in both hands. "Who the sorra's that?" she asked, in low, astonished tones, 'it's not Gillespie, for she hasn't the manners to clap at anybody's door. Och, I'll bate you what you like it's the ould fella that comes round lookin' jam-pots. He's a heart-scald!' She raised her voice and called shrilly, 'I've got noan the day, so you may gwan away out of that with you and give us peace.'

"It's your dream read," said Jinanna, with a sudden trembling.

"De'il a fear!" There was another brisk knock. 'If you quit rappin', whoever you are, and come on in, it would be no harm at all,' called Mrs Murphy easily, 'the door's not locked that I know of and if you're sellin' pins and needles, or any other mortal thing, you can get out of this as quick as you come, for I've something else to do with me money than to be keepin' the like of you up in style and grandeur – Lord look to us! it's Terency O'Grady's woman, as sure as a gun.'

Mrs O'Grady stood for a moment on the threshold and looked from one woman to another. There was a deadly silence in the kitchen. Someone was standing outside in the shadow behind her.

"I'm comin' in," she said grimly, 'I didn't expect to be asked. Come on, Jane. This is my sister Mrs Sloan, and one of the childer you've robbed. I've seven more at home and four buried and in a better country, where thieves do not break through nor steal, nor delude the dyin' in their beds for the matter of that.'

"Just so," replied Mrs Murphy vaguely.

Mrs O'Grady advanced into the kitchen and looked round for a seat. She was a tall woman with a long, blue nose. Her lips, which were thin, met in a straight line over a discoloured remnant of teeth. She wore a black bonnet with angular bows and black strings tied tightly under her chin. Her sister, who was shorter and stouter, came smiling behind her.

"Sit down Jane," said Mrs O'Grady, pointing to a chair, and Jane sat down.

"Take a seat and welcome," began Mrs Murphy, 'it's a fine day for the time of year. Maybe you'll take the sofa, Mrs O'Grady?'

"I will not," replied Mrs O'Grady, 'I'll sit on the chair I'm on, and no other. I've come down here on a matter of business, and not on pleasure.'

"Do you tell me that?" said Mrs Murphy ('thank heaven, I put away the childer's broken boots and Tam's ould trouser that I was mendin' at,' she thought, 'they'll never take notice to them stuffed alow the dresser. They can look till their hearts' content at me lovely chiney, and me tea-pot. Dear be thanked I have them out fornenst them!') 'Are you as bad as ever with the pains, ma'am?' she asked kindly.

"Did I come here to talk to you about my rheumatism pains, do you think?" said Mrs O'Grady, with lowering brows. 'I come here to see about gettin' back what is mine by rights and my sister's, and what should have went in the natural course of things to that innocent lamb there, and others like him, divided up. That's what I come about.'

"Do you tell me that?" repeated Mrs Murphy.

"What brought *you* up interferin' with a dyin' man, and sendin' him to his Maker with a sin on his soul that's something la*ment*able to think of? What had *you* to do with Andy Sloan? How dare *you* interfere with a poor old man, dyin' peacable in his bed, and leavin' everything right and proper, and as the Lord intended? You think anything becomes you, so you do."

"I did nothing at all, Mrs O'Grady dear. I didn't do half as much for him as I would have liked. The poor old crathur was wastin' away in his sins, and thank God I got him rightly stirred up before it was too late. Aye dear aye! There's nobody can say but Andy Sloan made a good end, whatever he was afore," and Mrs Murphy shook her head solemnly and continued to smooth her apron with a tantalizingly deliberate movement of her hand.

"Who's goin' to make up to me innocent childer, and me sisters innocent childer for the way you've robbed and stole on them?" asked Mrs O'Grady, 'that's what I come about. Maybe you'll tell me that?'

Mrs Murphy laughed scornfully. "Who's goin' to make up to Jinanna for the years of slavery she put in over that bit of a debt her man run up to Andy Sloan? He had her near murdered payin' it back till him, the ould villain! But he was dacent in the end. I'm not sayin' a word agin him, but he should have left her the farm as well, and all on it. That's what he should have done."

"The farm was promised to my wee Willie John the day he was christened," exclaimed Mrs O'Grady, 'you've done enough harm, but if you'd done *that*...'

"Do you think I'm afeerd of you, Martha O'Grady?" crescendoed Mrs Murphy, 'feth, I am not. I know you too well and all belonging to you. I know the dirt you've come from...'

"You know a good deal about dirt, I'll allow," retorted Mrs O'Grady, 'for you get your livin' of dirt – that silent, old sepulchre of a man of yours scrapin' it off the roads to keep you – dirt indeed! – you done well to mention dirt! I'd be ashamed of him if I was you.'

Mrs Murphy's eyes blazed with anger. Her face was scarlet. For a moment she felt like striking the other woman, who, in spite of the fierceness of her words, still looked cold and blue. They sat facing each other. Mrs Murphy was swaying backwards and forwards in rage when her eyes caught the gleam of the tea-pot on the table – the McSpeddan teapot – which was still full of half-cooled tea. In a moment the kitchen was full of dead-and-gone McSpeddans – grand people who had lived on decent farms, and driven down the windy hillside on sunday mornings to church in their own gig.

"Is it me, a McSpeddan, talk to the like of you about my family?" she asked in more level tones, 'or demean myself to rake up my ancestor's bones for you? You've said enough. You'd better gwan out of this.'

"I'm not goin' to budge an inch till I know what you're goin' to do to make up to my childer," said Mrs O'Grady. 'I'll see my childer righted, or I'll raise the town! I'll have it out of you some way or other.'

"You're talkin' like a fool..." began Mrs Murphy.

"I know you've nothing yourself, nor never had," interrupted Mrs O'Grady, 'but there's them that has. The McSpeddans of the Hillhead – ignorant, jumped-up people – hadn't a brass farthin' among them – and as for the Murphys,' she laughed 'the laste said about them the better. But this woman here – this wee, half-witted fool of a crathur sittin' shiverin' beside the crock of water – *she* has it. Maybe you'll allow that.'

Mrs Murphy suddenly became aware of a low, undercurrent of talk which had been goin' on behind her for some time. She turned her head to look. For a moment it seemed as if Jinanna had entirely disappeared, but as her eyes swept round the kitchen, she discovered her, shrivelled up in a low seat between the dresser and a crock of water which had been placed on a high stool. Mrs Sloan was sitting near her, leaning forward, with her hand resting on Jinanna's knee.

"What are you doin' there, Jinanna?" cried Mrs Murphy sharply. She realized suddenly where the danger zone lay.

Mrs Sloan looked up and smiled at her. She had a broad waxen face, pale, with a strange darkness showing under the skin. She spoke in a low, level voice, and her speech was strangely studded with the letter S. Indeed, when she spoke she seemed to fling them broadcast from her.

"We were speaking of the old sufferer," she explained, still keeping her hand pressed on Jinanna's knee, 'and what he s-suffered in his last hour, thinking about me and my childer. I hope he is forgiven. I hope his s-soul is at rest. In s-spite of his s-sins I hope so. I do indeed. I forgive him and I forgive you, Mrs Murphy, and I forgive you too,' she turned and looked with special sweetness into Jinanna's face. 'I care nothing for what happens to myself, for I'm safe for time and for eternity. But it's about my childer I come down here today.'

"Snake!" ejaculated Mrs Murphy.

"When I think of all that old s-sufferer s-suffered in his last hour," continued Mrs Sloan, 'I feel s-sorry for him, and when I think of what you'll s-suffer when it comes to *your* last hour, I feel s-sorry for you too. I can't help it. The last hour's a s-solemn hour...'

"It is that!" interrupted Mrs Murphy. 'Jinanna, quit lookin' at her. Look at me. What's come over you woman? Do what I bid you at wonct.'

Jinanna seemed to turn away her eyes with difficulty.

"What's that woman sayin' to you?" demanded Mrs Murphy.

"I'm to give her so much out of the money every year," said Jinanna slowly, as if repeating a lesson, 'it's what Andy asked himself to have done, in his last hour.'

"He s-said to tell her to give back the half to me every year," Mrs Sloan hastened to say, 'it was his last words. If you don't believe me, ask Mr Sloan. Ask them that was with the old s-suff...'

"Lave my kitchen this minute, ye pair of thieves!" cried Mrs Murphy, springing to her feet, 'get out of this, ye reptiles ye! I'll call the polis! I'll have you lifted! It's in jail you ought to be. Jinanna, you're a fool – a perfect born fool! I'll take a stick till you when I get done with them ones! Walk out, Mrs O'Grady. There's the door there fornenst you.'

"I'll go when I get my rights and not till then," replied Mrs O'Grady firmly.

"I'll throw you out on the street there, and the wee fella after you!" exclaimed Mrs Murphy, 'I'll hould you it will not take me long.' She turned and made a dive for the poker, and the little boy who had sat still in Tam's chair all through the interview, rose in terror and fled through the door.

"Mr S-sloan s-said..." began Mrs Sloan.

"I'm not used to serpents hissin' in my house," interrupted Mrs Murphy, 'and I want noan. Gwan now, the pair of you! And never darken my door again, nor offer to spake to me the longest day you live.'

"Spake to you!" exclaimed Mrs O'Grady, moving towards the door in spite of herself, 'is it *me* spake to you? I wouldn't spit on your tongue if it was afire.'

"Go 'long, ye dirt!" cried Mrs Murphy, brandishing the poker wildly in the air, 'gwan for your life.'

When the kitchen had been cleared of visitors she closed the door and turned to Jinanna. "Well!" she said breathlessly, 'well, well! That was over *all*!'

Jinanna was leaning back, white and faint against the wall. Her eyes were wide with terror. She could not speak.

"It wasn't long till I got me dream read," said Mrs Murphy. 'I'll make a sup of tea when I get me breath. You'll be rightly in a minute or two, daughter. I'm far through meself. I find me heart beatin' in me breast. Them's a pair of boys! Since God framed me I never heerd more nor I heerd the day! What are you doin' there, you dirty, wee rascal...'

She had turned to the fire to find the kitten licking the last of the butter off the potato-cake which had been left to keep hot on the hearth. As she raised her arm it sprang adroitly out of reach, and spent the rest of the evening watching her with green, triumphant eyes from the top shelf of the dresser.

"Jist you wait till I get at you, my brave boy," she said angrily, 'I'll give you the quare murderin'! My good bread! and it ruined! The kettle's comin' up to the boil, Jinanna. I'll have you a sup in a minute.'

She sank back in the chair exhausted. There was silence in the kitchen for a few minutes.

"When I seen thon blue neb comin' in at the door..." said Mrs Murphy faintly.

22

Old Ann opened her door and peeped out. The wind had risen in the night and the trees were rocking hilariously to and fro.

"It's the cuckoo-storm," she said to herself as she closed it carefully, 'it's heartsome to hear it after all. It brings the cuckoo. We'll be hearin' her now afore long. My-a-my! it's wonderful how the time goes round!'

"I'm sure *I'm* not keepin' him back," thought Mrs Murphy, a few doors away. 'I'm never done fillin' him with good eggs that I ought to be sellin' by rights. I wish he'd put an inch to his step. If he doesn't look out, she'll rust and not take him at all, and it would serve him right too, the little atterkap! – but it would be the quare come down till me. Sure I thought I'd have had them married and all by this time. And now here he's away tourin' and gallivantin' to Killarney his lone, and the Lord only knows who he'll fall in with there! I'd Killarney him if I had him this minute.'

Mrs Murphy was becoming anxious. Andy John came to the house with unfailing regularity, he looked at Mary, he talked to her, he brought her boxes of sweets, he took her for walks, but he said no word of marriage. Yet Mrs Murphy was convinced he was in love. She saw it in his eyes she said, as plain as a pikestaff. She left them alone when it was possible, she planned messages for them, she drove them before her up the aisle on sunday evenings, and saw that he sat beside Mary in her own pew. Michael never came to see her now. Occasionally she wondered why, but she had no time to think of Michael. She had to see this thing through. She was thirsting for the hour when she would sail down the village street, saying coolly to this one and that one, "Our Mary has tuk Andy John at last. He's fair dyin' off his feet about her!" She had rehearsed the speech more than once to an empty kitchen and it sounded well. 'Bad scran to that little fella for keepin' me waitin'!' she muttered impatiently.

There was nothing of the adoring lover about Andy John. There never would be. But he meant to marry Mary. She was so young and soft and fair. He wanted a wife and he meant to take one back with him to the States. But there need be no hurry. He wasn't going just yet. Towards the end of his visit he would arrange everything quietly. Of course she would be crazy to get him. He would give her what she had no right to expect – a fine house, a solid income, a position entirely different from her own, and a splendid husband – yes certainly, a splendid husband. She would be a very happy woman. He felt sure of that. But there need be no hurry. He loitered from one watering-place to another in the south of Ireland, and enjoyed himself exceedingly. Presently he would go home and bring her a nice present, and meantime he sent her a picture postcard when he thought of it.

A couple of times through the winter he had gone to Liverpool where some of his American friends had settled, for a ten days' visit. Mary was happiest when he was away. She liked to think of the grand marriage she was going to make, the money she would have to spend, the lovely presents to send home. But when he came back and sat on the other side of the fire, and talked in the bouncing, self-satisfied way he had, she wondered why she felt inclined to cry. Once, when her mother was praising him extravagantly, she ventured to say, "He's not a bit well lookin' at any rate – a wee short, stumpy fella like that!" and Mrs Murphy, eyeing her coldly, had strongly advised her to get one made in the pottery to her measurement.

"When is he goin' to pop the question?" the anxious mother asked herself a dozen times a day. 'That's what *I* want to know. Such a match! It's like a leaf out of a book!'

April came and went. May put on her beautiful garments. The poplars shook out a million leaves, and the birds went mad with happiness. One afternoon Mary came home early from her work looking white and tired and complaining of headache.

"It's the close work in the town has done it on you," said her mother kindly, 'and you used to the fresh air of the fields round you day and night. You'll have to stay at home and rest yourself for a couple of days, daughter. For mercy's sake, don't take bad now, *whatever* you do!' and she gave her a strong cup of tea and sent her to bed. 'It's no wonder she's lossin' her colour,' she thought moodily, 'that little fella will have us both astray in the mind before he's done, and I daren't say a word to hurry him either.' She turned the children relentlessly out of doors and moved softly about the house, lest Mary should be awakened out of the grand sleep she had fallen into. But Mary was lying very still and white, her hot eyelids pressed into the pillow, and she did not tell her mother that she had met Michael riding home on his new mare, looking very handsome and debonair, or that he had passed her with a curt nod.

She stayed at home for a couple of days. Her mother who was curiously irritable, would scarcely let her help with the housework, but would have her sit idly by the fire all the time. Idleness was the last thing Mary wished for now. Once, when Mrs Murphy was out, she got a bucket of water and a scrubbing-brush and began to scrub the table vigorously. She could not understand her mother's sudden wrath when she returned.

"I'm only scrubbing the kitchen table," she began defending herself. 'Sure it needed a good scrubbin'.'

"Am I tryin' to get the kitchen table married?" asked Mrs Murphy fiercely. The next day, she went cheerfully back to her work.

The morning after Andy John came home from Killarney, Michael walked across the farmyard and into the kitchen to look for a tool. He heard his brother whistling in his room. An open portmanteau was on the floor, and a few scattered articles on the table. Something bright gleamed on the corner of the dresser. He went over to look at it.

It was a little gold wristlet watch, with a gold, flexible band. He took it up and examined it, a smile spreading slowly over his face. "Caught at last, by Jingo!" he said to himself with a chuckle. Who was she? Probably some girl among his American friends at Liverpool. Andy John was very reticent about his friends and Michael too proud to ask questions, but for some time he had felt in an inexplicable way that his brother was thinking of getting married. As he went about his work that morning, he could not help thinking with amusement of the important air with which he would tell him of his engagement. When he came in at dinner-time there was no sign of the watch, and Andy John had gone off to town. Perhaps he had gone to post it. Michael smiled broadly at the thoughts. He had always had his suspicions about those Liverpool visits.

A couple of days later, he was driving home from town in the afternoon. He had been up earlier than usual, and the quiet jogging motion of the cart made him sleepy. The trees in the plantin' slipped dreamily past. He came out into the broad sunlight, and was only half-aware of it. The road lay winding, white and wide, before him.

"Hi mister! Hi there Michael!" a shrill little voice called. 'Give us a lift.'

Michael opened his eyes and looked over the side of the cart. Ned Murphy's keen, sunburnt little face was peering up at him.

"Hullo Ned! Jump in. Give me your hand – right you are!" as Ned climbed nimbly over the wheel, 'well, man, and how are you doin'?'

"The best!" answered Ned, as he settled himself on a couple of bags in the corner of the cart. 'I say, Michael, will you let us drive?'

Michael handed him the reins. He and Ned were old friends.

"Jimmy Forbes says he drove his uncle's milkcart the whole road to town one day last week," remarked Ned. 'Do you mind that?'

"Did he now?"

"Not at all, man! It's a lie! You couldn't believe a word come out of wee Forbes' head. He can drive no more nor the cat. Sure he'd coup any horse and cart he got a hoult of – that's what I told him. He's never done braggin'."

"Would you like to come in the cart with me some day?" asked Michael. 'I'd let you drive to your heart's content.'

"Man, but I would! I'll tell that to wee Forbes before he's much older." He thought deeply for a minute or two and then meeting Michael's kind eyes he said, 'I might be a wee thing frightened at the crossin's.'

"Never mind the crossin's. I'll look after them for you."

"I'll go the morra," said Ned, with sparkling eyes. 'I'll be waitin' for you at the corner.'

"All right. Be sure you don't forget."

"Feth, I think I'll not forget!" He fell into a satisfied silence. Michael's eyes rested on him with pleasure. There was something about his thin, freckled little face which reminded him of Mary, and it was sweet to be reminded of her.

"Mrs Gillespie fell down off her feet last night and hurted her leg," he announced presently. 'Mamma says maybe it's as well for her to have something to yammer about. It keeps her goin'-like.'

"Dear me," answered Michael, 'that was a pity.'

"Och, I dunno. Wee Wullie Gillespie was kept in nearly every day last week. He's the right bad scholar! He'd rather be runnin' the country, tearin' the clothes off his back as gettin' his lessons. Mamma says he needs a good batein'. Did you hear what happened our Bella's white dress?"

"No, I did not."

"Well, sure, they had it washed and put out on the hedge to dry for sunday, and what do you think, but McIntyre's big calf come down the field and ate the whole body out of it! Bella cried and cried, and when our Mary come home she promised her a new one if she'd whisht. It was a terrible pity."

"It was that," said Michael sympathetically.

But Ned did not wish his story to be all tragedy. He leaned forward, bursting with pride. "Our Mary has got a nice wee clock for her arrum!" he said eagerly.

"Our Mary" – how sweetly the words sounded in Ned's childish voice! Our Mary. The rest of the sentence did not reach Michael.

"Our Mary has got a wee clock – a lovely wee gold clock for her arrum," Ned repeated. 'I seen it myself,' he said with some indignation, as Michael did not answer. 'She had it on her arrum, and then she took it off. Mamma says it was a present from her boy, but I wasn't to let on to anybody and sure neither I am, only to you. What are you takin' the reins from me for, man?' he asked indignantly. Michael had grasped them without thinking.

"It's all right, son, you can drive away," said Michael, relinquishing his hold. A horrible, sickening thought was struggling to find its way into his mind. It went on struggling – struggling – in pain.

There was a couple of minutes' silence. Ned looked at him in wonder. At last he leaned forward and said confidentially: "Do you know what Mrs Gillespie says? She says it's a quare good thing for our Mary to be gettin' your Andy John!"

Michael took the reins and pulled up sharply. His eyes blazed. "I'm going to drop you out here. No, I can't take you into the village. Run on home, like a good boy," and in spite of Ned's indignant protest, he lifted him out and set him down on the road.

"Mind and be lookin' out for me the morra," Ned called beseechingly after him, but Michael was silent. The mare started forward in answer to the whip.

When he got home he saw to his horse, and went into the house. Andy John was not there. He ate a few mouthfuls of supper, and whistling for Patch, went out. He took a quiet path over the fields which led finally to the top of the hill. Patch, scenting a long evening with his master, ran joyously in front.

He saw everything clearly at last. He had been a blind fool – a blind, weak fool, but now he saw clearly. He was no man. He had lost the girl he loved for the sake of his friend, as he thought – for the sake of honour. Oh, it was a fine thing to do! He had lost the girl he loved, and his brother had won her – a stranger and an interloper who had nothing to recommend him – nothing in the world to recommend him but his dollars. Neither kindness, nor gentleness, nor humility. He was his brother, but he hated him. He would hate him as long as he lived... Of course he had heard the gossip about them. He had heard their names coupled again and again. And he had laughed in derision at the thought. For Sandy and she were lovers. He had seen it with his own eyes. And he stood aside with a bursting heart, for the sake of his friend... And his brother had won her.

Patch and he wandered over the hill for the most of the night. It was a beautiful, warm night in early June. There was no real darkness, only grey, silver shadows everywhere. Blackhead light-house, guarding the Lough, flung out long arrows of fire across the grey sea, softly and steadily all night long. The curlews cried mournfully over his head. At last, tired out, he sat down below a hedge, and Patch crept into his arms and went to sleep. He thought of his mother. He remembered the long winter nights when they had sat together by the fire, planning all they would do when Andy John came home. He thanked God she hadn't lived to see it. And as he thought of her the warm tears fell.

He came home early in the morning, and went straight into the yard to his work. He breakfasted alone as usual. His brother did not like country hours.

Later in the morning, he was passing through the yard when he heard a window being suddenly pushed down. He turned his head and saw Andy John. He called to him to come in at once. Michael shut his teeth. Better get it over quickly. In another minute he was going up the narrow stairs.

A trunk was pulled out in the middle of the floor, and several travelling-bags were lying about. Andy John's possessions were piled on the table and the bed. Marget was going to and fro, her arms full.

"What's up?" asked Michael shortly, 'where are you goin' now?'

Andy John lifted a bloodshot eye. 'I'm going back to my *own* country,' he said.

"Why, what's takin' you off in such a hurry?"

"The treatment I've got from some of *your* friends!" he shouted, stooping over the trunk.

Michael closed the door. "We needn't be tellin' all to the neighbours. What's happened to you?"

In another hour or two Andy John would probably have recovered himself enough to have given a more dignified but perhaps less truthful account of the story. But his self-esteem had been so cruelly wounded, his dignity so crushed, that for the moment he could think of nothing but that Mary should appear in as bad a light as possible.

"I had the ill-luck to take up with some of your friends," he began violently, 'and like a fool, I made up my mind that sooner or later I would marry Mary Murphy. I can't think what possessed me. I liked her fairly well, and she led me to believe she was crazy about me. I didn't like to disappoint her. I'd never have gone so far only for that. I couldn't pass the door but that wretched mother of hers was calling me in. She was no match for me, of course. I knew that, but I was willing to take her, and do well for her. And when I was in Dublin on my way home I bought this watch for her, would you believe it? – where is it? I hope to goodness I haven't lost it,' he searched frantically under a pile of clothing on the bed, 'there it is under these collars. Look at it, Michael. It's a regular beauty – cost me fifteen pounds in solid cash. Well, I bought it and brought it home and gave it to her, and she was delighted you may be sure, and when I kissed her' – Michael winced as if someone had struck him – 'she was delighted too, and she said she would marry me any day I liked – any day – and come out with me in September.' He paused for breath.

"Well?" said Michael. His lips were dry.

"And when I went down there last night – what had happened in the meantime I don't know – the ungrateful little hussy gave me back my beautiful watch," he held it out in the palm of his hand – 'and said she didn't want to marry me. She actually said that! And me lifting her out of the gutter, and setting her on a throne, you might say. I was willing to overlook her poverty and everything else about her, and this is my thanks. She has made a fool of me before everybody. I won't sleep another night in this damned country. I'm off by the afternoon mail.' He made a dive at a bundle of clothes and threw them into the box.

"Why did she do it?" asked Michael.

"I don't know and I don't care. I could have got plenty far above her. I wish I had never come home."

Events had followed each other so quickly that Michael's head was whirling. But he knew that the bitter hatred of his brother had suddenly died out of his heart.

"I'm terrible sorry," he said.

"Look at what I paid for that watch! I'll try to get them to take it back, but it's very awkward for a man in my position."

"I used to think she was fond of Sandy," said Michael steadily.

"That freckle-faced, red-haired chap? Not at all! She played with him too. Then she thought she'd fly at higher game when *I* came along – the heartless little devil! I'll catch the five o'clock mail to Dublin and stay there the night. I've a couple of important matters to see to – in fact going off in this unexpected way is most inconvenient. Do you think they'll take back the watch?"

"I'll drive you to the station," said Michael 'and if you like I'll go with you as far as Dublin.'

"No need," replied his brother, 'you've plenty to see about at home. Give me a hand with this bag, will you? I'll guess I'll be delighted to wipe the dust of this country off my feet. The little devil!'

"I wish you weren't goin' off like this," said Michael kindly. 'I'm terrible sorry this happened at all. You'll find you'll soon forget all about her. She's not worth thinkin' about.'

"I'll not be long in forgetting *her*, I can tell you, but I won't forget the way I've been treated in a hurry," he replied bitterly, 'making a laughing-stock of me before everybody! – a bit of a girl like that – and she so delighted to get me the night before. She drew me on, Michael, she did indeed, or I never would have been so foolish. She made me believe she was madly in love with me. I was sure of it, perfectly sure of it, and I was sorry for her. You've no idea of the depth of her. She's a bad one, I tell you.'

"I believe you," said Michael harshly, 'she's all that. For very little I'd tell her what I think of her.'

"I wish you would," returned Andy John, with fervour. 'I wonder will they make any difficulty about taking back the watch?'

As they drove quickly through the village early in the afternoon, there was an ominous silence and emptiness about the Murphy doorway. Not even a chicken was in sight. Michael wondered grimly what Mrs Murphy had to say on the subject. He thought she would be

equal to dealing with any number of refractory daughters, and he
knew his brother had been in high favour with her. For the moment
he felt glad that Mary was in such capable hands. She had made too
many people suffer – Sandy, himself, and now poor Andy John. His
brother's battered appearance touched his heart. After all, he was his
only brother, and he thought he must often have misunderstood him
since he came home. He felt nearer to him now in his trouble than in
all the months of his visit, and every hour his indignation with Mary
increased.

23

M ary opened the half door, and came out into the clear, golden
heat of the afternoon. It was sunday, and the street was very
quiet. Sammy's dog, lying on the hot, stone doorstep opened one eye
and wagged a courteous tail. No other living thing was in sight. Gape
Row was out in the June lanes, or nodding itself to sleep in the cool of
the house.

She closed the door gently behind her and crossed the road. Her
head was bare. She had felt cold in the house, but here the hot
sunshine blazed and shimmered above her, and sent delicious little
streams of heat down the back of her neck. She walked slowly along
the road, and presently turned into a field. Who that could walk on
soft springy grass beside a June hedge would stay on the dusty road?

Her face was white, and her eyes deadened with many tears. She
would never be happy again. She was sure of that. Oh, she had had
such a dreadful time! She had behaved badly. She had taken the little
gold watch Andy John had brought her home from Dublin – and it a
perfect dote of a watch – she had let him fasten it on her wrist – she
had even let him kiss her – and she had promised to marry him. Her
mother was wild with joy, but she had cried all night, and the next
evening she was alone in the kitchen when he came in, and without
waiting to think what she was doing, she jumped up and ran into the
room, and got the watch out of the drawer and almost threw it at him.
"I can't get married," she had repeated again and again with sobs. 'I

can't, I can't!' She wondered how she had had the courage to say the words. And at last he had gone to the door and sent for her mother, who was out among the neighbours telling the grand news. Mary shivered to think of the next ten minutes. But Andy John had cut it mercifully short. He had suddenly grabbed the watch and stuck it in his pocket. 'You'll rue this day, miss, I'll see to it that you do!' he called, glaring at her with angry, bloodshot eyes as he rushed out.

And afterwards when he had gone, her mother turned to her quietly and said, "this is my death, Mary." Oh, that was by far the worst of all! Her voice was so small and lifeless, and she had gone straight to bed and stayed there ever since. Ann was sitting with her now, and every time she went into the room she turned away her head and would not speak. Oh, she was so unhappy! She would never feel light-hearted and merry again. If only her poor mother would get well, and scold them all round. She did wish she could have married Andy John. She supposed what her mother said was true – that she was a *really* bad girl, and would be sure to end her days in the workhouse. 'I wisht I was dead and in my grave!' she moaned, 'I wisht I had never seen Andy John. I wisht I had never seen that lovely wee watch – och annee annee!'

She lifted her eyes from the green bank, jewelled with wild pansies and speedwells, and clear-eyed, cool-cheeked primroses. And she saw Michael in the distance, coming along in the shadow of the hedge. He was taking a near-cut through the fields out to the road. A flood of joy washed suddenly over her, wiping out in one swift moment every trace of fatigue and sorrow from her face.

For had she not seen Andy John driving away through the village with his traps a couple of days before? She had watched him furtively between the geranium-pots in the window. And was not Michael coming to her quickly across the sunshiny field? She did not wait to think. But she was happy again. Her feet felt like dancing along the grass.

When Michael came up to her, he saw a girl with the radiance of spring in her face. He remembered his brother's woebegone appearance when he had said goodbye to him in the Great Northern Station. And he hardened his heart. Mary turned and pulled a bit of red-tipped thorn out of the hedge. She suddenly felt shy.

Michael's sunburnt face was very stiff and hard under his straw hat. She looked up at him in wonder. It had not occurred to her that he would think badly of her. In her mind she kept the two men leagues apart. She could not connect them.

"Isn't it the grand day, Michael?" she began softly.

"I wonder you have the face on you to look at me at all. But I suppose you take credit to yourself for playin' off the one against the other so cleverly."

"Is it Andy John you're thinkin' of? Och, Michael, I'm that sorry..."

"I don't want to hear your excuses," he interrupted, 'keep them for them that will listen to them. It's not me. I wouldn't be talkin' to you at all only I was wantin' to tell you I'm heart-thankful my brother escaped you this day – and I despise you for the way you treated him.'

"Oh Michael, wait a wee minute! Let me tell you how it all come about."

"I don't want to hear," said Michael shortly. 'I know enough.'

Mary did not speak. It occurred to her that she had very little to say for herself. She had encouraged Andy John. She had promised to marry him, and she had broken her promise. Her eyes filled with tears.

"I'm that sorry!" she repeated helplessly.

"That won't make up to anybody," returned Michael, 'you can be as sorry as you like, but I'm not goin' to forgive you in a hurry. You're not the girl I thought you were, that's one thing I'm sure of.'

"Och, but Michael, maybe I'm not as bad as you think. Wait till I tell you..." again that hopeless pause.

"Didn't you know he was after you all winter?"

"I had a kind of notion..."

"Aye, I'm sure you had!" Michael laughed, 'and you kept him hangin' on and danglin' after you, and you even promised to marry him when the poor foolish fellow asked you, and then you threw him up and made a laughin' stock of him before everybody, you can't deny it.'

Mary was silent.

"Were you ever fond of him at all?"

"I was not then!" she said, breaking into indignant speech. 'Fond of him? How could anybody be fond of the like of thon? Sure he thinks of nothing nor nobody from mornin' till night only himself! I tell you I'd sooner never be married at all...'

"How dare you!" exclaimed Michael, his face flaming with anger. 'How dare you say a word against him! What are you I'd like to know? – a wicked, heartless flirt – a silly, light-headed...'

"I can be angry too!" cried Mary shrilly. 'I can call names and barge as well as you, my young man...' she stopped suddenly. She remembered the Lady Ermyntrude, and the excessive dignity with which she bore herself in circumstances of the kind. She drew herself up and spoke through scarcely-opened lips.

"You forget yourself strangely, Mr McCready, to speak to me in any such-in-a-manner. I will ask you to withdraw." She waved her arm towards the meadow gate.

"I'm goin'," said Michael grimly, 'and all I wish to say is that I'm heart-thankful Sandy escaped you, too. I suppose you thought I didn't know anything about that either?'

"What is between Alexander and me concerns noan of you," replied Mary, with immense dignity. She did not know in the least what he meant, but she was convinced the Lady Ermyntrude would never allow a vulgar name like Sandy to cross her lips. 'I must ask you not to interfere any more in my affairs...'

"I don't care a damn what you ask," said Michael roughly. 'I'll say goodbye. Thank God you're not comin' into *my* family...'

"Oh dear!" laughed Mary, in her shrillest and silliest fashion, 'I wouldn't have the name of McCready tacked on to me for life...' She stopped abruptly.

"Maybe you'll not be asked again," he said. 'Did you think you would?' He looked at her contemptuously.

Mary was furiously angry. It is true she remembered to make one or two frantic clutches at the retreating skirts of the Lady Ermyntrude, but that good woman must have been scared out of reach, for the last words she screamed across the field at Michael were, "Look, see Michael McCready – if you waited till you were blue-mooldin' I wouldn't take you!"

24

"Are you feelin' any better the day, mother?"
"I am not. I'll never be better in this world."
"Och indeed you will. If you could get away to the shore for awhile, you'd soon mend."

"Have wit, child! It's the shore on the other side of eternity that I'll soon be at, I've a notion."

"Och, but sure you've said that many a time before," said Mary cheerfully. 'You'll soon be rightly – wait till you see! Is your back bad the day?'

"It couldn't be worse!"

"Well mind you, you *look* a queer lot better..."

"I'm dyin' I tell you!" interrupted Mrs Murphy angrily, 'but you'll none of you heed me. You'll be sorry before you'll be much older. There's that father of yours walkin' in and out of the house as cool as pump water, and me tellin' him mornin', noon and night that I'm not long for this world, and he never as much as lets on he hears me! He's an awful mystery of a man, that!'

"I'll bring you home a nice wee bit of meat for your tea," Mary was standing in the middle of the floor, pinning on her hat, 'take good care of yourself till I come back.'

"Mystery and all, there's them would be glad of him, if I was gone," continued Mrs Murphy, leaning forward in her chair with a sudden return of energy. 'Mind you, daughter, if I happen to drop off, I'm lookin' to you to see that he doesn't go and get himself married secondly.'

"Mother, I wish you wouldn't say such things! Sure he'd never think of the like of that."

"Maybe not, for as far as I can rightly see he thinks of nothing. (What I've suffered with that man!) But sure somebody else might think of it for him, and where would you be then?" She paused and shook her head gravely. 'Mind you there's times I have me doubts about Gillespie!'

Mary threw up her hands and laughed.

"Aye, you can laugh, but, if you remark it, I never have the laste dwam but she's in here hot scud, makin' him his supper and fussin' round him till all's no more! The Lord knows I don't believe the man as much as sees her in his road, but he might be the innocenter ketched for that. I could die with the laughin' if it was anybody else."

"But would she take a man with a parcel of childer..."

"Would a cat lick milk?" asked Mrs Murphy scornfully, 'take him, indeed! What kind of foolery will you be talkin' next? Look you here, Mary, if you let her get him when my back's turned, or if you let him marry secondly on any other woman, you'll have to answer to me for it in another and a brighter world – mind I'm tellin' you.'

"If I was you I wouldn't die so handy then," said Mary, 'for you're better at managin' these things nor me. Take your meat, and try to keep up your heart a bit better.'

"Heart indeed!" grunted her mother, 'what kind of a fool is he at all? Any woman could have him at the church door unbeknownst to himself, I do believe. And that Gillespie's a brave deep one.'

"But it's all rubbish, mother dear...

"Rubbish!" Mrs Murphy rose and poked the fire unnecessarily. 'Rubbish, and her waitin' for till step in my very shoes the minute I drop off! Do you call that rubbish? The low, dirty, lazy strap! I could break her back when I think of it. After all I done for her when the man died, too! Rubbish? Aye, indeed! quare rubbish.'

"I must run on, mother, for Ann will be waitin' on me down the road. Mind and lie down on the sofa and rest yourself when you feel tired."

"I can't lie on the sofa. My brains won't let me. Sure you know that as well as me."

"Well, take a turn out by then. The air would..."

"If you're goin' to town the day, *go*," interrupted Mrs Murphy tartly, 'and quit standin' there, givin' directions to the mother that rared you. If I'm near my grave you know rightly who done it on me. I'll say no more. I'll get what'll do me my day. It's a wonder to goodness I'm here at all after what I've come through. I'm wore away to nothing! Me clothes is hangin' on me. I believe in my heart I've the impitentist, upsetinest, crookedest pack of childer that ever faced the sun...'

Mary closed the door hastily and ran down the street, her face was brighter than it had been for many days. "That's a grand idea about Mrs Gillespie," she thought, 'it has done her good already.'

An hour later Mrs Murphy came to the door, and looked out. The air smelt fresh and sweet after a rainy night. It blew against her face, and the gloom in her eyes lifted. Unfortunately she turned her head, and looked up the road and saw Mrs Gillespie spreading clothes on a hedge at the far end of the village.

"Ned," she called sharply, 'come here, I want you.'

Ned, who was shooting marbles with Jimmy Forbes, rose reluctantly and came towards her.

"Go round to the back of the house this minute, and see if the marly hen has laid and get her egg, and watch yourself and don't break it."

Ned may have had some thought of procrastinating, but changed his mind on coming in closer contact with his mother's fiery eye. He sped round to the yard and came back in a couple of minutes with a warm, brown egg in his hand.

"There's three of them sittin' on the ould delf nest egg, clockin' like mad," he said breathlessly, 'here, take your egg, I'm in a hurry.'

"You've got to stay in the house this mornin' and help me, you impitent little witch..." but he was out through the door and down the street before the sentence was finished.

"Of all the souple wee crathurs!" she thought indulgently, as she put a small saucepan on the fire to boil the egg, 'he bates all! He's the grand wee fella, so he is!' A smile hovered about her lips for a few minutes until some darker thought seemed to enter her mind and chase it away. 'I'll ate an egg every day of my life, I don't care who's angry or well-plazed,' she muttered, 'I'll not die so aisy! Feth, I'd look well.'

Mrs Murphy was beginning to recover from a heavy blow. When Mary was in the house, she sighed as often as she could remember, and kept rigidly to the role of invalid which she had hastily thrown aside in the excitement of entertaining the American. It was well for her daughter to be made to realise what she had done to her own mother. When Mary pleaded to be allowed to stay at home and take care of her, she assured her sorrowfully that the sight of her constant before her eyes would be more than flesh and blood could stand, for it would remind her of the downfall of all her hopes and plans. She was bitterly disappointed. The day before the catastrophe had happened she had gone in to almost every house in Gape Row, and had talked to her heart's content. She had seen jealousy in the faces of other women and she had rejoiced to see it. She could hold up her head again. The long-lost glory of the McSpeddans was flooding back on her. And then in her hour of triumph, someone had come to the door and called her back to her own house, and she had found Mary almost in the act of flinging the little watch in the face of the man she had promised to marry the day before.

"It was a mercy to goodness but she knocked an eye out of him!" she said to old Ann.

"And him not too purty as it is," murmured Ann.

"Let her wait!" sobbed Mrs Murphy, 'let her wait till she gets another man to offer her a gold watch and a two-storied house and a drawing-room to sit in like any lady, and her tea in a restaurant every time he took her to town, and the band playin', though God knows, I think that was goin' *too* far, it was too like the theatre for me – I'd rather have me sup in peace. But there was nothing under the sun, he wouldn't have got her. He thought too much of her. He committed a sin. Let her wait! The obstinate, good-for-nothing littly hussy.'

"Maybe she'll get somebody else," said old Ann.

"Aye, but maybe she'll not! And sure if she does, will he be a man like this man? It's a labourin' boy she'll end up with – wait till you see..."

"As like as not."

"I never got such a gunk in all me days," continued Mrs Murphy, wiping her eyes with the corner of her apron. 'You could have knocked me down with a feather. I couldn't believe it. And I could do nothing. The power of speech left me, clean and clever. And then, when I was tryin' to gather meself together, and makin' tracks to go up the hill and see him and talk to him, and maybe get round him again, didn't I hear my brave boy had cut his stick and was off to America. His heart must have been clean broke on him!'

"Maybe it wasn't so aisy broke," muttered old Ann.

"And now the ocean rolls between him and me," wailed Mrs Murphy, 'and man nor mortal can do no more. The young tinker! When I think of the way I wrought and slaved and brought them all up dacent and respectable, and had them schooled and larned – and hard enough it was to keep shoes on their feet, and plenty inside them many a time. Why, she should have gone down on her bended knees, and thanked the Lord for sending her a man that could offer her riches and vanities and pomps, and the dear only knows what! The little scut! And she threw the watch in his very face.'

Ann did not speak, but her lips seemed to move in a faint smack of satisfaction.

At that moment the door opened and Jinanna stood on the threshold. When she saw Mrs Murphy's tears, a scared look came into her eyes and she withdrew hastily. They heard her timid footstep hurrying down the street.

"That wee crathur's not at herself," observed Ann. 'What under goodness would be wrong with her now?'

"I'll soon tell you," said Mrs Murphy savagely. 'I'm fair mad when I think of it. There's *more* of my good work destroyed on me! The way I wrought over that woman, and pulled her out of the grave with my own two hands, and set her up in the wee house and shook that ould sinner in his bed till I shook the money out of him – and look at her now! She's away to nothing. Her clothes is hangin' on her. The flesh is peelin' off her before my very eyes. Her nerves is workin' her something desperate. If one of the childer lets a screech out of them behind her back you'd think she'd lost her life.'

"She was never like other people, anyway."

"She was rightly I tell you, till them two blades come down the hill, and give off their ould lip in my kitchen. I wish I'd threw them out on the street at the first. She was the image of death when I minded to turn and look at her, and she's never right come to her colour yet. Dear save us! I'll not forget that day in a hurry. The brazen tinkers!"

"A bad breed," said old Ann wearily, 'a very bad breed. Near hand as bad as the Darraghs – and I couldn't say no more for nobody.'

Mrs Murphy sat meditating by her own fireside that evening. Tam was out. Little Ned, on his stool beside her, leaned his head sleepily against her knee. In the opposite corner Sammy smoked his pipe in silence.

"I do not know under the sun – what I'll do," murmured Mrs Murphy, half-aloud, as she stroked Ned's fair little head.

"What's in your mind now?" asked Sammy.

She sighed heavily. "The brains is battered out of me, and that's the truth! If it's not the one thing aggravatin' me it's another. Jin-anna looks for dyin'."

"She's not lookin' well at all."

"That I may never spake again," continued Mrs Murphy, in accents of gloom, 'but if she drops off in some sudden dwam – and as like as not that'll be the next thing – it was open murder done! If she dies, there's two weemen at the top of the hill should be hanged by the neck till they're dead.'

"It was that done it, I suppose."

"*You* suppose!" snorted Mrs Murphy. 'You've a dale to do with your supposin'! I tell you she has never quit trimblin' since. You'd think the cup would drop out of her hand and her only takin' a mouthful of tea. She's gone to scrapin's this last month. It's my belief she spends most of her time lookin' behind her when she's by her lone. She still deems them two straps is after her.'

"She should have more wit. They'll not concern themselves again with her, or you either. They didn't make that much out of it the last time."

"If ever they darken my door again," exclaimed Mrs Murphy wrathfully, the light of battle rising in her eye. 'If they dare to come down this street as much as, I'll put them round the corner with the half-clocked eggs of the ould buff hen after them! Feth I'll send them home quicker nor they come, I'll promise them that!'

"It was very ill-done of them," said Sammy, 'very ill-done. But I would expect no better of the parties. Jinanna's a lonely bein', like myself.'

"She hasn't one of her own to come near her. Sure that's what's wrong with her, for when anything's on her mind it works in on her inwardly for the want of company. If I had nobody to talk to, it would kill me dead."

"You needn't tell me what I know," replied Sammy. 'But that crathur would be the better of a dog in the house with her.'

"A dog? Nonsense, man! What call has she for a dog atein' all before it?"

"There's a power of company in a brute beast."

"A kitten would do just as well. Maybe I could get the fella of ours off Mrs McIntyre if she hasn't it give away already."

"No, no," said Sammy, stooping down to stroke Ned's kitten who was rubbing itself against his leg. 'You would be no use at all, pussy. It's a dog Jinanna wants – a good watch-dog.'

"Maybe you're right," said Mrs Murphy, who felt relieved at the thought of action of any kind. 'A terrier's the thing for her. It has the wit of a man (and more than some, dear knows!) and it's the right size. If I could get a hoult of Michael he could maybe tell me about somebody that wanted rid of a terrier-pup. He's the sorra for dogs. I don't know when on goodness earth I seen that boy! He has his knife in me for what happened, I know rightly. He blamed me,' she put her apron to her eyes, and sniffed audibly, 'and me as innocent and unguilty as that child at my feet.'

Ned had not spoken for half an hour. He was looking into the fire with sleepy, half-shut eyes.

"A wee terrier pup," repeated Mrs Murphy, resuming her cheerful tones, 'the very thing! And not too crabbit a one or she'll be scarred to death – but a good sharp bark in its head for all that – and if them ones ever dares till annoy her it'll rise a brave disturbance, and I'll be in with the poker in my fist before you could say Jack Robinson.'

"That child should be in his bed," declared Sammy.

Mrs Murphy bent lovingly over little Ned and pushed back the soft hair from his forehead. "His eyes is dyin' in his head with sleep," she said, 'sure he had himself run off his feet, the wee son! It's time you were in bed, lovie.'

A few days later Jinanna, sitting alone by her fire, heard a shrill, trembling little voice outside her door.

"Jinanna! Jinanna! Open the door for your life!"

She ran to open it and Ned staggered in, panting and breathless. A little tawny-haired puppy was struggling in his arms.

"Here's your pup! Sit down and catch a hoult of him."

"My alive! Who is he? Where did you get him from? Your mother will have your life for bringin' home a dog. Who does he belong to, son?"

"He belongs till you, I tell you," panted Ned. 'Here, catch him by the back of the neck.' But Jinanna retreated a little distance. 'Sure mamma and Sammy were sayin' the other night in our house that you were like for dyin' and you needed a dog to keep you company, and Sammy said you were all away to scrapin's, and mamma said it was the tinkers done it on you, and she said maybe a kitten would do as well, and Sammy he said no, and she said she'd bid Michael get you one, it's to bark if them ones comes near you, and mamma'll come flyin' in with the poker, and she said something more about them hangin' themselves up somewhere but I don't mind it.' He paused, and drew a long breath.

"The dear save us and bless us!" ejaculated Jinanna in bewilderment.

"I got him off Jimmy Forbes' aunt," continued Ned. 'I heerd word off Jimmy about the pups. So I just run up to the Six Road Ends after my dinner – I'd like to see *me* waitin' on Michael – and sez I to her, 'will you give me a pup? It's for a neighbour woman,' sez I, 'and it's to scare away the tinkers, and she's like for dyin',' sez I, and she grabbed this one by the back of the neck – they were all sleepin' as nice as ever you see by the other at the fire -. 'Take him and welcome,' sez she, 'get him out of the road before he comes home from the market for fear he rues.' 'Can he bark?' sez I. 'The best,' sez she. 'What do you call him?' sez I. 'The childer has him called Shindy,' sez she, 'for he's riz more disturbance about this place than anybody ever heard tell of. He's a perfect heart-scald of a dog, pullin' the tails out of my good hens, and atein' my very shoes on me. Gwan your best, and if you meet him comin' home in the cart, take the pad across the field and never let on you!' and with that I ketched him by the back of the neck and run.'

"Oh my!" cried Jinanna, with shining eyes. 'You're a wonderful child! You're the best-hearted wee crathur...'

"Hould your tongue! Sit down on the chair there, till I put him on your knee."

"Would he bite?" she asked, with timid joy.

"Bite, your granny! Sure he's only three months old. He's the quare good pup, I'm tellin' you."

Jinanna sat down in her chair, and Ned put the puppy on her lap. Either from excessive weariness after its tumultuous journey down the hill in Ned's arms, or from the sympathy it felt in the touch of her gentle hands, it ceased to struggle and curling itself up went comfortably to sleep.

"Och, the wee crathur!" she exclaimed, 'the wee man! Are you sure you wouldn't like to keep him yourself, Ned?'

"I would not," said Ned, 'he might ate the cat.'

"Aye, so he might. Och I'm that glad. A puppy's that heartsome a thing. You couldn't feel lonesome, and it runnin' about the floor. He'll be the right company for me."

"Aye, that's what Sammy said."

"Sit down, son dear, and rest yourself. You're done out. It's a queer length to the Six Road Ends for a child like you to be runnin'." He sat down on the sofa and leaned back. His hair was sticking damply to his forehead.

"I don't know what under the sun I'd do without you, Ned. I'd be lost entirely. You're the terrible clever child."

"Hould your tongue!" replied Ned, in embarrassed tones, 'never name it.'

"Do you know what I have in the drawer, hid for you? A wheen of lovely cakes and a wee paper of brandy balls. I got them in the town yesterday. That's an awful queer name for a dog, Ned. Shindy. Shindy..."

"It's a right name. Listen here," said Ned anxiously. 'I'm thinkin' Jimmy Forbes will be wantin' his pup from you. If he asks it, hit him on the mouth. I run my best the whole road to the aunts, for he had a notion of goin', only the mother sent him to the shop at the Arches. Don't you be givin' him to wee Forbes, for, mind you, he's fit for anything, he's that bad-hearted.'

"Do you think I'm astray in the head altogether?" asked Jinanna indignantly. 'I think I'll not let anybody get my wee pup from me. He's tired, the wee crathur, he's sleepin' as sound as a top. Shindy.'

She stroked the puppy's head thoughtfully. 'Shindy. It's an awful queer un-Christian sort of a name. If it was Rover now, or Scamp. I used to put names on all the calves at home – Spot and Daisy and Clover. But Shindy – I never heard the like.'

"Look here," said Ned patiently. 'You might be forgettin' what drawer you put them brandy balls in.'

"My, but it's well you minded me, son," replied Jinanna solemnly, as she rose and crossed the kitchen with the puppy still in her arms. She opened a drawer in the dresser, and after what seemed a long time came towards him and dropped two paper bags on his knee. He felt the cold, hard feeling of coins in his hot little hand. For the first time in his life two silver shillings were his.

"Och, but he's the right wee man!" breathed Jinanna, touching Shindy's little forehead gently with her finger-tips. 'We'll have the queer fun now, Ned.'

In the days that followed, she and Ned seriously undertook the puppy's education. They washed and brushed and fed him. They taught him to beg and to die for his King. When he was not following Ned in his long rambles over the fields, he was playing mad puppy games through Jinanna's prim little kitchen, or lying exhausted on the edge of her skirt, or in her lap. Sometimes he lay on the warm hearthstone in front of the fire, his eyes following her with love in their brown depths, but always lifting his eager little head at the faintest sound of Ned's bare feet on the street outside.

"My wee Ned's the wonderful, pushin' wee fine fella!" said Mrs Murphy, 'he takes it after me!'

The cobble-stones were glancing with heat. Old Ann felt it pleasantly through her list slippers as she walked slowly down the street, leaning on her stick. The hot sunshine beat down on her thin shoulders, and quivered over the fields. Here and there a bird sang in the hedge. The meadow-sweet shook out its flounces sedately, and the poplars crooned their mystery day and night, day and night.

Mrs Murphy loomed abruptly in her doorway.

"Do you hear this they're all sayin'?" she asked. Anxiety was in her voice. Her face was grave. 'Did you see the paper last night?'

"Blethers and Nonsense!" said old Ann cheerfully.

Ten days later the Norfolks hung their flag in the cathedral, and sailed away to France.

25

M ichael and Sandy walked up and down the lane behind the
farmhouse. Michael had had a heavy day in the cornfield, but
he seemed to feel no fatigue. They were talking in low, eager tones. It
was a night in the middle of August. The moon looked down through
the ash-trees, and watched them with chill indifference.

They were going to join at once. They were burning with eagerness
to join. Michael, the elder, was if anything the more excited of the
two. He chafed at the delay which he knew was inevitable before he
could leave the farm. There was a fire in his blood.

He said more than once that he thought it would be a good thing if
they were trained in some camp at a distance from home. He said it
hurriedly, but with a certain emphasis which made Sandy feel he
meant it. He gave no explanation and Sandy asked for none, but
thought he was probably feeling sore over the undignified exit of his
brother, and he assured him he would go anywhere he went. There
was a fine old Irish regiment stationed in Holywood, not so many years
ago – Michael said. Many a time the officers had hunted over these
fields – and terrible fine gentlemen they were... For half the night they
walked backwards and forwards making their eager plans.

When Sandy left him, he stood still for a few minutes. He could
hear the ring of his feet on the dry road long after he had faded down
the hill. He stood looking out over the dim, silver country – his own
country, his own fields. He had never thought to rise up and leave it
like this.

He had no one to leave behind him – neither wife nor parent nor
child. That was a splendid thing, he told himself as he turned and
walked towards the house. He would be able to get a couple of hours'
sleep before milking time. The little, low house lay in shadow, with a
great belt of silver light in front of it. The trees flung ghostly phantoms
on the grass. A bird moved sleepily in the hedge. Away in the valley a
cow lowed. And the rest was silence.

Except for Patch, who was spending the night in agitation behind the kitchen door, and his old servant asleep in the attic, the house was empty. He had closed Patch up before he went out with Sandy, and ever since he had lain there, crouched and listening with a fast-beating heart for his master's return.

There were deep heavy shadows hung about the door, from the thatch which jutted out above, and the tall fuchsia trees growing close to the wall on either side. They were his mother's fuchsias – the small, delicate, Irish fuchsia – and they were in beautiful bloom. She had often told him how she had brought them from her old home on the other side of the hill, on the evening of her wedding-day. He thought of her now, a semi-invalid as long as he remembered, of the gentle, lined face that had been like a light in darkness to him all his life, and he wondered if she had been sitting there inside, how would he have gone in and told her he was going to join? Oh, it was a fine thing to be going out from an empty house, and leaving no woman to cry her eyes out beside a lonely hearth – and suddenly the cold, cold chill of the moonlight passed into his very soul.

He stood motionless, his feet on the rough grass in front of the house. Enthusiasm died away. He felt stripped of all heat and warmth. And the moonlight fell round him, drenching him with cold, inhuman brightness, beautiful and unperturbed.

He lifted his eyes, and in the heavy shadows between the fuchsia trees he saw the faint outlines of a woman's figure. He saw her pale face. It was turned towards him and seemed to be asking something of him. The eyes were heavy with tears.

"Mary!" he said huskily. "Mary!" He moved a step further, and she was gone.

Patch whined joyfully when he turned the key in the door a minute later. His hand shook though he did not know it. He took off his boots and tried to quiet the little terrier who was leaping round him frantically. Then he went to his room, and lay down for an hour or two without undressing. He was deadly tired, but he thought he could not sleep. Patch curled up beside him and he laid his hand caressingly on the wide, beautiful little head. Before long both of them were sound asleep.

The next morning when he went out to his day's work, he remembered the night before as one remembers a dream. The strong, reassuring sun came up out of the east, and burnt away the shadows from the door and made light of the ghostly things of night. Mary crying, and in trouble. He had never thought of that. He thought of her always as she was when her anger had been roused and she had flung ugly words at him across the field. He had forgotten that she looked broken and beseeching at first. All his sympathy had been given to Andy John.

Lately he had gathered from a careless speech of Sandy's that he and she had never been lovers. He was considerably surprised, and was still puzzled as to their relationship, which seemed unusually intimate and confidential. She had not played with Sandy. At least she had not done that. But she had made Andy John miserable and ashamed before his friends, and Michael, who had grown fonder of his brother since he went away, had not forgiven her. He kept the fires of his indignation alive and glowing with constant prods of encouragement.

And he never dreamt that the real root of his soreness was her twice-repeated assertion that in any case she would not have married him. She had said it with the utmost emphasis, and he made no allowance for her anger at the moment. She meant it, although she would not have said it so cruelly at another time. It was the feeling of her heart, and it had found expression in an unguarded moment.

He had barely spoken to her since that sunday afternoon in the meadow. Once or twice they had met in the churchyard after service, and he had passed her with a curt 'fine day.' He hoped he would not see her again before he left. He was anxious to go as quietly as possible. He hated the thought of fuss and farewell, and he bade Sandy tell no one he was going.

An elderly bachelor cousin, who had an annuity, and nothing particular to do in the world, had promised to come and look after the farm in his absence. He was waiting every day for a letter from him to say when he was coming, and at last one morning as he came out of the byre, the postboy met him with a letter. Jacob wrote that he would be on the train that evening from Dundalk.

Michael's going away was very quiet. Sandy had gone a week earlier. A couple of days before he left, he passed Tam working on the road, and obeying a sudden, blind impulse, went back and told him what he had done. "You're right, man!" was all Tam said, for in friendship as in all else he was inarticulate, but he gripped Michael's hand and wrung it shatteringly. He was fond of the boy, and stood watching him till a twist in the road took him out of sight. Michael went on, his heart cheered, he did not know why. There were still three whole days before he left. Something might happen in three days. He did not ask himself what he wanted to happen, when he opened the door to chance.

Tam went home thinking what a wonderful thing it was to see John McCready's son going off to the war. But he hid the thought so carefully in a dim recess of his brain that his wife only stumbled on it by accident when she was searching vigorously for something else. And that was two days after Michael had left.

His saddest farewell was with Patch, whose eyes begged and prayed to go too. He had watched his preparation for a long journey all that day with a dumb agony of entreaty and many a furtive, side-glance at the stranger who was making himself so unaccountably at home in the house and about the yard. When Michael was settled in the corner of the evening train for Dublin what gave him the deepest pang was the thought of the soft, chestnut-brown eyes that had watched him go down the road.

His going away was perhaps a little lonely. There was no one to make a fuss over him. If only Mary had loved him how different it would have been! But he would have gone all the same. Something in him, as strong and wonderful as his feeling for her, was calling him away. He remembered certain spring mornings early in the year, when the gulls followed his plough, and the sharp sweet air of the hills blew round him, and the strange mood that came and went with the morning. What was it that was rising up between him and these narrow, green fields of his? At times he almost seemed to see them from a distance. It haunted him all through the spring, and he resented it and blamed Andy John's visit for unsettling him. But now he understood. The war had come, and made everything quite simple.

The early morning of the day he left home was very bright, and a flood of sunshine pouring in through the window wakened him. He lay still for a few minutes, listening to the familiar sounds in the yard below, while Patch slept lightly at his feet. A strange detached feeling had already taken possession of him. Then he rose and dressed, and went out and saw the red eastern sky. It would rain before night, he called cheerfully to Jacob.

As the Dublin train moved out into the country he turned away, and looked steadily out of the window. His eyes were used to scanning long distances and he was glad when they left the patchiness of the suburbs behind, and the long, level fields, the hills rising and falling, and later, the high, blue outlines of the Louth mountains came into view. Soon the fields took a grimmer look and stone ditches replaced the autumn hedge. The mountains came nearer, and the train swung out through the Gates of the North. The clouds grew darker and lower, and great, heavy shadows lay along the fields. In five minutes a thick storm of rain was beating against the windows, and the view was blotted out.

"I never seen such weather," came in fretful tones from the far end of the carriage, where two small boys were wrangling over a paper of sweets. It was their mother who spoke. A stout woman of a better class sat opposite, and felt constrained to offer her occasional advice on the bringing up of her children.

"Sure I can do nothing with them since the father went and listed," Michael heard her complain; 'he's in the Rifles. I was agin it from the first, but he wouldn't listen to me. And now mebbe he'll go and get kilt, and me heart-broke with these childer and four more at home, forby three I buried, and everything the price it is.'

It grew darker outside. A peal of thunder rattled overhead, and passed on into the mountains. The children stopped fighting, and crept nearer their mother. "There now!" she said, satisfaction in her voice for the first time, 'there now! Mebbe you'll get kilt in a minute or two! Mebbe you'll be quate now.'

A cold mist gradually crept into the carriage and wrapped them in its damp and chilly folds. The rain lashed against the windows, and when its fury was spent and they could see out again, the train was close by the sea. They slid in and out of Malahide in a twinkling. A couple of villages seemed to run away behind them and then the lights of Clontarf came into view.

At Amiens Street Station he took his bag in his hand and waited patiently until the other passengers got out. The woman with the two children tore them forcibly from each other with a running commentary on war, and men who went to war without their wives' permission, and the punishment that was like to befall them for such obvious neglect of duty. He made his way through the crowded station and out into a dirty, dismal-looking street. The rain had cleared off, but the thick mist made it difficult to see the opposite houses. He had arranged to stay with cousins for the night, and to go south to his depot in the morning.

He walked on slowly, more or less uncertain of his way. Once, under a lamp-post, he stopped to look where he was, and a dog with brown eyes came and sniffed at his knee. "Patch, old boy!" he said, as he bent to touch his head. He took several wrong turnings, and it was

almost an hour later before he found himself in Rosapenna Street. He
knocked at number twenty-seven. The door opened instantly and half
a dozen soft voices seemed to speak at once.

"Glory be to goodness, is it you at last! We had nearly given you up.
Your train was very late surely, come in cousin Michael, come in out
of the wet. You're lost entirely!"

He found himself in a dark little shop. Someone held aloft a small
lamp with a hole in the chimney, and the flickering uncertain light
threw grotesque shadows on the figures of the women who grouped
themselves round him.

"You're as welcome as the flowers in May, Michael," said his aunt,
kissing him hastily. 'Your uncle went to bed an hour ago – he came in
wringin' wet – for the Lord's sake, don't fall over the potatoes! – they
tumbled out of the sack, and they're all over the floor. Your uncle
nearly broke his neck over them. I tell him to look where he's goin',
but sure I might as well not. Mind the lamp, Bridget. Come in here
and get yourself warmed. You must be famished with the cold.'

She drew him into a little sitting-room behind the shop, where a
large fire blazed, and the supper table was laid. His cousins fussed
round him. One brought him a pair of dry slippers, another felt his
damp coat and insisted on his changing it, his aunt disappeared and
presently came back carrying a dish of ham and eggs, followed by
Bridget, the youngest girl, with a huge teapot. They spoke with a
curious softness that made everything they said sound gracious and
kind, and which would have put colour and warmth into the stoniest
words. He thought they smiled more than the people he lived among
were accustomed to smile, and they moved in a gentle, leisurely way as
if to say there was plenty of time, and why hurry? He noticed that even
his aunt softened her double t's, and dragged her words here and
there, in spite of her northern upbringing. It was very warm and kind
in that little room, and the cold loneliness that had lain on his heart
since he left home gradually lifted.

"How long is it since you were here, Michael?" asked Sophie, his
eldest and largest cousin.

"Spring was a year," said Michael shyly.

"And where's the nice boy that came with you?"

"He's listed too. He's in the same regiment as me."

"So you're going off to the war, Michael," said his aunt, nodding
her head. 'These are wonderful times, and no mistake.'

"I'd be going myself, if they'd take me," said Sophie, 'it's a grand

thing to be a man now, isn't it? We're awfully proud of you, Michael!'
and they smiled and beamed on him, and made him feel for the
moment that he had done something rather fine, and the feeling did
poor Michael good.

"I wondered many's the time why your poor mother was taken away
so soon," his aunt went on. 'Your father had reached the age when it's
to be expected, but she was young. She would have broken her heart
fretting about you. Maybe it's well she went when she did.'

"Maybe," said Michael briefly.

"I say, Michael, can't you stay longer than just one night?" Jessie
began in a coaxing voice; '*surely* you'll not be after going off in the
morning. Couldn't you stay for just a wee-ney visit?' She smiled and
dragged the adjective persuasively.

"I've got to report myself to-morrow at Ballykilty," returned
Michael. "I'm afraid I must be movin' off in the mornin', Jessie. It
takes the best of a day to get there, by all accounts."

"The Lord help you, is it away there you're going!" exclaimed his
aunt. 'Sure that's a terrible long journey. And the trains are very
slow-going down that side, I've heard them say.'

"We'll pack a basket of nice things for you to eat on your journey,"
smiled Sophie, 'for it's dead with cold and hunger you'd be before you
got there. And mind you Michael, the first leave you get, you *must*
come and stay here. I want to show you off about the town, you know!'
and Michael laughed and promised.

His housekeeper had packed a hamper of eggs and butter, and a
couple of his best chickens for his aunt, but in that embarrassing
moment when he found himself sliding over potatoes in the dimly
lighted shop, and surrounded by cousins who looked as if they might
kiss him at any moment, he dropped it into a dark corner and said
nothing. "They'll find it in the morning when they're reddin' up," he
thought, and even when town eggs and country butter were under
discussion he was too shy to speak of it.

"Can you eat what's before you, son dear?" questioned Mrs
Mehaffy anxiously; 'these eggs aren't as fresh as you're used to, but
the like of them we couldn't buy for love or money.'

"The eggs are grand," said Michael, taking a second mouthful with
rare courage.

"Dear be with the time when I could gather them in the nests in my
own yard," sighed his aunt; 'you never know the want of the water till
the well's dry, Michael.'

"That's so," he replied sympathetically.

"You know very well you hate the country, mother," said Jessie. 'Don't I hear you blessing your stars many a time that you married into the town. I prefer a countryman myself, you know Michael,' and she lifted her head and smiled at him innocently, 'but mother's different. She likes excitement. She would die of loneliness in the country.'

"Michael dear, it's the gas-ring in the kitchen," interrupted her mother apologetically, 'there's nothing like the country of course, and the good, clean smells and everything – but it's the gas-ring in the kitchen that has me reconciled to the loss of nature – and a very great loss it is. And then there's a dry pavement under your foot, summer and winter.'

"And water laid on," said Sophie turning to him triumphantly, 'three taps in the scullery.'

"I'd just love the country if there was a tram in it," confessed Bridget in her slow, rich voice, 'and I do love it as far as the tram goes...'

Michael laughed. He thought of a little corner of the world that was all his own, of the early summer mornings when he had opened the door and stepped out into a delicious world, flooded with the first, cool sunlight of the day and wet with dew, of the blackbird singing year after year in the old apple-tree in front of the house, of the sound of cattle feeding over the hedge, of the smell of brown earth. He thought of these things with something like a lump in his throat, but he was too heartsore to talk about them. When supper was over, his aunt, seeing how tired he was, made him go to bed and he slept almost as soon as his head touched the pillow.

When he was leaving the next morning Sophie pressed a small wicker basket packed with eatables into his hand.

"I've put a couple of candles in as well," she said. 'I'm a bit of a traveller myself, and have been down that line more than once, and the lighting, I may tell you, is something surprising. Be sure you get a corner seat, and give it up to no woman, old or young, and when you want to read your paper light your candle and drop a taste of grease on the window-ledge at your elbow, and bang the candle into it for all you're worth while it's hot – and there's your grand reading lamp for you! What on earth are you laughing at? You couldn't see the road to your mouth, I tell you. It was a Dean I saw doing that with my own eyes. In fact it was from him I got the wrinkle. Excuse me, Jessie. He *was* a Dean. I knew by his legs. And mind, Michael, and don't let the grease get on your clothes, and me not there to look after them!' and Michael laughed and promised.

His cousins kissed him in the privacy of the shop among the strewn potatoes.

"It's your mother would be the proud woman if she was here to see you today," said Mrs Mehaffy tearfully; 'come back as soon as you can, son dear.'

His cousins came out and stood round him on the street. They looked at him admiringly with their kind, bright eyes, and patted his coat, and said, "God bless you, cousin Michael," in a way that amazed his northern reticence. When he had gone a few yards Sophie called after him, 'be sure you think of me when you're lighting up, dear!' and he laughed and called back that he would. At the corner of the street he turned and waved his hand, and then hurried cheerfully on to catch his train.

26

Old Ann was not greatly interested in the war. Her mind was too feeble to fasten itself for long on so vast a subject, although the ancient fires of resentment burnt as vigorously as ever. Young Ann's troubles seemed to have kindled them afresh.

"If all of the name of Darragh got bullets put through them it would please me well," she said to Mrs Murphy, 'but sure it would be too good to be true: I hear Johnny is for bringin' home the wife. If he does, I'll set the polis on them.'

"I wouldn't bother myself. I'm only hopin' and prayin' for them to get what they've worked for, in this world and the next. There's the right scarrifying before them, if they but knowed it."

"Take my advice, and lave them ones to the Almighty. They'll get their deservin's yet, never you fear! And don't vex yourself talkin' about them. The cold's rightly lifted off you and you're lookin' a quare lot better, if you'd only take peace to yourself. Come on out for a bit of a turn up the street..."

"Feth, there's a coolin' in store for them that's not canny!" Ann chuckled.

"There's a heat in the air the day would do you good," began Mrs Murphy.

"I'm not goin' out by, I tell you. Let me alone." She leaned forward, peering into the fire, while lurid prophesies, as far removed from anything in the nature of a 'coolin',' as could be imagined, fell from her lips concerning the ultimate fate of her enemies.

"You'd make a body's flesh creep, Ann Rainey!" expostulated Mrs Murphy. "Come on up to Jinanna's for a bit. It's pausin' and musin' over the fire by your lone that has you destroyed. She's made the loveliest wee wool mats ever you seen for the flower-pots in the window. That woman has terrible good hands, the more you mightn't think it."

"She'd a dale to do! Wool mats indeed."

"And wee fancy capers for the back of the chairs in the room, wrought in silks, and them all the colours of the rainbow."

"What do I care about her, or her capers? My own house is good enough for me. What call has she for such fooleries?"

"A taste of the fresh air would be a queer help till you," continued Mrs Murphy, 'why the very stones on the street is warmer, the day. Sure you haven't been out of the door this weeks. You're that hard till shift woman!'

"You want to shift me intil my grave, that's what you want," answered Ann perversely. 'I'm not goin' out of the house, I tell you. I'll maybe never be goin' out of it again.'

"All right, you can sit there. I'll bother my head askin' you no more," and Mrs Murphy got up, and went back to her own house. 'She's that ill to work with,' she muttered, 'and her rightly too.' And she did not go near Ann for three whole days.

But the next sunday afternoon, Happy Bill came out to preach at the pump. He harangued a scanty audience with ear-splitting vehemence for some time, and afterwards hastened from one door to another in Gape Row, asking cheerfully if the inhabitants were saved. It was tea-time with Mrs Murphy, and although her mouth was full of soda-bread, she managed to say she would scald him with a kettle of boiling water if ever he took the light from her door again. Old Ann was sitting forlornly alone, and he went in and sat down beside her and gave her a tract. He told her she was going straight to hell, but she shook her head and said he must be meaning people of the name of

Darragh. When he tried to make her repeat the words, "God be merciful to me, a sinner," she answered, speaking from the depths of bitter political feeling, 'If you'd go and larn that to oul' Asquith, it would answer you better!' After a long theological skirmish he left her, and she rose immediately and went up the street in wrath, to check Sarah Murphy for sending that fool fella down to her. Mrs Murphy, while stoutly denying the charge, was delighted to see her, and said it took Happy Bill to get her hoked out of the house.

One morning, soon after Christmas, Mrs Murphy got a letter from America which threw her into a violent state of agitation.

"What's wrong?" asked Tam, when he became conscious that his wife was swaying backwards and forwards with her apron to her eyes.

"It's Charlie!" she sobbed. He put out his hand for the letter in real alarm.

"He's comin' home to list!" she gasped, 'he's on the water now!' Tam took the letter, and began to read it.

"Didn't I always tell you what he was? You never believed me. You didn't think there was that much good in him."

"I never said that," replied Tam, somewhat shamefacedly.

"No, but you thought it and that's worse. And him a boy that anybody might be proud of, with the manners and the notions of a gentleman born! Och annee annee! You'll be sorry when he's kilt dead."

"I can't make out his writin'!" said Tam, turning over the pages.

"I can hardly make it out myself – there's that many curley-cews about it. But who could expect our Charlie to write plain and straight like a common man? To the best of my belief he's on the water now."

"Dear-a-dear! It's no wonder you're proud of him, Sarah," said Tam, going out of the door a little later. There was more life in his voice than usual. As he walked down the road to his work in the biting air of the morning, he almost felt as if he too were keeping step with marching and heroic men.

In the intervals of her work that morning, Mrs Murphy ran in and out of certain favoured houses in Gape Row. "My Charlie's comin' home to list!" she repeated from door to door, 'he's on the water now!' There was all the pride and sorrow of motherhood in her voice.

When she had tidied up the kitchen after dinner, she sat down to rest in the old-rocking-chair. She was a little tired after the agitation of the morning. "I think maybe I'll read a bit of something good," she thought, 'for dear knows, this is a forby day,' and she rose, and took the Bible from the shelf where the children's sunday-school prizes were kept in a neat row. She opened it at one of the gospels and read how a mother brought her little son to the temple, and when she came to the words, "a sword shall pierce through thine own soul also," she leaned her head down on her hands and wept for Mary, the mother, and all the mother-Marys whose souls were pierced that day.

But solitude and inaction were as ever distasteful to her, and before long she dried her eyes, and went out of the door and up the street to see if she could be of any use to Mrs Morrow, whose husband had joined, and left her with a handful of young children on her hands. Mrs Morrow was baking bread and talking cheerfully to the baby in the cradle when she went in.

"Billy will be home for a couple of hours on sunday," she said, 'the childer and me will be heart-glad to see him.'

"Aye, you will that!"

"I think I feel it the most when I'm turnin' the key in the door at night. I never get it right out of my head that I'm lockin' him out."

"I think the like of him had no business for to go and 'list, and you here with all these childer to mind."

"But it was his duty," said Mrs Morrow, with eager pride, 'that's what he said himself, and I never said him no.'

"Well, I trust he'll be spared to come home along with my own child."

"We can't die till our time comes – noan of us," returned Mrs Morrow earnestly, 'that's my great comfort.'

"Aye, that's what they say, but..."

"There was a man came in here the other day, and sez he, 'If Billy's goin' to be killed, he'll be killed just the same, if he was sittin' in his own back yard. So you may take aise to yourself,' sez he."

"Aye but..."

"My mother always said if you were to get a man, you'd get him if you sat in a bandbox, and never come out of it."

"I wouldn't like to say that," said Mrs Murphy hastily. 'My alive, I wouldn't like to go as far as that! I ratherly think if it was me, I'd be makin' a bit of a push if I seen what pleased me. Dear save us! That's an awful dangerous doctrine, Mrs Morrow. 'A horse in the stable will never get sold,' that's what *my* mother used to say, and she knowed a thing or two.'

"I don't know," replied Mrs Morrow thoughtfully 'I like to think it all be to be.'

"Nonsense, woman! Do you mean to tell me providence intended me to sit the whole length of my days in Gape Row? Not at all! I missed my foot – that's what landed me here. Sure I might have made the best of a match if I'd had any wit. And our Mary has done the same. She's clean mad! She's fit for the asylum any day."

"She didn't care a rap about Andy John."

"And why didn't she care about him?" asked Mrs Murphy indignantly, 'a match like that! But sometimes, mind you, I think she did care and only intended to put him off a bit, but went too far unbeknownst to herself. It's aisy done. I done it more nor wonct myself. You can dilly-dally and shilly-shally, and tig-toy too long. Mary's not lookin' well, whatever the sense of it is. Maybe she's frettin' in secret about Andy John.'

Mrs Morrow shook her head. "I don't think it." 'If I dare mention such a thing to my own daughter!' went on Mrs Murphy moodily, 'I could tell her how to bring it on again, as nice as tuppence. A bit of her hair, now, in an envelope, and maybe a wee verse of poetry – and there you are! He'd lep at the chanct, for he was fair mad about her. But she'll do nothing.'

"Let the girl alone."

"I done all I could for her. I even took at the father and tried to get him to do something with her, but I might as well talk to the hen in the corner. Such a man, I never seen since God framed me! But what am I talkin' and ravin' about? she broke off suddenly, 'what's matches, and marryin' to me this day, and my Charlie comin' home to 'list, and maybe him drowned dead afore he gets this lenth! Och annee, annee!' and she put her apron to her eyes and wept.

Mrs Morrow lifted her baby out of the cradle for comfort. She pressed her face against his soft, warm, little neck. Her tears fell on his tiny shoulder.

"Och, that dirty, outrageous, old villain of a Keeser!" sobbed Mrs Murphy.

When Mary came home in the evening, she managed to read Charlie's letter from beginning to end, and found that he did not mean to come home until later in the spring. He was saving up for his passage, he said, and hoped to be on the water some time in the month of March. Mrs Murphy wept afresh to think she would not see her darling until then, and even little Ned was overcome with grief, and sat down on his stool by the fire and cried with her. Jimmy Forbes' big brother had brought Jimmy a penknife that was the envy of the

village, and when his mother read out of the letter, "tell Ned I have a
present for him," he was persuaded it was something that would take
the pride and impitence out of Jimmy Forbes. He had even hinted as
much to him. Mrs Murphy was touched and pleased by his tears, and
promised to give him a penny if he would quit. He dried his eyes with
an adroit sweep of his little sleeve, and when she had fished a penny
out of the depths of the big, bulging pocket in her petticoat, he hurried
down to the shop, determined to wring more black balls out of Maggie
Maguire for that sum than had ever been done before.

27

From the hills, the lamps, which came out as far as the plantin',
looked like a ribbon of light twisting through the dark fields. A
huge lamp stood at the very edge of the trees and threw pale fingers of
light into the darkness. Sandy stood in the shadow, waiting for the
tram.

He had not seen Ann since he came home on leave a couple of days
before, but Mrs Murphy said she was well and as full of notions as an
egg was full of meat. Only goodness knew where she got such notions
from – but it was her belief that she had forgotten all about that poor
cat of a crathur in Glasgow, who was fighting rings round with the wife
already. That she could not, or did not care to verify this statement,
mattered not at all to Mrs Murphy. She was used to sailing lightly over
difficulties of the kind.

Sandy thought both girls looked pale as they stepped from the tram.
He went forward to meet them and for a moment they looked at him in
surprise. They had not seen him in uniform before.

"Och, you red-headed crathur, is it you?" exclaimed Mary. 'I didn't
know a bit of you. Why man, you look grand! Would you know him
Ann?'

Ann looked at him kindly. "We're delighted to see you Sandy," she
said, 'you're lookin' well.'

"I'm the best," replied Sandy, 'and I hope you're the same. Don't
be standin' here in the cold – it's a bit fresh the night. Come on and I'll

leave you through the plantin'. It's as dark as pitch.' He turned and walked between the two girls.

"How is Michael?" asked Ann.

"Michael's grand."

"Didn't he come with you?"

"No, he didn't, but I was to say he was askin' for all old friends, and he told me to bring back particular word how the dog was and if he had settled down at all. Michael thought terrible long about that dog."

"Why didn't he come home too?" asked Ann, 'did he not get leave?'

"Aye, surely he did, but he only come the length of Dublin. He's taken on queerly with the cousins he has there. After all, what has he to come home to? The girls will give him the right lively time of it. There's three of them, and as affable girls as you'd meet with in a day's walkin' – terrible well-lookin', too."

"Does he like the soldierin'?"

"Like it? I tell you, he's took to it like a duck to the water. He's queer and well-thought of down there, too."

Afterwards on thinking it over, it almost seemed to Sandy as if the two girls had changed places. They were curiously altered. Ann did not make the mad little jokes that used to fall so readily from Mary's lips, but there was something soft and steady and bright about her, and Mary was for the greater part of the way silent.

"Mary," he said at last, 'what's come over you? Are you quit talkin' altogether?'

"When you shut your mouth, I'll begin," she replied quickly.

"Faith, I never saw you stoppin' for that! It used to be I couldn't get in a word as thin as a sixpence with you. But it's a queer improvement, mind you!" And she laughed and answered him pertly.

But that night in a tiny bedroom, packed as full as it would hold of Murphy children, there was a sound of stifled sobbing. When the Orange drums played past the door on late July evenings the children did not even stir in their sleep, and it was scarcely likely they would hear Mary's quiet crying, or catch her low, muttered words: "Sorra take them! Terrible well-lookin', I'm sure! I suppose they think they'll get him – schemin' black-hearted rascals and I nivir seen them."

Michael had been glad to accept his aunt's invitation to Dublin. He had made up his mind not to go north if he could help it. The farm was doing well with Jacob who seemed to have settled down for life. There was nothing to go home for. Patch was the only creature who loved him and he was getting over his loss. Before he went to the front he would have to go home and see to things, but he would spend as short a time there as possible. Mary would probably be engaged by that time. He hoped he would not see her. At present he was absolutely determined he would not see her.

Perhaps Mary would have been somewhat consoled had she overheard a conversation between Michael and Sophie one afternoon. Sophie who had taken him out for a walk, kept to the crowded streets he hated, in the hope of meeting acquaintances. She was proud to walk with this tall, handsome soldier-cousin whose uniform became him so well, and felt that the chief charm of the afternoon would be lost if she did not meet some of her dearest girl friends. Her head and Michael's were very close together, for the subject was of the most confidential.

"Would you advise me to run away, Michael?" she breathed. 'Pa says he'll *never* consent. I do be getting very tired of the dressmaking, and it's high time I had a home of my own. There's nothing wrong with him whatever – I know a good fellow when I see one. I met him at a dance last winter, and he said he never closed an eye that night. I wore pink. He said I was a picture. Of course I don't believe him. When he comes in, Pa sits there with a scowl on his face would frighten a horse from his feed. But it doesn't frighten Jim. It only makes him more determined to win me.'

"Why does your father object?"

"How do I know? I'll show you his photo when we go in. You'd know to look at it that opposition would only strengthen love in his case. I have such a beautiful coloured one, and I used to keep it on my bedroom mantelpiece, but now I have to keep it under the mattress. Pa threatened to throw it in the fire."

"But what's his objection?" again asked Michael.

"He has no real objection – he only thinks he has. Of course Jim hasn't very good pay. He's in a bicycle shop. He was in the fish trade for a while, but the smell disagreed with him and he left it. I can tell you I was glad! He changes about a good deal, I will say. He was partner in a little shop for a good while, but that burst up too," she concluded cheerfully.

Michael was considering the matter rather gravely when she spoke again. "To tell you the truth Jim's mad on horses and that sets Pa crazy. But then, so am I. We go to the races together and have a lovely time. Sometimes he does put more money on a horse that he should. Would you advise me to run away, Michael?"

"I would not," replied Michael decidedly. Sophie sighed.

"Look at that girl over there – the one in the red hat. The paint's an inch thick on her face. I suppose she thinks she looks well. Do you believe in love?"

"I don't know," said Michael cautiously, 'maybe I might.'

"I do," she hesitated for a moment. 'But Michael – the worst of it is there's another one! – and Pa keeps pushing him down my throat morning, noon and night. He has a barber's shop of his own, and three men under him, and you couldn't endure him to come next or nigh you. He's one of those people that always gets on. Don't you hate them? Jim's far more exciting, and it's him I love and I'll have him!' She turned to him with wet, sparkling eyes.

"The lucky devil!" exclaimed Michael.

"I'll tell Pa you approve," she whispered afterwards as they went in to tea through the topsy-turvy little shop.

That night he lay awake for a long time, thinking. Sophie's love difficulties came and went through his mind. In spite of his northern caution he did not think them insurmountable. The women of his family had often been strong, and if she cared so much for her Jim she would probably handle him very successfully. If he came back from the war, what would happen to him? He would go home and work his farm of course. But although he tried, he could not look forward. Something seemed to have barred the way.

The few days of his leave passed very pleasantly. He had never in his life been faced with so many problems of the affections as his cousins laid before him. Jessie and Bridget had long confidences for him as they sat round the parlour fire at night when their parents had gone to bed, and Sophie chanced to be out at the picture-house with Jim. He grew very fond of his cousins with their kind ways, their soft, drawling speech, their innocent candour. It never occurred to him to tell them anything of what filled so much of his thought. It lay too deep and sore for that.

"Will you be getting married when you come home, Michael?" Bridget asked him one evening.

"Not at all!" he replied lightly.

"Oh, but we think you will. Jessie and I were talking about it last night. We think there's some girl about your place at home, that's desperately in love with you – you're so good-looking you know, cousin Michael – and she cries every time she looks at the moon and all that sort of thing. And then when you come home, you'll get married to her and live happy ever after."

His tanned face did not show the colour that flashed into it. "Woman dear, but you've little wit!" he said uneasily, 'did anybody ever hear such a pack of nonsense?'

"It isn't nonsense at all," persisted Jessie. 'Wait till you see.'

That night he dreamt about the north and home. It was a bright, warm day, and he and Patch were in the nutwood field. Suddenly Mary stood before him, her face all smiles and tears. He held out his arms to comfort her, and she came to him just as he wakened. For one dizzy moment he thought it was true. And then his aunt's cuckoo clock in the parlour below struck four, and he heard the swish of sleet against the window. The room was very cold. Summer and the nutwood field and Mary were far away.

Up in the far north, on the last evening of his leave, Sandy spent an hour with the Murphys. "See here, Sandy," said Mrs Murphy, leaning forward impressively, her hands on her knees, 'will you tell Michael from me that I think it very ill-done of him not to come till see his friends – and us all waitin' on him – and tell him to watch himself, and let nobody nabb him, for there will be plenty after him up the country, I'm certain sure.'

Sandy laughed. "All right, I'll tell him."

Mary sat knitting a grey soldier's sock by the fire. Two little sentences were darting about in her mind – "Give Michael my love – tell Michael I was asking for him." She would follow Sandy to the door when he was going away, and she would say one or other to him. She was trying to make up her mind which would be the best; suddenly her heart gave a thud, for he had risen to his feet and was saying good-bye. He shook hands with them all, and they wished him good luck and bade him come back soon again. Mary went to the door and opened it. Mrs Murphy was standing in the middle of the floor, her hand on Sandy's arm.

"Don't come near the door, mother," said Mary hurriedly, 'the wind would take the nose off you the night.'

"Tell Michael," repeated Mrs Murphy earnestly, 'that I've givin' up buyin' bottles for my inside since the war begun, though dear knows the constant pain has me near astray in the head, and nothing will sit on my stomach. Mind them ould guns, son. I'm quare and onaisy about you many a time.'

"You'll get your death of cold if you stand here any longer," said Mary, for Mrs Murphy had moved nearer the door. Sandy wondered at the solicitude in her voice. Was something the matter with her mother after all? Mrs Murphy turned away, and for one precious fraction of time Mary and he faced each other. She opened her lips and the words trembled on them, and then from the shadow behind, Tam moved between them.

"I'll lave you up the road apiece," he said.

"Righto! Bye-bye, Mary. I'll send you a picture postcard when I get there."

"You might," said Mary huskily. She leaned out over the half-door, listening to the sound of their steps on the soft, muddy road. At the end of the street they paused for a moment. Her heart leaped with a sudden hope. Was he coming back to say something he had forgotten, to give her a message perhaps? But in a moment the sparkle of a match told her he had only stopped to light his pipe. The steps moved on and died away. Her eyes strained out into the grey of the night.

"Come on in out of that with you," grumbled Mrs Murphy, from the fireplace, 'it's time we were getting to our beds. I don't know what took that man out at this hour of the night.' But Mary did not hear her...

Every evening when she came home from her work, her mother was accustomed to give her, with microscopic detail, an account of all that had happened that day in Gape Row, and expected to hear in return something of the gay doings of the town. But at times Mary was dull and tired, and had not much to say.

"I never seen the like of you," said Mrs Murphy, complainingly a few days after Sandy's visit. 'If it was me goin' in and out of the town constant, I think I'd have a bit of narration in my mouth when I'd come home. I'm seldom or never across that door, and I declare to me goodness if I don't see more, and hear more nor you. I'm thankful I was born with brains. Didn't you hear me sayin' many a time that them cousins in Dublin was after Michael?'

"Aye, I did."

"Well, sure, Betty-fly-around was here this mornin' and she was tellin' me that she was up lately at the farm for a while of a day, and Marget was tellin' her that Michael writes brave and often to Jacob, and he's tellin' about the cousins sendin' him things constant – socks and cakes and baked bread, and one thing after another. I know rightly what was in their heads the more I never seen them. I'll bate you what you like one of them ones will get him."

"Well!" said Mary indifferently.

Mrs Murphy laid down her knitting for a moment and looked at her severely. "I've stood a quare lot in my day Mary, and I expect I'll have to stand a quare lot more, but nothing in my whole life has aggravated me more than the way your Da has of sayin' 'well' to me when I tell him anything that's extra forby. I believe in my heart if I told him a fire had burned down the Orange Hall, he'd say 'well' as cool as pump water and go on atein' his supper. But what I take from him I'll take from no other body, and I'll ask you to 'well' me no more!" Mary laughed and her mother resumed her knitting.

"Aye, you can laugh and poor Michael at the mercy of them straps!" she said indignantly, 'dear send that he mayn't come home with one of them hangin' on his arm. I was ragin' when I heard it.'

"He can marry whom he likes," replied Mary loftily, 'it's immaterial to me.'

Mrs Murphy dropped into melancholy thought for a minute or two. Then she sighed deeply, shook her head, and seemed to wipe away a tear from a dry and tearless eye.

"He never came near me before he went away at any rate," she said, 'and we know rightly the whys and the wherefores of *that*. He blamed me for the way you carried on with the brother. But I wasn't to blame. Feth, I wasn't to blame! All I am to blame for is bein' too anxious-minded and too kind to my childer – not that I care now if they come to begging and want. Deil a hair I care! They can do what they like. And it's my firrum belief, you'll get nobody.'

"I don't want anybody," exclaimed Mary hotly

"No, but maybe you will when you're a weazened old maid, earnin' your livin', tight and sore, and wishin' you'd taken your mother's advice, that's dead and cold in her grave. The thanks I get! When I bid you go and buy a bit of a fur for your neck this winter, after I'd seen them something beautiful on the Newtownards Road, either cat or rabbit, at four and six apiece, what answer did I get? You wanted the money for the soldiers. My alive! And you'll wait till you're past your market, that's what you'll do."

"Well!" said Mary, unawares; 'Oh, I'm sorry, I forgot.'

But Mrs Murphy rose with great dignity, and went out of the door and down the street to Ann Rainey's. As she went in she heard Jinanna's timid voice saying: "I wisht I hadn't bought the blue dress."

"Come in, Sarah Murphy, and sit down," said old Ann.

"Aye, it was a queer piece of foolishness. You'd no call for it at your time of life."

"I only wore it four times," Jinanna spoke wistfully, 'and they said I looked middlin' well in it too. But I'm awful sorry I bought it. If I'd knowed the war was to be, I'd never have done it. It was a great sin for me.'

"It's a queer pity and a great misfortune altogether," said old Ann sharply, 'that you hadn't something sensible to yammer about, for you're past the common good at it! Hould your tongue, for mercy's sake! You have me deeved listenin' to you.'

"I can't help it," answered Jinanna meekly, 'it's that gay lookin' and that blue...'

"Feth, it's blue enough! What ails you, Sarah? It's new 'uns to see you so quiet." Mrs Murphy had seated herself on the other side of the fire without speaking. Her knitting was in her hands and she seemed to be counting stitches. She held a needle firmly between her teeth. 'I mostly hear your tongue goin' like a hand-bell long before I see you.'

"Wait till I lift the heel," mumbled Mrs Murphy.

28

Jacob Holden, Michael's cousin, was driving home in the tax-cart from town one morning, and as he passed through the village an enormous woman with a red, agitated face tumbled out of a door and signalled to him to stop.

"What's wrong?" he exclaimed, pulling up hastily.

"It's the kitlin'!" she gasped. 'I seen you goin' by, and I run, and it run, and it got between my feet and nearly whummelled me. It's a fashion it has, bad wind to it! How are you, Mr Holden dear? I'm glad to see you.' She recovered her breath, and they shook hands gravely.

"It's not the first time I tried to get a hoult of you," she went on, 'but somehow-in-other I always just missed you – and a minute ago wee Ned run in, and sez he, 'there's he's comin' – run for your life!' for the child was watchin' for you like a fox, and it the market day. So I dropped the griddle out of my hand and run. I told Tam to get acquaint with you many a time, but I might as well not. He's like a monument on the side of the road, that man of mine – he spakes to noan. But we're all as God made us Mr Holden, that's what I say. How are you likin' this part of the country, at all?'

"I like it well," said Jacob, his eyes on the mare's twitching ears, 'it's a fine country.'

"Aye!" returned Mrs Murphy fervently, 'you might say that! You'd travel a long road before you'd light on a wee farm of land like Michael's. And a terrible fine fella he is too! Why on earth didn't he come home when Sandy was comin'?'

"I couldn't right say."

"What I'm afeerd of is that he'll be nabbed."

"Nabbed?"

"Aye. Ketched. They're all mad about soldiers now, no matter what size or shape they are. I trust in goodness he'll have sense."

"I doubt the mare's not for standin'," said Jacob, 'she knows she's on the road home.'

"I'll not be for delayin' you either," replied Mrs Murphy graciously, 'there's a kickin' divil in her, and always was. I told Michael to get redd of her many a time. But what I was wishful to say to you, Mr Holden, is that *I* was Michael's greatest friend in the country, and it was to me he always come when he wanted a word of advice on one thing or another, and I'll be the same to you and more.' She extended her arms as if to embrace mare, tax-cart and driver. 'Drop in to my house any night, and welcome.'

Jacob was at a loss for words, and there might have been an embarrassing pause had not the mare swerved violently at the moment, whereupon Mrs Murphy with a hasty "Lord save us!" retired to her own door. Jacob gripped the reins and nodded over his shoulder.

"I got him for you mother, didn't I?" said Ned, turning quickly from a pot of jam on the table, 'Give us a penny.'

"I will not, indeed, you young rascal! I've something else to do with my pennies."

"Well, give us a ha'penny."

"Not likely! Gwan out of my road this minute, and let me get on with my work in peace."

But Ned, with a persistence peculiarly his own, followed her hither and thither, repeating, "you might give us a ha'penny, so you might," until at last she dived into her big pocket and produced the ha'penny, with the words, 'get out of my sight, you young heart-scald.'

Sandy had gone back to his soldiering a good deal happier. He was not, in any degree, Ann's lover, but he was more her friend than before. Mrs Murphy spoke of 'notions,' and 'foolishness,' and told him of the girls who came out to stay with her, sometimes for a few days, sometimes for weeks. "It's more of that Johnny Darragh's work," she said. 'She's not right in the head. Many a one has went to the asylum before now through love.'

But Sandy knew better. He was glad Ann was giving her heart to this sort of thing since she would not give it to him. She was so kind to him now. He knew she wanted to show her sympathy because he was serving. He never misunderstood for a moment. When she turned on him that softened look he loved, he felt it was worth while to go away, even if he never came back. If he had not known it was his duty to go, the look in her beautiful eyes would have sent him. The vision of service that had come to Ann that rainy night, outside the public-house in Ballymacarrett, had been intensified a hundredfold by the war. A passion to serve and to endure rose in her and burnt like a flame. Mary and she had nothing but scorn for the crowds of fur-becoated women they saw day after day, studying the finery of the shop windows while boys were dying in droves in the battle-line. But the difference in the two girls was that one saw a great sacrifice being made for a great cause, and the other thought only of one man going out, perhaps to die.

Jacob Holden, finding the time hang rather heavily on his hands with only Patch, and an octogenarian house-keeper to speak to, bethought himself one evening of Mrs Murphy's invitation, and wandered down the hill right into the heart of the group sitting round the Murphy hearthstone. They made him very welcome. After that he came often, and a curious friendship sprang up between him and Tam. Both were of a silent habit. Sometimes when Mrs Murphy was out, they sat and smoked on either side of the fire without speaking. If they talked, it was in monosyllables and yet in some subtle way they came to understand each other. When Jacob rose to go, Tam invariably accompanied him, which was his custom only on the rarest occasion. Jacob would turn and leave him back to the village, but even then it could not be said that they added much to the huge welter of conversation that eternally beats round church and state. Mrs Murphy merely said, "men bate all."

"The end of the world's comin', there's no doubt," remarked
Sammy Soretoes one evening as they sat round the fire, 'it's as plain as
the nose on your face.' 'My alive. Do you tell me that!' exclaimed Mrs
Murphy, dropping her knitting hurriedly, 'are you sure, Sammy? I
always had a great dread on me of that time.'

"Aye, I think I'm sure."

"There used to be a man that had great pieces in the paper about the
end of the world," said old Ann, who seldom joined the company; 'he
let on he knew the very day and hour, and it never come yet. He was
another windbag! The world's full of them.'

"I trust in the Lord I'll be happed in the green grass afore that,"
shivered Mrs Murphy.

"The old lad, he's to be chained a thousand years," said Sammy,
musingly; 'man, but that will be wan good riddance.'

"The world has turned clean upside down in my day," said old Ann
mournfully. 'I said it when I seen the bicycles comin' in at the first –
for surely them that the Lord has blessed with legs should use them –
and look at them ould engines they're runnin' on the roads now. Why
it's as much as your life's worth to cross over to that ditch thonder.'

"Feth, aye! It's a terrible time altogether."

"I don't know how we're goin' to live at all?" remarked Mrs
Murphy despondingly, 'with the price of everything riz the way it is,
and my family that ill to feed. There's wee Ned with not a crow's fill on
him, and it's my belief that child has an atin' devil in him.'

"They're sayin' in the town the war will soon be over." Mary lifted
her head from her knitting to say.

"The war's only kindlin'," replied Sammy sombrely.

"Och, dear-a-dear!" sighed Mrs Murphy, 'when I think of them
young boys that used to come down the Holywood Hills singin' and
marchin', and the band makin' lovely music – them Norfolks – I could
cry my fill. Their faces would be like the risin' sun – och, the young,
young faces they had on them! Och, annee, annee!'

"I'd like to be a young fella the day..." began Sammy.

"There's a change come over a body if you remark it," interrupted
Mrs Murphy in her ruthless fashion. '*I* find a change in myself. The
things that used to have me put out! Why, if the kettle boiled over it
annoyed me, and the cat broke my heart.'

Jinanna, who seldom spoke when men were present, suddenly
broke into the discussion. "What I'm sorriest at," she said, lifting an
earnest face, 'is that ever I bought the blue dress...'

"Look see here!" exclaimed Mrs Murphy, turning on her vehemently, 'if you don't quit mournin' over that ould dress, I'll put a match till it myself! I'll hould you I'll make a bonfire for you. I'll give you something to mourn for...'

"My lovely dress!" exclaimed Jinanna, incredulously, 'my lovely dress that's fit for a queen to wear...'

"I wouldn't be seen dead in it," returned Mrs Murphy hastily, 'it's that wild in the colour. Sure you have me near astray in the head with your mournin' and lamentin'. Wear it for goodness' sake, for nobody wants it off you.'

"Oh, I'll never wear it again," she said humbly. 'I couldn't now – it's that gay and lively lookin'.'

"You look queer and well in it, Jinanna," interposed Mary consolingly, 'don't you heed a word mamma says.'

"You've no son goin' out to the war to be breakin' your heart over, so wear your dress, woman dear, and content yourself."

"That's the truth!" replied Jinanna, and she bent her head meekly over her knitting. But soon a smile had come back to her face, for Ned and Shindy were playing subdued games in the corner, and she could not help watching them. She had grown easy in the life of Gape Row, but she did not talk freely to anyone but Mrs Murphy and Mary and Ann. Her face had gradually lost the frightened look it had worn for years. She got up every morning at seven, but took immense pleasure in the thought that she might have lain till ten. Her days had long, delicious gaps of idleness in them. She read in the paper of women who went abroad for rest and change, but to her it was a heavenly thing to lie back in a chair and do nothing. Every day of her life she thanked God for the riches He had sent her – how rich she felt – but more than all she thanked Him for the idleness. On this side of the grave she had not dreamt of it – these long, magnificent idle hours. Hints of her girlish prettiness began to come back to her face. The hard years were all forgotten. Everything was a festivity to her. Jinanna had gone back to her youth.

"Any word from Charlie, lately?" asked Sammy presently.

"Aye, I had a letter from him last week. He'll not be home for a couple of months yet, and I'm just as glad – there's that much annoyance on the water."

"Aye, them submarines is the devil. I wouldn't say but he'll be a good bit changed agin we see him again. America'll have knocked some of the notions out of him."

"Do you mean brains?" asked Mrs Murphy indignantly. 'I would like to know what would knock the brains out of Charlie! He's full of them. He takes after me.'

"Do you mind the time he wanted to do something or other in the church, and he wasn't let? He was clean mad."

"I think I do. I was ragin' myself."

"I don't mind it," said Jinanna inquiringly.

"You don't mind it, my dear, because you never heerd it," returned Mrs Murphy, 'for it happened when you were livin' in the wee house down the loanin' and might as well have been in Derrydramuck, or at the back of Slieve Gallun for all the neighbourin' was in you, till we took and hoked you out. Well, Charlie was helpin' to decorate the church for the harvest thanksgivin' and mind you he was quare and good at it, and he took and filled the big windy in the porch with moss, and wrote on it, 'when the roll is called up yonder, I'll be there,' in potatoes, wee, tooty potatoes. And if you please they wouldn't let him! And them our own potatoes too, and grew in our own garden.'

"It must have been the quare grand sight," said Sammy smiling, 'I was always sorry I missed it.'

"The trouble he went till," lamented Mrs Murphy, 'if you please he dyed the potatoes red, white and blue, and the blue run into a kind of a spruce on him, and there was no end of a confusion.'

"It would have been a change from chrysanters," chirped Jinanna.

"You'll think the queer lot of Charlie when you see him, Mr Holden," said Mrs Murphy.

"I'm sure I will," Jacob hastened to say.

"I'll show you his likeness some time in daylight. I've a whole drawerful of them in there." She jerked her head towards the room door, 'the father used to be ragin' at him for puttin' the money in them. Poor Charlie! He was the sorra for gettin' his countenance tuk! And now he's far away from all belongin' to him.' She wiped her eyes with the corner of her apron.

"Do you mind the time when he joined the Salvation Army?" asked Sammy.

"I think I do that! I hardly spoke till him the night he came in here and told me about it, and the good he got and all," replied Mrs Murphy, in disgusted tones. 'I just said till him 'didn't I carry you three long mile, and it the winter day, to get you baptized into the church, ye pup ye!' My mother was failin' at the time, and I was stayin' with her at the Hill-head. 'Let me hear no more about you, and your armies,' sez I, and he was that affronted he got up and walked out of the house. And before a month was over, I heerd word he was for comin' out to preach one sunday at the pump – him and Happy Bill – and I sent the father in, fut for fut, the whole road to Ginger Street, and bid him tell him that before I'd let him stand up there and disgrace me afore the whole parish, I'd brake every bone in his body! And he knowed rightly I'd have done it, too.'

"If he's anything to his mother, I wouldn't say but he'd be the right preacher," observed Sammy. 'What do you think, Tam?'

"Hould your tongue, man!" said Mrs Murphy, with unconcealed pride, 'wait till I tell Mr Holden the piece out. There was a man come in here one day after that awhile. He was on his road home from the market, and he left the horse and cart standin' there to come in and tell me. He'd heard our Charlie preachin' in some gather-me-up sort of a place in Ballymacarrett – some gospel hall or other – and he thought terrible well of him. He said he never heard the like in all his livin' days. The swate was pourin' off him before he'd right started – he got himself that worked up – and never a note nor nothing in his hand the way the real ministers has – but it all come warm from the heart.'

"He always had a great notion of himself," remarked Ann, 'from he was the size of two turf. I mind that.'

"He has the quare headpiece on him," replied Mrs Murphy proudly, 'he takes after my side of the house.'

Afterwards when old Ann and Jinanna had gone out, Sammy said, "that wee woman's well mended," and Mrs Murphy, pleased to handle a subject with which she was so familiar, turned to Jacob and gave him a long and detailed account of her tragic history.

At the end of May, Michael accepted a pressing invitation to spend a week's leave in Rosapenna Street. He had thrown himself into soldiering with eagerness, and had managed to extract a good deal of pleasure from it. He was keen to go to the front and expected to be sent before long. Later on he would go home for a few days. Jacob was continually writing for him to come and take a look at the crops, and see what he thought of the cattle. Presently he would go, but for this week, probably the last leave he would spend in Dublin, he would throw care to the winds and enjoy himself thoroughly.

He reached Westland Row Station in the middle of the day, and was conscious as the train left the sweet, green-leaved country and slid in between rows of houses, of the strange, captive feeling that always assailed him in cities. His cousins gave him a vociferous welcome, and before the evening was over he had seen with his own eyes what a significant wink from Sophia had tried to tell him – that the barber had turned his blighted affections to Jessie and was making good progress with his love-making.

He was sitting in the little back parlour that evening, idle for the moment. Jessie and her lover were looking at pictures of Killarney through a stereoscope. Sophie, who had slipped out of the room a moment before, came back and whispered to him that Jim was at the corner waiting to speak to her, but she would not be away more than a few minutes. The barber remarked twice that Killarney seemed the very place for a honeymoon, and Jessie giggled across the table at him. A sudden longing for the open air came over him and he rose and slipped out through the empty shop. It was nine o'clock on a May evening. As he came up in the train that morning he passed the May hedges white with hawthorn. The foam of the bog-cotton was over the purple bogs, and he saw all the familiar, bright-eyed little country things flowering on the banks beside the train. Here the children were playing on the hard pavement.

"God pity them!" thought Michael the country-man.

As he walked aimlessly along, he found himself on a wide, noisy road. Trams rattled past with their peculiarly hideous noise, cars and drays came and went, women and perambulators jostled him. He turned into a side road and quite suddenly found himself under trees.

He looked up gratefully into the thick, leafy net-work over his head, and the leaves knocked against each other and made exquisite little noises as all leaves do in May time. The city seemed far away. As he went on, a fresh soothing delight fell on his heart. On either side of him stretched a few small fields, with the hedges a little tumbled and tossed, and overgrown with the luxury and light-heartedness of May. There were trees to shade you from the sun – heavy beeches and wych-elms so pale and beautiful in their first green and long-fingered chestnuts. He stood for a while leaning over a gate and a little black cow came and pushed her head through the bars to him. He fondled her lovingly. "Och, the crathur!" he said, 'the crathur!' And then an old man in his shirt-sleeves opened a gate at the other side of the field, and at the sound she turned and ambled leisurely across the grass to him. The good smell of cattle – how it brought back home and milking-time.

The road narrowed and twisted suddenly to the left. It led to a terrace of houses – high, grey houses with many windows. He stood leaning against the fence under the heavy, overhanging trees.

There was a curious stillness everywhere. Behind the houses there were gardens and orchards. The old earth was very busy and the long, brown plots were filled with young, green things springing into maturity. He could see the apple trees stretching back – the lovely bridal white and pink and green that lay as lightly as a cloud over the gnarled old branches. Michael stood still. The curious silence held him...

29

As he walked back the sounds of the city came nearer, and with each step they jarred more on Michael's mood. Suddenly his heart lifted with a great longing for home and the sight of his own green fields. If he went away now, his cousins, who had been so good to him, would be disappointed. But without waiting to think, he knew he was going. He could not stay. The wind was blowing over the hills with a touch of the sea in it. And Patch was hungering for the sound of his voice. He would take the morning train and be home by midday.

Sophie met him with reddened eyes, and they went into the parlour, which was empty, together.

"Look here, Sophie," he said awkwardly, 'I doubt I'll have to be off brave and early in the morning.'

"Why, I thought you were going to stay with us all week? We have planned lots of high jinks for you. Where are you going?"

"Off home."

"I'm very sorry, Michael..."

"It's awfully good of you to want me," he began earnestly, 'and I never will forget your kindness, but there's things I ought to be seein' about at home – cattle and things – and Jacob's never done writin' for me to come on. I doubt I ought to be goin' this time. Jacob's not so well used to handlin' cattle and the like of that, you see.' He had reddened considerably during his speech.

"I understand," said Sophie, in a low voice, 'I understand perfectly. You couldn't have told *anyone* on the wide earth who would sympathize with you as I do. I'm in the same boat myself. Don't be afraid, no one will hear us. I hope she'll be good to you. I'm sure she'll be glad to see you. Stick to her, Michael, through thick and thin, and if she's worth a scallion, as mother would say, she'll stick to you. That's my motto – stick! Oh Michael, I'm in such trouble! Jim's out of his sit, again.'

"Och, no," he said sympathetically. He had felt greatly drawn to Jim since he met the barber. 'I'm terrible sorry to hear it.'

"That's why he sent for me this evening, the poor fellow, it's unfortunate he is altogether," wept Sophie, 'and we meant to get married before long and now I suppose we'll never be married at all. Does anybody mean to tell me that *I* am to be the old maid of the family? Oh, my poor Jim, what's going to become of us at all! I wish now I had taken the schoolmaster.'

"The schoolmaster?"

"That was the one before Jim and the barber," she explained, drying her eyes.

"Were you fond of him?"

"Fond of him!" she echoed scornfully, 'I hated him; but what about that when your heart's broken.'

"Sure Jim will drop into some other job one of these days."

Sophie sighed. "Yes, but he'll get out of that too. Wait till Pa hears this."

"I'm queer and sorry," Michael repeated.

"I think if he'd a little house of his own to work for he'd do better, don't you?" She turned and looked at him and he saw in a moment that her eyes were fixed on something far away. She did not speak for a moment.

"Michael, Michael!" she gasped suddenly. 'I've got it! We'll get married first and look for something after! Why didn't I think of it before?'

"But what will you get married on?" asked Michael.

"Fiddlesticks! Jim will do splendidly when he has *me* to work for. Of course he will. He was so down-hearted when I left him, not twenty minutes ago. Oh, I am so happy! Won't it be fun, Michael? And you'll come and stay with us, and no matter how little we have we'll share it with you, for thank God that's the kind of Jim." And she looked so proud and happy, and her eyes sparkled so radiantly that he had not the heart to discourage her.

"We can get married any time now," she repeated joyously, 'anytime – and down at the corner, a couple of minutes ago, poor Jim nearly cried because it seemed further away than ever. I don't know how to wait till the morning to tell him. Isn't it wonderful how things settle themselves, Michael dear, when you are positively at your wits' end?'

Michael thought it certainly was, but said: "Think it over, Sophie, if you take my advice."

"I'm tired thinking it over. Oh, Michael," she leaned forward and pressed his arm between her hands. 'I hope with all my heart you'll soon be as happy as I am! I wish you the best of luck when you go home to see her, indeed I do.'

"You're talkin' foolishness, woman," Michael protested. 'I'm not going home to see anyone. I'm going to see about the land. You think everybody's like yourself.'

"I saw it in your eye as plain as plain can be," said the experienced Sophie, 'and you to be putting it off on cattle and the like of that.'

"Lord love you," exclaimed Michael, 'you don't know what you're talking about.'

"I do and I don't," retorted Sophie. 'I don't know her name, or the colour of her eyes or her hair, though I might make a very fair shot at both. But there – I won't tease you any more. I'll make it all right about your going with mother and the girls. I'll say it's pressing business – *very* pressing indeed if they but knew it,' and she put her hand to her heart and sighed.

That night as he was going up to bed, he met her on the stairs. Even the dim, blinking light on the landing could not hide the gaiety of her eyes. She put her arms round his neck and kissed him.

"Just for luck, dear," she whispered.

Michael felt conscience-stricken at leaving the kindly little household so abruptly, but Sophie had evidently impressed them with the importance of his business, and they threw no obstacle in his way. It was a relief to him when he found himself in the corner of a third class carriage of a train going north. Sophie came to the station to see him off, still talking cheerfully of Jim and her future, and he was grateful that she did not attempt to kiss him, in spite of an exuberant farewell. He stood up and leaned out of the window to see the last of her. She was making desperate efforts to find a handkerchief to wave to him, and the search failing, she tore a stringy bit of ermine off her throat and waved it instead. Michael laughed out and waved his hand in return.

"Good old Sophie!" he thought, 'she's the heart of corn.'

As the train rushed up into the north, he thought he felt, even in the carriage, a touch of the cold, sweet sharpness he loved in the northern air. He got out of the train at Belfast, his heart leaping to be at home again. As he walked along the street, he noticed, for the first time in his life, a curious little snip-snap in the voices of the people. And there was the blue head of the Cave Hill peering down familiarly into the town.

At the Junction he got into a tram which brought him within a few miles of the farm. He left the road and made his way home through the fields. As yet he had not met a soul he knew. He went straight across country, climbing over gates and fences and pushing through holes in the hedge. If only Patch was with him! It warmed his heart to think of the frantic welcome that awaited him.

At last he came out on the road near his home. His eye roamed over the fields. The smoke was rising, clean and blue above the ash trees that brimmed round the little house. He saw the whitewashed gable of the barn, and heard the familiar 'caw-caw' of the crows. In the turnip field he saw Jacob, who seemed to be mending a gap in the hedge. There was a white speck lying on the grass beside him. He whistled. The speck unfolded itself alertly and sat up and listened. He whistled again – and with a cry of rapture, Patch was bounding across the field and was upon him.

Jacob, who could not see so far, but who knew as well as if he had seen, straightened himself and followed a long way behind.

"Good old boy." Michael was saying for the hundredth time as he came up. 'Good old fellow! You didn't forget me, did you Patch?' and Patch leaped round him frantically, catching his coat or his hands in his mouth, when he was not uttering wild yelps of joy. At last Michael took the tense quivering little body up in his arms and carried him on his shoulder. He was almost as pleased as Patch.

"You're welcome, man dear," said Jacob, 'sure this is grand! But why didn't you let me know you were comin', and I'd have been in to meet you with the mare.'

"Sure I didn't know myself till last night," replied Michael truthfully.

"Marget will be queerly put about, for she's been layin' off the dinner she'd have ready for you this queer while. You're lookin' well Michael, I wouldn't say but the life agrees with you."

"I'm the best," said Michael cheerfully, 'and I'm heart-glad to be at home again.' He wondered now that he had stayed away so long.

In the evening he grew restless, and went out by himself. Jacob was content to sit smoking by the fire. With Patch running beside him, he took the field-path that led sooner or later to the village. He did not mean to go there yet. He might have to meet Mary while he was at home, but he would not hurry the day.

Presently he turned into a rough, narrow bit of road known as Dempsey's loanin'. Mosses and ferns grew in the wet hollows on either side and the hedges above were starred with foamy clumps of hawthorn. Cuckoo-flowers were growing timidly in the shade, and the blue-eyed speedwells and the soft, faint gold of the primroses gleamed on the grassy banks. May had made a heavenly thing of Dempsey's loanin'.

"Daughter," Mrs Murphy had said an hour before, 'what ails you? You're the colour of death! Take the can, and go up to Pat's Mary's, and get a taste of buttermilk off her. Maybe the air will put a bit of colour in your cheeks.'

So Mary took the can and went over the stile into Dempsey's loanin'. Before she had gone very far, she sat down on a little bank beside a gate. She put the can down on the ground and listlessly watched a spider crawl into it, and although she did not know it, she sat there and waited for Michael to come.

She laid her head down on her hands and thought. Long, long thoughts. Something of bitter sadness must have crept into them, for soon the tears slid down between her fingers. Then to her horror she heard a soft pattering beside her, and Patch's cold little nose was pressed against her hand. There were steps coming behind. She took out her handkerchief, and dried her eyes quickly. How fast Jacob was walking this evening.

Michael did not see her from a distance, for she was hidden by a thick clump of low-growing thorn. He came on with great strides. Mary, whose heart was beginning to beat in thick, heavy jerks, looked up. There were traces of tears still in her eyes. Her face had a new gravity that gave it depth and softness. She looked up, her hands clasped nervously on her knees.

Michael, coming on her, stopped suddenly. In one moment he forgot everything except that he wanted to kiss her. She rose and looked at him, her face flushing to the roots of her hair. And neither of them spoke a word.

He held out his hands to her.

"Darling," he said 'I love you with all my heart!' And to comfort her he said it again and again, for she was clinging to his shoulder and crying as if her heart would break.

30

"**I** might have knowed!" said Mrs Murphy exultingly across the hearth to old Ann. 'I might have knowed when I heard Sammy Soretoes comin' down the street like the half of Newry.'

"Aye, it was new-uns for him to be hurryin' himself."

"Thinks I to myself, 'bad wind to them childer,' for I thought, sure enough, it was one of the wee Morrows chokin' – they're the sorra for chokin' on fardens and marbles and one thing and another – she has a bad fashion of givin' them all they ask for – I rared mine different – and I riz off my chair to run. And with that Sammy come up to the door, puffin' and blowin' like a steam-engine. 'Come on out,' sez he, 'till you see who's linkin' your Mary down the road. My alive, it's wonderful! Praises be to the Lord this day!'"

"Aye, it was a quare surprise."

"Surprise!" Mrs Murphy echoed the futile word with scorn. 'Surprise! Why, woman dear, it's the wonder of the world! Michael and our Mary! However it come I never thought of puttin' them two together in my mind's eye. Never once. It was the last thing I thought of. It bates all! I'm queer and thankful to the Almighty this day.'

"You weren't so thankful a while back when she wouldn't take Andy John to plaze you."

"Feth, I was not. But did ever I think she was goin' to get Michael? I tell you, I never deemed it. All I was afeerd of was that she'd put herself past her market like many a one afore her."

"It's time for you to quit cockin' yourself up as if you knowed everything," said old Ann severely. 'It's a very bad fashion you have and always had, Sarah Murphy.'

"But, woman dear…"

"There was you on one side of me, deevin' me, mornin', noon and night about Andy John McCready. You'd think nobody ever seen a man afore. And that fool crathur – has she all her wits about her, do you think? – on the other side of me, lamentin' about the blue dress she bought that she didn't ought to have bought – sure we all knew that from the first day she had it on her – and me, with my own troubles that *were* troubles…"

"But I tell you I-didn't-know-she-was-goin'-to-get-Michael, or you'd never have heard a word out of my head about Andy John," interrupted Mrs Murphy.

"Lyin' heavy on me," continued Ann firmly, 'and me never namin' them, I may say. Well, thanks be to the Almighty, we'll hear no more about Andy John McCready now.'

"I think not!" returned Mrs Murphy joyously, 'is it the like of him? I wouldn't bother my brains talkin' about him. Sure you wouldn't think he was a drop's blood to Michael – a fat little tub of a fella, neither shape nor make – and Michael the grand lookin' boy he is.'

"Well, well! It didn't take you long to change your mind anyway."

"But sure I tell you I hadn't the laste notion *this* was comin' off. If Mary had it in her mind she kept it brave and close from her own mother."

"She showed her sense that time."

"I had to do the best I could for my childer. I'm a dyin' woman, and have been this twenty-year and more, and if anything happened to me, look at the man I'd be lavin' behine me? He's a good man – in a sense – and a hard-workin' man, and as sober as Buttermilk John himself, but sure you know rightly he'd be no good wantin' me. What sort of a debate would he make for the childer?"

"His tongue's not goin' like a hand-bell the day round the way some people's is, I'll allow."

"He's more like a monument than a man, that's what I say many a time, but I don't care. When I see my family goin' up in the world, that's all I want. *I* never liked Andy John – *I* never liked a bone in his body – but he was the right match, and what could I do when I seen him throwin' sparks at our Mary? Sure I didn't know she was goin' to get…"

"He had a wife and family in America the whole time – I know that as well as if I'd seen them. Maybe you'll believe me now."

"I wouldn't just like to say that…"

"And him runnin' every night of the week intil the town to them theatres and them music-halls," continued Ann disgustedly. 'That's a queer sort of a character for you. Them bad places!'

"It made me onaisy many a time, I'll allow. My father and mother would have riz in their grave if they'd heard word of it."

"You're just as bad as him yourself. I see no differs in you."

"Oh no, Ann dear," said Mrs Murphy, raising her eyes piously. 'I am not. I hope I'll never be nearer the Bottomless Pit than when I'm passin' the Grand Opera House in Great Victoria Street. I hope and trust in the Lord I will not. That's near enough for me.'

"I knowed rightly what he was when I seen him comin' down the street with a watch-chain on him would tether a goat," said old Ann, 'sure anybody might have knowed.'

"He was dyin' about our Mary, fair dyin'. It's my belief he'll never get over it."

"Man, but you've a head of wit! He's over it rightly afore this," said old Ann, with a short laugh. 'Our Mary's workin' for a coolin'. Our Mary's refused the biggest match in the country! Biggest match, indeed! I was deeved listenin' to you. Many a time I wonder if he wanted her at all. There's the tea-drawer at your elbow,' she added hastily, as Mrs Murphy showed ominous signs of going off in a huff, 'set it on the fire and make a cup of tea. My mouth's dry.' She leaned forward, and held out her thin, wrinkled hands to the blaze.

"I never had a day to do well since the day I married," she went on moodily, 'never a one! If I had my life to live over again I wouldn't be so aisy ketched.'

"It's all in the Lord's hands, Ann dear," Mrs Murphy bent down, and stirred the fire as she spoke. 'It's all in the Lord's hands, and it's not for the likes of you or me till interfere.'

"You were brave and busy interferin' a while back there yourself."

"And it's all sent for till show us this is not our home," continued Mrs Murphy jubilantly, 'here the day and away the morra! (I'll make you a brave strong drop when I'm at it.) What's this world and the things of the world, as I many a time tell Tam. What's riches to a dyin' woman? If we had too much sure we might forget oursleves.'

Ann grunted. "I'd like to see Ann settled before I drop off."

"And I trust in the Lord you will too. She's that lovely lookin' a girl! Sure it would take the light from your eyes to see her goin' by the door."

"She's not a patch on her mother – not a patch! But who minds Mary Ann now?"

"The first time I ever come intil this house, and that was afore I was long married," said Mrs Murphy, 'she was sittin' there in the corner with the child on her knee and it the livin' image of her. I mind it like yesterday. Aye, she had the lovely face on her.'

"She took her death soon after that."

"She did, indeed. Well, I trust and hope Ann will do better nor her mother done. I declare to goodness, you'd nearly be better wantin' altogether, as gettin' a bad one! But it's the mercy of goodness she missed Johnny Darragh. The woman's not born that could keep the harness on *him*."

"Feth, and I'll bate you what you like the one that's got him will do it. I bate you she'll trounce the very life out of him."

"Well, I trust in goodness Ann will fall in with a good match, and get the worth of herself yet. There's not a girl in the country I think as much of. She's haughty and she's distant, and I wouldn't say till her what I'd say till many a one, but if I was in trouble it's her I'd turn till. She's a sincere one, that's what she is!" concluded Mrs Murphy.

"She's Mary Ann's daughter," said old Ann, with a tremulous movement of her head.

"Just such another. Praises be to the Lord, for one here and there you can depend on. And there's my new son-in-law that is to be, if it's the will of the Almighty." The words burst from her as from a pent-up dam, 'he's another one! You could lay your last farden on Michael.'

"I believe you," said old Ann thawing rapidly under the influence of tea and conversation, 'for wonct, I believe you, Sarah Murphy.'

The golden week of Michael's leave went by. The day before he left Mary was sitting in the kitchen, her head bent over a sock she was trying to finish for him. Mrs Murphy moved gently to and fro in the rocking-chair. Her eyes were fixed on her daughter.

"I do declare," she said, after a prolonged study. 'I do declare, Mary, you're gettin' to be the image of your Aunt Maria McSpeddan, and she was the beauty of four townlands! Actually to goodness you're gettin' well-lookin'.'

Mary laughed. Her face was a radiance these days. "I wish I was," she said and she coloured a little, remembering certain stupid, exquisite things that had been said to her lately.

"But you are – that's what I'm tellin' you. Daughter dear, I'm queerly pleased about Michael! There's not his like in the whole country."

Mary's eyes filled with tears. "Mother – sometimes I'm that frightened about him."

"I wouldn't be a bit frightened, dear. He's in God's good hands and no harm can happen him there. Sure there's plenty of them will come home without as much as a scratch."

"I saw in the paper last night – about a soldier – and him only three weeks married..."

"If I was you I wouldn't believe a word's in them papers," said Mrs Murphy firmly, 'sure they put in any sort of gorbage to make them sell. Gwan and get on your hat. Michael will be here any time now.' He had gone to town, and was to call for her on his way home and bring her up to the farm for tea.

And a few minutes later he did come, looking so handsome and debonair, that it was impossible to be sad or apprehensive in his presence.

"Which way will we go?" he said, after a few minutes' chat with Mrs Murphy, 'by the road, or the fields?'

"Oh, the near cut through the loanin' and the fields?"

"You can please yourselves," remarked Mrs Murphy, 'but if it was me, I'd go by the road and let the people see me.' Michael laughed. 'What takes you up that dirty old loanin', for dear sakes? You'd meet nothing there except maybe a goat.'

"It's not dirty at all. It's the nicest road in the country, isn't it, Mary?" She smiled but would not look at him.

"Dempsey's loanin' nice? It would take you to the neck in gutters the last time I was there – but that was near-hand Christmas Day. Maybe it has dried up by now." She wondered why they laughed, as if they shared some happy secret.

When they had gone, she stood looking after them until they were out of sight. "Dear send that he may come home safe!" she thought, with a sudden sigh, and old Ann peering out of the shadows of her doorway, murmured, 'Lord love them, the foolish childer! Lord love them, the poor, foolish childer.'

They made it into a long walk – that near cut up Dempsey's loanin'.

31 ▟▙▟▟▙

"**D**arling, the war will soon be over. Don't fret."

"But they say..."

"Never mind what they say. Promise me you won't fret."

She pressed her lips against his coat, but did not speak.

"At any rate we'll be married the first leave I get. Sure you'll have me, Mary?" He drew her closer. The minutes were racing past.

"Certain sure."

"I'll be off home to you the very first minute I can. Dear knows how soon I may be home."

"Michael, do you mind that day in the field when I was so angry?"

"I was angry too, dear. More shame for me."

"No, no, but I said the *hatefullest* things to you, Michael. You won't be rememberin' them and you out there away from me?"

"I've clean forgotten them long ago. Sure you *know* I have."

"You'll never, never think of them once? Sure it wasn't me that said them at all! I'll be breakin' my heart thinkin' of that day, and you far away. But you'll not remember it, Michael? Promise me faithful."

"I promise."

They clung to each other for a long time without speaking.

Michael and Sandy went out with a draft in the middle of July. They rushed home for a few days' leave, and Gape Row clustered round them with affectionate farewells and much sage advice. Old Ann told them to watch themselves and keep out of the road of the guns.

Michael and Mary spent their last hour in old Ann's kitchen. Ann had gone to bed at seven o'clock saying war or no war, she be to get her sleep. Mrs Murphy sat in her own house, bursting now and then into tears and lamentations. The children who were ranged round her were waiting impatiently for Mary and Michael to come in, and enjoying the situation with true Murphy instinct for drama. But the lovers who had gone out for a last stroll together, had at young Ann's suggestion slipped into the empty kitchen, and they sat clinging

together on the little sofa, covered with shiny American cloth. Ann
and Sandy stood talking outside the door.

"You'll not be forgettin' me altogether when I'm away, Ann," said
Sandy lightly.

"Forgettin' you! As if any of us could! We'll be thinkin' of you night
and day till you come home," and she took his hand and held it
between her own, and looked at him with kind, moist eyes.

"Till the boys come home!" he repeated jovially. He wanted above
all things to put his arms round her and kiss her. But he did not dare to
do it – not yet. Somewhere deep inside him an unexpected hope
warmed and gladdened him. It took the sting of parting away. Till he
came back, he would ask no more.

Presently he opened the door a chink, and called "Michael" in a low
voice. Time was getting on. They would have to be going soon. And
he held Ann's hand for a minute and talked cheerfully of his return.
Mary shivered as his hand touched the latch. He called Michael's
name a second time.

She would be brave, oh she would be brave – for she was almost a
soldier's wife... She laid her forhead against his coat speechlessly for a
moment... and then she lifted up her head and they kissed each other
with the long kiss of farewell.

Michael had been the gayest of the gay those few days at home. That
strange mood that had touched him at intervals as he went about his
work a year ago, and which had driven him home from Dublin in the
spring had wholly disappeared. He had the highest hopes for the
future. Before long he was coming home to be married. Meanwhile he
was glad of a chance of being 'in it.' Who wouldn't be glad? He was
eager to be off.

His letters, full of the same ardour, began to come regularly. Mary
kissed the thin little envelopes and locked them safely away in a box
she had bought specially for them. Her bedroom swarmed over with
children, and she was afraid they might be seen by other eyes than hers
during her daily absence. She hid the box carefully in a small, tin
trunk below her bed.

Soon Michael wrote that they were moving up nearer the fighting-
line, and then that they were going into the trenches the next day. For
ten days there was no letter.

"No news is good news, granny always says," said Ann, one
morning on their way to the tram. 'Sure there might be a letter any day
now.'

"It's aisy talkin'! replied poor Mary, 'when you know rightly there isn't anybody like him.'

"Indeed I know. I think the world and all of Michael. But you must try to be plucky. He'd like you to be plucky."

"I *am* plucky, I tell you," said Mary crossly, 'and if I'm not an iceberg or a refrigerator or any other sort of a stone, how am I to help it?' And the next day a letter came, saying they were going back for a short rest and she wasn't to worry. He was quite well and wouldn't be out of it for the world.

She used to lie awake at night, thinking of him, and praying with an agony of earnestness she had never dreamt of before. "Oh, cover his head in the day of battle." She, who had always been so full of healthy young sleep, lay awake and heard, for the first time in her life, the horns and syrens blowing along the sides of the Lough. They punctuated the long, slow, heavy hours of the night.

At six o'clock the mail car passed through the village. It slowed down at the post office, where the mail-bag was thrown in, and then rattled on to the nearest town. Her mother would be stirring quietly in the kitchen after that, getting her father's breakfast ready. Earlier still she would hear a few snatches of bird music in the garden – all that was left of the high revelry of spring – and when it was time to get up, she was tired and could have fallen into a sound sleep.

She and her mother and Jinanna were sitting chatting and working in the kitchen one saturday afternoon. Ned and Shindy were far afield. Sometimes lately Mary had been struck with the ardent, ungrudging sympathy Jinanna had shown to her over her engagement. She thought it was so good of the poor, lonely little thing. They had finished tea, and Mary had washed the cups and put them away. She took her work and sat down in her father's chair in the corner. A fever of knitting had taken hold of the village, and each of them had a half-finished soldier's grey sock in their hands.

There was a strange agitation about Jinanna at moments. She dropped her knitting on her lap and then took it up feverishly. She began sentences which she never finished. She fidgeted until at last Mrs Murphy, who had been eyeing her critically for some time, said:

"Jinanna, what kind of a wee crab of a man do you intend that fut for?"

Jinanna jumped. "For dear sake," she exclaimed, holding up the sock, 'is it too wee, do you think?'

"It is that. It would maybe fit some wee cricket of a fella that I wouldn't be bothered knittin' for. I always like a man I could take a decent sunday out of when I was young, and mind you, Tam wasn't a bad lookin' fella when I first seen him. It's hangin' over that shovel has tuk all the spunk out of him, I do believe."

Jinanna pulled out the needles and began to undo the sock hurriedly. Then without any warning she jumped up and ran out of the house. Mrs Murphy looked across at Mary with uplifted eyebrows.

"Dear bless us! Is she right, do you think?"

"Maybe she's affronted about the knitting."

"She's aisy affronted then. She can get better the way she got bad, for I'm not goin' near her. My, but she was in a hurry. She's the best mended wuman I ever seen."

"Yes," said Mary absently.

"Do you mind the die-a-loney wee crathur she used to be?"

"Yes."

"She's looked up quarely since she got the money. There's them that despises money, but feth, it's not me."

"Yes," said Mary, in the same absent, gentle voice.

"You're a great hand at the talkin' the day, so you are!" ejaculated her mother, 'you're queer good crack.'

Mary blushed and laughed. "I was thinkin' of something else," she said. 'Jinanna wouldn't have much only for you mother. I don't know how you managed it.'

"I take no credit to myself, whatsomever. But I'm thankful many a time I was born with brains."

"You were indeed."

"And you take after me, Mary. You've a right, good head on you." In these days Mary came near to ousting Charlie from his place in Mrs Murphy's admiration.

Jinanna had not been gone more than ten minutes when she came back suddenly and closed the door. She stood in the middle of the floor and looked from one to the other.

"Oh, let me tell you!" she cried beseechingly, 'Oh Mary dear!' and she burst into violent weeping.

"God bless me! She's bad again!" exclaimed Mrs Murphy, 'sit down woman on this chair at the fire. Are you sick? Would you like Mary to run for the doctor? Will I make a poultice for you?'

But Jinanna swayed to and fro, and cried with an intensity that would not let her speak.

"Quit cryin', woman dear, and tell us where you're bad. Sure we're here to look after you. This is queer and sudden. Run your best Mary up for Mrs Morrow." But Jinanna put out a frantic hand and caught her skirt.

"Well, well, then, we won't send for anybody," and Mrs Murphy patted her shoulder soothingly, 'don't you fret, Jinanna. If you feel a fresh sickness comin' on, or if you're in any other sort of trouble, just lave it till me. I'll manage for you.' She looked at Mary over the little woman's bent, grey head and said grimly: 'This is more of the fortuitous ways of providence! It's not for us to complain, but I did think we had her settled for life.'

"That's it!" gasped Jinanna, 'that's the very thing.'

"Would anybody be wantin' to shift her out of her wee house, do you think?" Mrs Murphy spoke across to Mary in puzzled tones and to their surprise Jinanna's head seemed to nod a violent assent.

"Wait now! Wait till you get your breath, woman dear. There's not one dare touch you, and *me* here! Don't you be afeerd of nothing, Jinanna."

"Och, Mrs Murphy! Och, dear-a-dear!"

"I couldn't have believed it," exclaimed Mrs Murphy, who was beginning to enjoy herself. 'Och, but the people's heart-bad. Quit cryin', like a decent woman and tell us the name of the dirty blaggard that wants to shift you out of your wee house. It'll be a pity of him when *I'm* done with him! And sure Red Abel would never stand it either.'

Jinanna sat up and dried her eyes. Perhaps it was her tears that had washed them to such brightness. She glanced from one to the other like a timid bird, and then for some reason she turned to Mary.

"It's Mr Holden himself," she said.

"Jacob Holden?" repeated Mrs Murphy blankly, 'Jacob Holden? What under the sun would he be wantin' with your bit of a house?'

"Och, Mrs Murphy, dear, it's not the house he wants at all," she cried, clasping her hands, 'sure it's *me* he's awantin',' and she looked at Mary shyly.

There was a moments stupefied silence. Then Mary suddenly clasped her hands and laughed. "Oh, mother, Jinanna's goin' to be married too!" and she jumped up, and ran to her, and put her arms round her, and kissed her. 'Oh, mother, isn't it splendid?' she cried, 'isn't it grand?'

"Lord bless us!" breathed Mrs Murphy, 'for dear sakes! Jacob Holden. Who'd have thought it?'

"I couldn't help it, Mrs Murphy," said Jinanna, flushed and apologetic, 'though what he seen in a wee done crathur like me...'

"Why, you're gettin' younger lookin' every day," declared Mary, 'oh my, but I'm glad – I'm heart-glad!' and she laughed and beamed at her in frankest sympathy. 'Isn't it nice to be engaged, Jinanna?' she kept repeating, 'isn't it grand? And the fine, good man you've got and all!' And she patted her knee and told her again how young she was looking.

"Well, well!" said Mrs Murphy from the sofa where she had subsided, 'you're a great pair of girls altogether! There's not much sense lost between the pair of you. Jacob Holden! My alive!'

"Listen to mother, and her just as glad as I am. When did it happen, Jinanna? Did you know it was comin'?"

"One evenin' down the road he said to me, 'a wee bit of a crathur like you should have somebody to look after her' – that was the first of it," she said with a significant nod at Mary. 'I thought he was terrible kind.'

"And him sittin' there in the corner by the hour together, talkin' of this, that and the other thing, and never lettin' on to me he had such a notion in his head. He's as deep as a draw-well! I never heard him as much as namin' your name, except once, I mind, after he come here he asked me who you were."

"Oh my!" fluttered Jinanna, 'did he ask that? Isn't it wonderful?'

"Feth, it is."

"I had no notion of gettin' married at all. Sure I never thought anybody would be wantin' the like of me! But you never know Mary, sure you never know?"

"No," returned Mary, all sympathy and understanding. 'You never know. That's the lovely part of it. And then one day when you're not thinkin' – it happens! Isn't that it Jinanna?'

"I believe that stuffed duck on the fire board is knowiner nor me," soliloquized Mrs Murphy in depressed tones on the sofa. 'I am a lamentable fool! I worked day and night to get Andy John for our Mary, and Michael breakin' his heart about her all the time, and him twict over the man Andy John was or ever will be – and I trailed you out of the grave, with a dale to do, and here you go and make a match at my own hearthstone unbeknownst to me! I *must* be a lamentable fool.'

"Indeed you are not, Mrs Murphy, dear," said Jinanna fervently, 'you're the best and kindest friend ever anybody heard tell of. That's what I was sayin' to Jacob the other day – when him and me fell in with other – down the road – by chance-like.'

Mary laughed softly, and Mrs Murphy went on in more cheerful tones. "I will allow I'm a bit proud of takin' the money out of poor Break-o'-day Andy. Man, but it was grand. Jinanna, do you mind the piece we had with them two weemun?"

"I think I do! I'm scarred to death yet when I think of them."

"It would take a sight more to scar me! But when thon one began to hiss like a serpent or a snake in the corner, it was over all. It gave me a turn. They were a pair of the worst tinkers I ever came across, but she was the cuttinist of the two. They went off home out of the village speedy-heels that day at any rate."

"Where would I have been only for you, Mrs Murphy, dear," Jinanna's pale earnest little face turned to her. 'The friends that have been raised up for me – and now – him! Isn't it wonderful?'

"Feth, aye."

"It's not right for me to be so happy – but sure I couldn't get him put off. And now I'm afraid of what the neighbours will say and me the age I am. I'm nearly forty-two."

"If anybody passes remarks afore me they'll get my tongue on them, and thanks be to goodness, some of them's ratherly afeerd of *that*."

"But everybody will be glad," Mary assured her.

"I would like everybody to be glad," said Jinanna wistfully, 'and I would like everybody to be as happy as me.'

"So would I," responded Mary, thinking how idle and absurd a wish it was, since there was only one Michael in the world.

"Isn't it well now I bought the blue dress?"

"It will do you to be married in."

"Aye, it will indeed. I was married in pink before and now I'll try blue. It comes in handy, after all."

"Bless my heart, I hope you won't rue the match, the way you rued that dress! I'm not one for givin' advice, Jinanna, or for interferin' between parties that's goin' tegether – but one piece of advice I'll make free to give you afore you flit out of here – and it's this – if you tell a lie, or if you tell *ten* lies – or if you break his mother's tea-pot – or lave the gate open and let the cattle out over the crops – never say you done it. For the Lord's sake never say you done it. For whatever the sense of it is, when you get a rhyme in your mouth you can't get redd of it, and you'd drive any man astray in the mind. *What* we've suffered over that blue dress. Why, if you'd been married the man would have taken his fists to you."

"Oh, no, no, Mrs Murphy dear, indeed he wouldn't!" protested Jinanna with shining eyes, 'the good, kind, peaceable man he is. He wouldn't hurt a fly. He'd mind you of Michael there – only older and solemner.' She glanced apologetically at Mary.

"Well, maybe that. But don't deeve him whatever you do. Men don't like to be deeved. It's a miracle to me you're gettin' anybody."

Jinanna glowed quietly in her chair without speaking and then the door opened and Sammy Soretoes hobbled in. She rose and slipped out past him, and in a few minutes Mary followed her into her own house, and they had a long conversation behind closed doors. That night she wrote to Michael and told him all about it.

Mary wakened one morning out of a vivid and alarming dream about Michael. She had been expecting a letter for several days, and as she wakened she heard, faintly in the distance, the familiar double beat of the horses on the mail car. She had grown used to that sound now, for on many a morning she had lain awake listening intently for it. Her ear had grown so acute and sensitive that she knew the exact moment when the horses passed out under the trees of the plantin' – when they were at the Forked Roads – when at the loanin' leading down to Jinanna's old cottage. Her dream still held her, and as the sound came nearer and nearer, she felt that those great heavy hooves must pass over her, trampling out her life. Then the car passed through the village, and fully awake now, she took it for a sign and lay trembling and waiting for the post-boy to bring her a letter to say Michael was dead. But presently he went past the door whistling 'The Boyne Water', and she almost cried with relief. After that she slept better. She would not heed signs or dreams any more, and she comforted herself with writing long, loving letters to the front, and in sending parcels filled with every good thing she could think of. She carried them down to the General Post Office and posted them herself. That was as near as she could get to him how. Even if they were handled by cold, official fingers afterwards, she thought Michael would be sure to feel her touch on the paper and string. Dear, dear Michael. "O cover his head in the day of battle."

It was early in October. Mary wakened to hear unusual sounds in the kitchen. Someone seemed to be reading aloud in a low voice.

"Mother," she called sleepily, 'what's the matter?'

Mrs Murphy came into the room. She came very slowly towards the bed.

"Don't waken the childer," whispered Mary, rubbing her eyes to get the sleep out of them. There was someone moving in the kitchen. It must be the post-boy. She heard a shuffling sound, as if he stood first on one foot and then the other.

Mrs Murphy's face was grey and ashen. She held a thin wisp of paper between her fingers. Mary raised her head and held out her hand. Michael's letter.

"Och, daughter dear – we must submit – it's the will of God..."

She put up her hand and touched the band of her nightdress. It had suddenly tightened round her throat.

Also available from White Row:

The Most Unpretending of Places
A history of Dundonald, County Down.

Essential reading for anyone who would like to find out more about the world of the real *Gape Row* – a place no less colourful or extraordinary than Agnes Romilly White's fictional creation.

"Sparkles with compelling detail... one of the most impressive local histories available for any locality on this island, north or south."
Linenhall Review

"One word could suffice to describe this book, magnificent! ...I cannot praise it too highly. Well illustrated with photographs, studiously annotated without overloading the text, a questioning of sources, a good index and the courage to express opinions of a controversial nature. This is what local history is all about."
Irish News

"Original, quirky...You may never have heard of Dundonald, but that will not prevent you from enjoying this book. This could be the story of any small town or village in Ireland."
Archaeology Ireland

"Opens with the formation of the Holywood and Castlereagh Hills five hundred million years ago, and comes screeching to an end, still full of repressed vitality, with a salvo at the DoE's 1987 Belfast Urban Area Plan... Great stuff."
Fortnight

ISBN 1 870132 00 9, 256pp, paperback, 160 illustrations, price £5.95. Available from bookshops, or in case of difficulty, directly from the publishers.

Coming shortly:

Yes, Matron!
A history of Nurses and Nursing in the Royal Victoria Hospital, Belfast

Dr Peggy Donaldson

If you have ever visited or worked in "the Royal", or would simply like to know what goes on behind the scenes in a large general hospital, this book will interest you. For the Royal is by any count a remarkable institution: a city within a city and a largely self-contained world, at the centre of which stood the formidable figure of Matron, the head of nursing; invariably an enormously capable woman, seen by callow would-be nurses as something akin to an earthly divinity.

Yes, Matron tells the fascinating story of nursing at the Royal, from 1797 to the present day, in a candid and entertaining way. It explores both great events and small, from the impact of wars and devastating epidemics, to the dramas, joys and disappointments of everyday hospital life. We hear of the "angels" and the awesome matriarchs, such as Sister Dynes, who was feared and respected by generations of nurses, patients and doctors alike.

Peggy Donaldson, herself a nurse for over ten years, tells their story with humour and compassion. Drawing both on her own experience and a rich vein of oral and archive material, she has created a fresh and readable narrative that will surely have a universal appeal.

ISBN 1 870132 15 7, 240pp, available spring 1989